The Society of Shadows
Dasha Tryon Wallace

Dasha Writes
LLC

Contents

Dedication   V

Chapter One   2

Chapter Two   11

Chapter Three   21

Chapter Four   29

Chapter Five   35

Chapter Six   47

Chapter Seven   55

Chapter Eight   64

Chapter Nine   76

Chapter Ten   86

Chapter Eleven   95

Chapter Twelve   103

Chapter Thirteen   108

Chapter Fourteen   113

Chapter Fiveteen   123

Chapter Sixteen   132

Chapter Seventeen   145

Chapter Eighteen   152

Chapter Nineteen   160

Chapter Twenty   172

Chapter Twenty One   179

Chapter Twenty Two   185

Chapter Twenty Three   193

Chapter Twenty Four   200

Chapter Twenty Five   205

Chapter Twenty Six   210

Chapter Twenty Seven   217

Chapter Twenty Eight   224

Chapter Twenty Nine   228

Chapter Thirty   233

Chapter Thirty One   238

Chapter Thirty Two   247

Chapter Thirty Three   256

Chapter Thirty Four   264

Epilogue   272

To those who have stuck with me and are still here.

I never considered how odd it is to look at a mirror. It is obviously the same person looking back, but everything is the opposite. The hat tilted to the left would then be tilted to the right in the mirror. The same image, yet contradictory to its original.

Journal of Arabella Cooper
Page 22, paragraph 3

Chapter One

Arabella, or Ella to her friends, stood in the grand ballroom scanning the entrances and exits. The Season had started, and she had been stationed in London to attend the balls. It had been five years since the riot, and Ella had been relegated to support duties, such as the case of this mission. Her goal was to help Eleanor gather information about a business deal between Baron Grey and an unknown person. It wasn't a particularly dangerous mission, or even one of great importance. Ella hadn't been given those sorts of missions since the last time she spoke with the Duke of Wellington.

A door opened and Ella caught a glimpse of Baron Grey entering the ballroom. Skirting around the edges of the dancers, she made her way to the exit. Now knowing he was out of his office, she slipped out of the room.

As Ella made her way Baron Grey's office, she strode confidently through the sparsely populated hallways. Faking a trip to twist the sole of her shoe, she "fell." From the corner of her eyes, she checked to see if anyone was coming. As she stood, Ella picked up the lockpicks. Absentmindedly, Ella brushed aside a fake blond curl from her wig as she went about picking the lock.

It took but a moment, and she was in. When the door shut behind Ella, she took in her surroundings.

"That took far longer than it should have, and you didn't check to see if anyone was in here first."

Ella gave a sigh at who was talking. It was Lady Nora, her mother. It had taken two years since she received the information from Adrian about her mother for her to be released from slavery. Now that she had recuperated from her ordeal, she had been sent to support Ella, while Ella helped Lady Nora understand the political field and regain contacts.

"Mother, I was hoping to see who left the party and if anyone would talk to him while Lord Grey was in his office," Ella explained as she moved towards her mother and started looking through the Lord's papers with her.

Ella loved her mother dearly, but things differed from her childhood memories of her larger-than-life mother, who was always vibrant and elegant. Giving a critical eye, Ella checked to make sure her mother was still feeling well. Ella noted her mother's red hair, now dull and threaded with grey, and her willowy figure interrupted by her permanently hunched shoulders from heavy work. She didn't look too tired, but her mother was good at hiding her emotions. As Ella continued looking through the papers, she kept a wary eye on her mother to make sure she didn't collapse, not focusing on her mother's lecture.

"I thought they taught you better at the academy. It is much easier to charm the man and get information from him. Lord Grey thought me dull-witted and harmless, letting me get close to him earlier," Lady Nora continued.

"Yes, mother," Ella said, holding back an eye roll. She didn't want to get into another argument with her mother. After her mother improved, Ella jumped at the chance to work with her mother. Now she was regretting it.

"Start looking through anything with numbers on it. That should have what we need on it." Lady Nora said, throwing out the comment and continuing to scan the papers.

"Or a letter discussing a business transaction with Baron Greenwood?" Ella asked, holding out the paper to her mother, annoyed that her mother still treated her like a fresh recruit.

Lady Nora perused over the proffered paper, a smile on her face. "That is it exactly. Well done, now the best way to not get caught is to always listen before leaving. Do it for more than a few seconds because a person might not be moving when you first listen. If they are not moving, you are not likely going to hear a noise."

Ella refrained from sighing; it would only prompt another lecture from her mother, which would make her mother more tired. As her mother continued her lecture, Ella was already heading towards the door. Paying little attention to her mother's condescending words that would only irritate her, Ella pressed her ear toward the door. After listening for a few moments and not hearing anything, she nodded toward her mother and opened the door. As the door opened, it revealed the back of a gentleman who had been leaning against the door. Startled that his backrest was no longer there, he turned around to look at her.

With a disarming smile, Ella spoke, "Oh my! I'm so sorry. I didn't realize anyone was there."

The man gave a smile back as he replied, "No problem. I seemed to have startled you as well, young lady." As he spoke, a realization of where they were lit his eyes, and he shifted uncomfortably. "I don't think you should be in here--"

Whatever he was going to say was cut off by Lady Nora, who had snuck up behind the gentleman and pricked his neck with her broach, causing him to collapse to the floor.

"As I was saying, it is better to leave in a different way from than you entered," Lady Nora said, pinning her broach back on and brushing her skirts flat. "Now, what to do with him? Humm. I suppose we could pour some wine or beer on him. Make it look like he got drunk."

Ella's stomach twisted at that thought. It was a good plan, but doing that would make people view him unfavorably. The older gentleman had been polite to her, and his smile had been warm. It didn't feel right to do it that way. Instead, she pulled him out of the room and shut the door behind her mother, who was watching Ella with a stern look.

Ella ignored her as she knelt next to the man and called for help. A servant came at her call and hurried to help the guest as both Ella and her mother slipped away in the confusion.

"You know that others will now consider him weak. You haven't done him any favors." Her mother whispered once they were out of earshot of passing servants.

Shrugging, Ella made her way to the ball. If she spoke back now, her mother would pour into yet another well-meaning lecture back home, which Ella would yet again ignore. Instead, she sought out Baron Clive, who had entered his name on her dance card. Now that they had finished their mission, exhaustion set in. The same exhaustion that had been pulling at her for a few months, but she couldn't let that stop her. Baron Clive had noted her entrance and was making his way over to her. Relieved as she was to escape the situation with her mother, she still wished that her husband was dancing with her instead.

Adrian sat next to his father's sickbed, reading a book.

"Why didn't you wake me up?

Adrian immediately looked up at the sound of his father's voice. Closing the book and putting it to the side, he sat next to his father on the bed. He helped his father into a seated position as his father hacked out a wet cough.

After his father regained his breath, he waved his son away, "Stop fussing over me. I get enough of that from the doctor. And stop it with that worried look on your face."

Attempting to relax his features, Adrian spouted, "I can't help it if I worry about you."

"Well, it's not helping me. Shouldn't you know how this feels?" His father said with a brow raised.

It was true. Adrian did understand how his father felt. After his childhood sickness and his more recent issues, due to the incident with the riot, that had left him with a permanent rasp to his breath, he would know better than anyone how his father would be feeling. The sense of your own fragility and hating how you were forced to rely on others. All with the hint of death breathing over your shoulder as you can see how your sickness is causing everyone around you pain.

"Then you can get better as I did," Adrian said with a plea.

"No, son. I am not getting out of this. But I will make sure to hang on until Drina is of age. So help me if I let her mother sit on the throne for even one moment." Fire lit his eyes as his father clenched his fists with determination.

"You should stay for longer."

"Death comes for us all," the king said, ending the discussion. "So, how is that wife of yours? How is she handling things?"

Worry over his father had distracted him from his family problems. A year after he had told his father the plan, Ella and Adrian were married. Things were rocky at first. Adrian had to change his own identity and life to that of a viscount. It was a drastic change from his life as a prince—not to mention everything that was the secret of the Fan Society. He had to keep everything from his father.

"She is handling it as well as possible. Though there are some societal pressures to have a child." Adrian replied. Things had gotten better when they found out that Ella was pregnant, but she lost the baby a few weeks later. In the past two years, they still haven't had another child.

Adrian was pulled out of his musings by his father's reply, "It may be better if you don't try. Pregnancy is risky."

Adrian, watching his father, knew his father was thinking of his mother. She had given birth prematurely several times before giving birth to twins early as well. His twin brother passed as soon as he was born, and Adrian didn't have good odds himself. But on top of the loss of his twin was the loss of Adrian's mother.

Adrian's touch on his father's shoulder broke his father's concentration. His father tried to clear his throat, but it turned into a wracking cough. Hurrying to the bedside table, he poured his father a glass of water.

After taking a sip and calming his lungs, his father said, "Cherish your wife, and don't let society push you to make a mistake that you can't take back. I was just so glad that Lady Nora was there for me."

Grateful for the change in topic, Adrian jumped at the chance to ask a burning question, "Who was Lady Nora? I mean, in relation to me. It feels as if I should know her."

His father smiled, "She was your mother's friend and confidante. She was the one who took you in and saved your life. If it weren't for her taking care of you, you would have died. I had just lost my wife and child, and I was waiting to hear about your death. I couldn't even look at you during that time. Nora forcefully gained my permission to raise you. And she did. By the time you had lived to be five, and though you still were a sickly child, you survived far longer than anyone expected and returned home."

"Is that the reason you granted the title to Lady Victoria after Lady Nora's disappearance? So that someone could take care of her daughter?" Adrian asked, as his memories and certain circumstances melded together to understanding.

"Yes," His father replied. "It was the only thing I could do for her daughter after everything she had done for us. If only I had known what a witch her stepmother was. Thank you for bringing her circumstances to my attention."

"Thank you for helping her."

His father's eyes were drooping with exhaustion, and Adrian then excused himself with a promise to visit later. As he exited his father's room from one of the hidden escape passageways, anxiety clutched at his heart. Struggling to shove his worries back, he walked in silence until Mathew came to join him.

"How is he doing?" Adrian murmured, knowing that while he was looking after his father, Mathew was talking to the doctors.

Taking a quick look around at the empty halls, he replied, "The doctors say he's not doing well. The pneumonia isn't going away. The doctors aren't looking hopeful. They are more surprised that he has lasted this long."

"Isn't that what they said about me?" Adrian said, with a smile on his face. The smile fell at the sight of Mathew's expression. "You don't think he is going to make it."

Mathew bowed his head in remorse.

"I see," Adrian said. His feelings tumbled inside of him. Tears threatened to well up as he struggled to control his emotions. His father wasn't dead yet. He was too stubborn to die. Adrian's thoughts turned back to his father's shriveling form and pale complexion. And he shied away from it. That was not his father. A cold could not bring a boisterous man like him down. There was no way that was possible, and yet his father's haggard appearance suggests otherwise.

Lost in thought, they made their way out of the passageway to a deserted street a little ways away. Adrian looked back at his home, thoughts still heavy as he struggled with the knowledge that his father might actually die.

"Do you regret it?" Mathew asked.

"What?" Adrian snapped out of his musings. Looking up, he saw Mathew was watching the manor. Shaking his head, Adrian answered in an instant. "No. I do not regret my decision. Drina is doing a marvelous job. I only regret leaving all the responsibility on her shoulders. But I know she will do a better job for these people."

Adrian turned to Mathew. The person who had been through every-thing with him. Adrian only had to watch his father turn ill these last few months, but Mathew has had a lifetime's worth of watching Adrian coming close to death. A question poured from his lips from the weight of his emotions, "Do you regret following me?"

"Your Highness, I will never regret following you," Mathew said just as quickly as Adrian had answered the same question. It lightened Adrian's melancholic mood.

Adrian laughed, "I'm no longer a prince. Now that things have become all moody, it's time to cheer up. Our ladies are waiting for us."

Chapter Two

Ella was listening to yet another lecture on how she could have executed the mission better when Adrian walked through the door of their London abode.

"Adrian!" Ella called, welcoming him with a smile. Grateful for the interruption, she hurried over to her husband. Catching the sorrow hidden behind the smile he gave her, Ella grasped his arm and whispered, "What's wrong?"

Ella knew that the king had been sick for months, and given Adrian's expression, he wasn't getting better. Worry filled her as she opened her mouth to speak. Adrian patted her arm, halting her words, as he gave her a wearied smile. A glance at her mother told her that he would wait to tell her when they were alone. Turning instead to her mother, Adrian greeted her with a bow of his head, "Greetings Lady Nora. Pleasure seeing you. How did your mission go?"

Her mother's mouth twisted at his question. She had made it very clear that she didn't approve of a member of the royal family knowing about the Fan Society. It was against all the rules of the Fan Society.

"It went well." Was all Lady Nora answered, with a tight but polite smile.

Jumping at the break in the conversation, Ella said, "You must be tired, mother. Thank you for your lesson, it was really helpful, but I think it's time to take a rest. Good night, mother."

Ella tried to make her escape so she could talk to Adrian, but was pulled to a stop. Adrian had paused to give her mother a deep bow, saying, "Thank you."

There was weight to his words as he said them. Confused at why he would thank her mother, considering she had mostly ignored him or said one-word replies since she had arrived. After his thanks, he linked his arm to Ella's and guided her to their room. Once they entered their room, Adrian sat on the bed with a sigh. Putting aside her confusion at the exchange with her mother, Ella sat beside him, taking his hand in hers. Adrian came first.

They sat in silence as Ella waited until he was ready to talk.

Voice even raspier than normal, Adrian said, "My father is dying." Tears dripped onto their linked hands.

"I'm so sorry," Ella whispered as she pulled him into an embrace and held him until the tears ran dry.

Ella woke up the next morning lethargic. Though Ella woke up early for a noble, her mother was already up and having her morning tea, a habit from her days as a slave. But instead of being forced to haul buckets of water, she could relax and read a book.

"Good morning, Arabella," her mother said as Ella attempted to leave the house without getting stopped.

"Good morning," Ella said, trying to hold back another yawn that threatened to escape. "I'm on my way to speak to Flora."

Her mother nodded. "What about your husband? When is he coming down?"

Remembering the long emotional night, Ella replied, "He is still sleeping."

"Humm," her mother hummed in thought as she took a sip of her tea.

"Goodbye, Mother."

Her mother nodded again, going back to her book as she said absentmindedly, "Make sure you give Flora my regards."

Ella was about to leave when Clementine came in with a tray of breakfast food. The smell hit her, and the nausea she had all morning grew.

Ella hurried out of the room with a muttered goodbye. She could hear the clatter of a tray being sat down as Clementine followed after her. Slowing her steps, Ella let Clementine catch up to her easily. She came close and whispered, "Are you doing okay?"

With a sigh and a shrug, Ella said, "Same as it has been." The worried look in her friend's eye did not abate until Ella continued. "I'll talk to Flora."

Clementine nodded, then made her way back to Lady Nora. Ella watched her friend go. The scar on her head was looking much better, but Clementine always made sure her hair hid it. Even though it had healed, it serves as a constant reminder of that horrible night five years ago. An incident that will never happen again.

Ella made her way to the waiting carriage that would take her to Flora's house. Her house wasn't too far from where Flora had been stationed. Fiddling with the blond wig that she had to wear for her cover, she spent the short ride looking out the window. The houses were buttressed up next to each other, shadowing the street in the morning light. Her mind drifted as she watched the early morning streets with a few people chatting as they walked in the chill morning air. Rather than enjoying the scene, she recalled a similar street ablaze, echoing with screams.

Startled out of her reverie by the carriage coming to a stop, she waited for the door to open. The footman helped her out as she made her way to Flora's house, which also housed her clinic on the bottom floor. It was actually another doctor's place, but being a Friend of the Society, Flora basically runs it. The red brick house was situated on the corner of the street, allowing for two entrances. One entrance allowed for the entry of her patients on one side, while the other side allowed visitors to head up to her parlor on the second floor.

As Ella entered the quaint parlor, she saw Flora waiting for her. Dressed in her nurse's uniform of a dark gray dress and white apron, she turned as Ella entered and smiled at her. Flora moved towards her with a smile on her face. Though they didn't really see each other much during their academy days together, they had become friends during the time they had been stationed there. Demure and calming, she called for Mary to get some tea. Once Ella was situated by a small table, with tea in hand, Flora placed a sign on the door and shut it. Ella knew by now that it was a signal to keep away eavesdroppers with the other Medics on her team.

"It's good to see you, Flora. My mother gives her regards." Ella said as Flora sat across from her.

"How is she doing?"

"Mother is doing very well. Thank you for taking care of her. Though she still gets tired in the evenings, she doesn't collapse. I've been making sure she doesn't push herself as hard. But my mother always wants to be part of the action." Ella took another sip of her tea and then asked, "What information did you find out?"

Flora's green eyes looked at her over the cup she had been sipping from. Setting her cup down, she folded her hand in her lap, "How are you doing?"

"I'm fine." The words slipped from her lips at the repetitive question

With a soft snort, Flora let her know just how much she believed those words. "Then you should be able to make a deal with me."

Wariness thrummed through Ella. "What is this deal?"

"Nothing complex. I will just ask you a question about yourself for every piece of information I give to you. I will even allow you to ask me a question in exchange."

"You do realize that you are *supposed* to give me the information. That is why I'm here," Ella said.

Flora just smiled and sipped her tea in that infuriatingly calm manner. But maybe this was for the best. She did promise Clementine that she would speak to Flora, and all Flora was doing was her job to make sure that everyone was healthy. Maybe she could even ask for information on how to help the king to help Adrian.

"Alright. It's a deal," Ella said. She tried to calm her nerves by sipping tea. Her stomach had finally started to settle after having something in it. Though the conversation was making her nausea rise.

"Baron Jones had an affair with the maid. Their baby is doing rather well."

Ella nodded. It was not uncommon to hear, but Baron Jones had been dipping his toes into the black market. The information on his child could keep him from stepping too far out of line. Committing the information to memory. Ella then asked the dreaded question, "What do you want to know from me?"

Ella winced at the waver in her voice as she asked, knowing that Flora would pick up on it.

Setting down the tea that she had been sipping, Flora asked, "Are you still having nausea? Still tired?"

"Yes, and yes," the answer was short. This was the same nausea and tiredness that she had had since her miscarriage. Not wanting to dwell on something she couldn't change, Ella asked, "Any other news?"

"Yes. Brigette, who works as a maid for the Greenwood family, asked for something to help her sleep at night. Upon further questioning, there is a reason she could not sleep at night. She claims to be hearing voices. I happen to know that she sleeps in the basement." Flora said that last statement with a raised brow.

From that, Ella could understand that the maid wasn't crazy and maybe hearing someone's voice. But if it is in the middle of the night, it was likely of nefarious implications. "I will let the Society know to have someone look into it."

"Are you still having trouble eating?" Flora asked.

Holding up a hand, Ella stopped her, "Not so fast. Didn't you promise me a question? And since you have asked me two, I get two questions."

Flora nodded. "As long as you answer my question, then ask away."

Remembering the tear-filled night with Adrian, Ella asked, "Is there anything that can be done for the king?"

"Not much, I'm afraid." Flora bowed her head. Flora was connected to all the medical information in the Fan Society and knew the nurse who was helping the king. "There is nothing much we can do. His age is working against him. His body is too weak to fight off his affliction. Even with all the medical knowledge we have, we still can't fight against time."

Ella was afraid of that answer, but if Flora said that there wasn't much they could do, then there was no hope. "How much longer do you think he has?"

Ignoring her question, Flora took a sip of tea, reminding Ella that she still hadn't answered Flora's last question.

With a sigh, Ella answered, "Yes."

"I doubt he has longer than a few more months, if he is lucky. It will be a sad day when he passes." Flora looked down at her hands sightlessly.

Pulling herself out of her own thoughts that had hounded her since this morning, and examined her friend. Her eyes were puffed from lack of sleep, and her hands were chapped from washing them frequently. She smelled of the harsh soap they used to clean up after patients. Even after taking care of the sick, she had always looked prim and proper. Something must be happening to have her look like this. "What is going on, Flora?"

Her normally calm face crinkled at the brow as she avoided looking at Ella, "It's nothing more than speculation."

"That is what we do."

"As you know, we have been getting more smallpox patients recently, and we are starting to get overwhelmed. If it goes any further, it will be an epidemic."

After speaking frequently to her, Ella knew she was holding back, "That has always been a concern. What is really bothering you?"

Looking around the walls, Flora stood and poured Ella more tea. As she did, she leaned forward and whispered, "It is nothing more than an observation and my instincts. But I feel as if someone is spreading it on purpose. It's not quite reacting like smallpox, though the symptoms are similar."

"What do you mean?" The whispered question meant she didn't want the watchers to hear and worry, but why would she think that someone was spreading smallpox?

Flora sat back in her chair, arms folded, "There are far more cases of smallpox than there should be at this time of year. Normally, the nobility don't fear it as much as the commoners do, but there have been more cases among the nobility."

"Any other reason?" It was strange to say with only that much information.

Shrugging, Flora said, "As I said, it is nothing more than a feeling."

A feeling that was usually correct. Ella sighed. Even though there wasn't much to go on, it would still be good to keep an eye on. Flora didn't want to worry her fellow members about someone purposefully spreading it, but they must know that there were far too many cases. That's probably the reason Flora even mentioned it to Ella at all. "Thank you for the tea. It was a pleasant visit."

As Ella got up to leave, Flora motioned her to sit down, "I believe you asked more than one question. It is my turn to ask you."

Ella had hoped to avoid that. She had pressed Flora for more information. Taking a deep breath, she sat back down.

"I will only ask you one final question," Flora said. "Have you thought you might be pregnant?"

"FLORA!" Since the loss of her child, Ella had had bouts of nausea and tiredness. For two years, this had been happening. Every time it got bad, they thought she was pregnant and sent her to Flora. And every time, she wasn't. This time would be no different. "I'm not pregnant! And it won't happen."

Eyes softening, Flora poured her another cup of tea. Grateful, Ella took the cup and downed the tea far faster than what was considered polite, but at the moment, she didn't care. Ella stood again, "Now, if you will excuse me, I have a mission to prepare for and reports to turn in."

Flora didn't stop her this time, but as Ella passed by Flora, she said, "You should mourn the loss of your child."

Turning to Flora, Ella felt her heart clench at those words, "My child is dead, and nothing is going to change that. I have things I need to do, and sitting around crying for a child that I've never seen won't help me get it done."

Sighing, Flora stood and opened the door. Walking her to the front door, she left Ella with her last words, "If you ever need me, my door is open."

Refusing to turn around, afraid that her agitation would cause her to make a scene, Ella stepped into her carriage and made her way back home.

We need to meet to discuss Justice. Please meet at the Academy through the secret entrance at midnight.

Note to codename: Phoenix
Original codename: Cinders
Sent from the Academy

Chapter Three

Adrian woke up feeling wrung out, but more at peace than he was last night. He sat up, rubbing away his crusted eyes, yawning. Reaching next to him, and feeling nothing, he looked to where Ella would sleep. Unsurprisingly, it was empty. He felt an ache in his hand and looked at the burned palm, a gift from the riots. It didn't hurt often, but it was a constant reminder of everything he lacked. Calming his breathing, he had started wheezing in remembrance, he rubbed his eyes and stood. The afternoon light was already peeking through the curtains, reminding him that it was late for most of the people in the house.

A knock sounded on the door.

"Enter," Adrian said.

Mathew allowed himself in and poured Adrian water in a bowl to wash his face, then set the newspaper on the table next to him. "I hope you had a good night's rest."

Nodding, Adrian stood and made his way to splash water on his face, "Yes, it was." Closing his eyes, he scooped up the cool water and rubbed his face. Holding his hand out, Adrian felt Mathew place a towel in his hand,

and he proceeded to dry his face, ignoring the tightness of his skin pulling on the palm of his hand.

"There is a meeting taking place. I thought that you would want to know."

Adrian dropped the towel, "What? Why didn't you tell me sooner? Hurry and help me get ready."

The whistle in his breathing grew louder as Mathew helped him get dressed. Helping Adrian put on his shirt, he said, "You know Lady Nora wants to keep you away from things like this, so why do you continue to try to help on these missions?"

Adrian could see how careful Mathew was at keeping his expression neutral, but Adrian wasn't buying it. He knew that Mathew continued to worry about him. Even more so since his lungs were damaged. Mathew didn't know all the details of the missions and didn't want to know. He feared that if he knew, he would worry more. But he did make sure to help in every way he could with knowing the details. He worried that if he would be captured, they could force him to reveal their plans. Mathew didn't want that to happen.

Not that Adrian thought such a thing would happen, but Adrian made sure not to tell him details as he wished. "I continue to help because, even though I am no longer prince, I still feel responsible. And if we help with these missions, Drina would be safer and in a more secure position. Considering how her family is, I feel better knowing that she has my support."

Raising his brow, Mathew didn't comment. He knew that Drina's mother had tried to kill Adrian several years ago and how controlling she was. Drina did help with investigations of some of the nefarious things her mother had gotten into and passed the information on to Adrian. It was difficult for her since she was just in her teens, and Adrian knew very well how hard it was going against your parent's wishes.

Finishing tying his cravat, Mathew said, "There is breakfast waiting for you in the meeting."

"Thank you, Mathew."

"Yes, your highness."

Adrian shook his head, giving up on correcting him. He had more important matters to attend to.

The meeting took place in the basement of the home. It was a secret room hidden beneath a rug with stairs leading to a rather large space. Clementine looked up at him as he came down, then turned back to the room. Ella and her mother were already seated and in deep discussion.

"We need to find a way to stop Baron Greenwood," Ella said. Adrian could tell she was trying to keep herself from raising her voice.

"We don't even know what he is doing yet. Our orders are to find a Ghost who could help us find information in this matter, nothing more." Lady Nora sighed as she sat poised in her chair.

It was a difficult situation. Much had happened between the time Lady Nora went missing and the time she was rescued. She was no longer in the same position she once was.

Adrian stepped forward, interrupting them before it became heated, "What is the mission?"

Ever the polite Lady, Nora spoke up, "Orders have been received that we need to place a Ghost within the Greenwood household. It will be an easy mission that you should not be needed to place yourself in danger."

Adrian knew where her priorities lay. As always, she would follow her orders explicitly and no more. Taking into consideration what his father had told him the night before, he knew that she was also worried about him. But Adrian also knew that protecting someone from everything wasn't always the best thing you could do for that person.

"With all these coincidences, how could it not be that he is doing something nefarious? Taking the time to find a ghost to get the information would take too long," Ella said.

Adrian furrowed his brow. Yet again, Ella wanted to go off on her own to take care of things. Her glances at Clementine and her mother showed her worry about hurting her friends again. She had gotten better over the last five years, but when her mother appeared, she fell back to old habits.

"What do we currently know?" Adrian asked. He had hoped that he could stop the growing tension in the room.

Sighing and pressing her finger against her forehead as she tried not to wince, Lady Nora said, "Lord Greenwood has made business dealings with Lord Grey, but it doesn't specify what it is. We also know that a young girl is getting nightmares from a rat infestation."

"Really, Mother?" Ella rolled her eyes, "Lord Grey had been getting into the black market with Baron Jones, and we know that he has been making shady deals with Lord Greenwood in the middle of the night in the slums. Why else would the letter say to meet there? And the maid is *not* hearing rats. She is hearing voices in a room that doesn't exist. Like how the basement we are currently in doesn't exist."

"All conjecture. A spy needs to keep her head at all times and *follow orders*. Don't make so many assumptions." Lady Nora folded her arms as she kept her feelings from showing on her face.

Ella couldn't see, but Adrian could see her fingers twitch whenever Ella spoke.

"Yes, but sometimes, if you don't pursue the information, some things could be missed. You could be too late to stop it." Ella was keeping her features controlled, but Adrian, who had been with her, could tell from the twitch in her eye and the clenching of her fingers that she was worried that she would be too late, just like how she was almost too late to save himself from the fire. He had forgiven her for that ages ago, but she still felt guilt for it. He could see it in her eyes whenever he caught her sneaking glances at him. It was a complicated situation for her; he shouldn't have been caught up in the fire or the Fan Society. But he had known too much and had ended up getting Viscount Edmund's attention, putting him in danger. Besides, Ella shouldn't have been doing things without the Fan Society's backup. Yet if she hadn't pursued the information, they wouldn't have known about Viscount Edmund, *but* if she hadn't been so rash, maybe there wouldn't have been as much collateral damage. Adrian could see both sides of the argument.

Between Ella's guilt and the worry that Adrian could see growing on Nora's face, he knew it was time to step in. "A Ghost would still be a good idea either way."

He could see Ella open her mouth to voice her objection, but Adrian continued, "Don't you have connections to Lady Hill, who is married to a Bobby? Since he is involved with the Metropolitan police, couldn't we gain more information that way? Then, if we get a Ghost as well, that would mean more information from different sources. If we gain more information, then we can see how we should proceed."

The ladies looked at each other. Lady Nora spoke first, "That is an acceptable arrangement."

Turning to his wife, he waited, giving her time to think things through. After a few moments, she nodded back.

"They have a ball tonight. We can start then," Ella turned to Clementine, "We will need any information that you have about the household. Can you get the information while I write the letter to Lady Hill, as well as have enough time to get me ready?"

Clementine, who had been watching the whole conversation, said, "Who do you think you are talking to? Besides, I will give Harriette something to do. She has been itching to help."

Standing, Ella turned towards her mother, "Now that we have agreed, I need to change into appropriate attire for this evening. Will you be joining?"

Lady Nora paused, gaze weighing heavily on her daughter. "No, you should be able to do this on your own. I have a meeting that I need to attend."

"What meeting?" Ella stopped herself and stood. "Nevermind, I need to get ready. Good luck at your meeting."

Then she turned towards Adrian. "Coming, dear?"

Eyeing Lady Nora, he answered, "I will be up in a moment. You can go ahead and start getting dressed."

She shrugged, then headed up the stairs with Clementine following after her, leaving him and Lady Nora behind.

Once the girls left, Lady Nora motioned for him to sit, sipped her tea, and said, "What do you wish to speak about?"

Taking his seat, Adrian faced Lady Nora in the chair that his wife had just vacated, "I would like to thank you."

Gazing at him from above her teacup, she raised her delicate brow, questioning him. Adrian was still in awe of this woman. After meeting her, he could understand how Ella grew to be an amazing woman. Lady Nora, after everything that had happened to her, showed her resilience just by sitting. That steady gaze burned with fire, the same fire that he had seen in Ella's eyes whenever circumstances were against her. Yet all of that strength was dressed in a beautiful navy dress with impeccable manners.

Adrian smiled, "I knew that you seemed familiar, but I couldn't quite place where I had seen you. When Ella said your name, it brought to mind a warm feeling and distant memories. After asking my father, I now know why. You were the one that saved my life as a child."

Setting her teacup down, a smile touched the edges of her lips, "I couldn't leave him to raise a child on his own. Besides, I owed your mother."

Unlike Ella's loss of her mother and subsequent loss of her father, Adrian had always had his father. Though overprotective, he always spoke fondly of Adrian's mother. His father could have been lost in his grief for a very long time or blamed Adrian for the death of his wife. But in all of Adrian's life, he had never once felt that. Even though his father didn't really listen to Adrian's wishes, he had always been there for him. The forcefulness was just his awkward attempts to protect his son. He had always been there for him. Sorrow pierced his heart. Soon, his father will no longer be there. He looked down at his hands, which had now started to tremble. Holding back the tears that now threatened to roll down his cheeks, he said, "My father *is* very stubborn.

A hand tentatively reached out and touched his. "I'm sorry for the illness that has befallen your father. He is a good man."

Adrian looked into Nora's blue eyes, ones that looked so similar to Ella's, and the concern held there. Those two really were so similar. Her touch pulled him from his sorrow as it turned into a dull ache.

"Thank you. That was what I had wanted to tell you, not just for raising me, but for raising Ella, whom I love."

"I have no part in raising Ella."

"Pardon me for saying this, but you are wrong," Adrian said, now holding her hand in his, grey eyes holding her blue. "You have had far more influence than you realize. And after seeing you, I know that for a fact. Everything that Ella has done was motivated by you."

After holding her gaze for a few more moments, he stood and gave her a bow, "Now I must bid you adieu."

As he started making his way towards the stairs, Lady Nora spoke up, "Is it too late to be her mother?"

Adrian stopped and turned towards her, "Nothing can stop you from being her mother."

Then he turned back around, leaving Nora to her thoughts as he readied himself for the ball.

Chapter Four

Entering the lavish ballroom on Adrian's arm released the last of the tension Ella had from speaking to her mother. Her stomach was still queasy, and the bright light from the chandelier did little to help her headache, which had been steadily growing. She wanted to itch her blond wig, but that would be inappropriate. Instead, trying to focus on the task at hand, she leaned over to Adrian's ear and whispered, "Remember your task?"

Whispering back, Adrian said, "Try to see if Lord Greenwood will make a deal with me and set up a meeting. Make sure that I say that I will use a representative."

"Perfect," Ella said with a smile on her face as her gaze wandered the ballroom, picking out people of interest. Keeping half her attention on the other people, they made their way to the host.

When they stood in front of Lord Greenwood, Ella focused her full attention on him. The feeling of danger flooded through her as she gripped Adrian's arm tighter. Memories of the smoky square filled with screams and a clash of swords on fan with an opponent who called himself Fox. A

29

man who looked very much like Lord Greenwood. Gripping her fan, she readied for an attack.

"Hello, Lord Greenwood. Thank you for inviting us this evening," Adrian said, not knowing the danger that they were in. Ella wanted to pull them away, but that wouldn't be polite, nor did she know if he would do anything in a public setting like this.

"Greetings, Lord Cooper," the fox-faced gentleman replied in kind.

"This is my wife, Priscilla Cooper," Adrian said, introducing Ella to the man as was customary.

Lord Greenwood turned to her. If he recognized her, he didn't show it. "Charmed."

Forcing a polite smile on her face, she bowed her head in greeting. Either the man was not the one she had met during the fight, or he was playing a game. After her greeting, he turned away from her and focused on Adrian, "Lord Cooper, now that you have become a new Lord. I know that you have come into some money now that you run the Cooper estate."

"Yes, I have," Adrian said, playing the pre-planned part as a Lord interested in spending his newfound money.

Ella calmed herself with the familiar motion of feeling the hidden emblem on her fan. She needed to make sure that he could make it out safely should this become a problem. Picking out a person she had noted when they came in, Ella flicked her fan open and fanned herself to get their attention.

The Lady, using her fan, signaled her desire to know what was needed by opening, closing, and then tapping it with her finger. Ella turned to Adrian, who was conversing with Lord Greenwood about a business proposition. He had learned so much and did so well with everything that Ella taught him. She had originally taught him to help him adjust to his new life, but he did better than he thought he did. Even Ella had been surprised at how he took to the lessons. Ella eyed Lord Greenwood. Even though she may be wrong about who the man was, considering how through the entire conversation he hadn't so much as glanced at Ella, Adrian still didn't have the strength needed to defeat a man as skilled as Fox.

"... we should take this to another room." Lord Greenwood was trying to move this business deal to make it private—just as it should be. Ella held back the desire to shuffle nervously and took stock of the situation. She knew that Adrian could protect himself should it come down to it and that he didn't want to be sheltered. But she had to protect him. Flicking her fan closed, she tapped him on the shoulder with it as she threaded her arm around Adrian, closing her hand on the other hand that was holding the fan, indicating to Lady Dorothy, a fellow Fan Society member, that she wanted him protected.

Adrian looked at Ella with a question in his eyes. He must have noticed her fan sign.

"Husband, please quickly finish with your business and hurry back. I wouldn't want to miss a dance with you." As Ella said that, she unwrapped her hand from his and tapped her face with the fan, indicating that he should be wary. Then she flicked her fan towards Lady Dorothy so he knew who was watching him.

"Of course. How could I leave my lovely wife all alone? See you soon, my dear." He gave her a kiss on the hand and followed Lord Greenwood with a glance back at Ella. Her emotions warred within her. Doubting herself, she worried about Adrian being away from her and wondering if she was wrong about Lord Greenwood. Adrian wishes to be useful and put himself in more dangerous situations, but he does not want to be over-protected. Knowing that her husband was capable, yet remembering his nearly dead body in her arms. A mistake that she promised herself she wouldn't allow to happen again.

As Adrian made his way to the meeting with Lord Greenwood, he was worried about his wife's reaction. She had signaled Dorothy to protect him and gave him a warning. And though she hid it quite well, her eyes held fear. Ever since her mother came back, she had fallen back to her old ways. It had taken him a while to relax his wife's overprotective sight when he first started helping her with her missions. But soon, they had a very trusting relationship. He would need to talk to her after this was all over. For now, he needed to focus on his part, and his wife sensed something about him. Adrian trusted her instincts. He would need to be careful.

"Please have a seat, Lord Cooper," Lord Greenwood said, motioning to a chair.

They had entered a private room that wasn't much bigger than an office. It only had a few chairs and a small table in the middle. He noticed that the thick wooden walls, like those in his father's office, made eavesdropping difficult. Thinking of his father's office touched a sore spot, but he couldn't have it messing up the mission. Giving a polite smile, Adrian took the offered chair.

"Lord Greenwood, you were speaking of a business proposition earlier? What was it that you had in mind?" After taking a few lessons from Ella, he found out that he was talented at playing various roles. Or at least he was not bad at it. It may have been due to being stuck in bed for most of his life and spending most of it daydreaming and reading a vast number of books. He had loved making up characters to fill the empty bedroom. Now that he was able to leave the house and learn of real life, he had learned how to tone down his overdramatic characters and put it into a more realistic setting. Settling into his role, he leaned back to relax. It wouldn't do him good to aggravate his wheeze. Anything could give the man seated across from him an advantage.

The man grinned, crossing his legs, "Do you know about racetracks?"

Adrian nodded, "I haven't been too many personally, but yes, I know of them. What does this have to do with the business deal?"

"A new Hippodrome in Kensington that specializes in horse races is opening up soon," Lord Greenwood said, opening a bottle of wine that had been left on the table. Pouring himself and Adrian a glass, he continued, "He built it to rival the current racetracks. It is a very promising venture, though we could always do with more funding."

Picking up the glass and swirling the wine around. Adrien didn't know what to make of the conversation other than the man wanted something from him. The character that Adrian was playing was greedy and impulsive enough to jump when Lord Greenwood said jump, but Adrian needed more, "Why would I care then? You have nothing to show yet."

Adrian added more snootiness than he had intended, but it got the point across. Why would a noble with new gains deal with a venture that isn't even out yet, even if it is promising?

"That is where you would be wrong," Lord Greenwood said, placing his glass on the table. "We are doing much more within the track other than racing, which has even higher gains, but it is only for the first few who help invest. We don't want a huge pot of investors. This is just for the VIPS."

Those words were like a siren song to a character like the one Adrian was portraying. It would show that he was special and also give him money. The one thing that would push him over the edge would be how much money.

"And?" Adrian questioned as he pulled out more information that would clinch the deal. "How much money could I earn from a new racetrack? Are you sure this venture would be lucrative? If it's not, I doubt a new racetrack would be enough to pique my interest."

Sitting back in his chair, Lord Greenwood smirked, "What if I can promise 100% return on investment? That is us being generous. I promise it will be a lucrative endeavor."

Thoughts flashed through Adrian's mind as he tried to puzzle out how they were planning on earning that much money against big-name racetracks. But his character wouldn't care about that. If he pushes further, he will make the man question him. And with Ella's warning, he knew that he wouldn't be able to handle it if things turned sideways. "How lucrative did you say the deal was?"

Lord Greenwood smiled as they started to bargain.

Chapter Five

As Adrian disappeared through the door, the worry for him didn't dissipate. Ella had been nauseous all day, and it was getting worse with the worry. Rubbing her fan, her thoughts frantically bounced about as she tried to think of what she should do when a voice said behind her. "Don't worry, your husband will be back soon."

Ella whirled around at the sound, flicking her fan open and holding it at the ready.

"You are a jumpy, little lady," the man said. Eyeing the newcomer, she held back her shock as she looked at the lean man with russet hair. He looked so much like Lord Greenwood, who had just left with her husband. Confusion filled her as she looked back at when her husband had just left.

Quickly falling back into character, Ella flicked her fan in front of her face to hide her features. "Who are you to scare me? What is your name?"

Giving her a bow, "Pardon my rudeness, I am Lord Fox."

The name resounded in her head as conflicting feelings arose. Fox was the name the soldier had given her when they sparred. Trying to keep her emotions from her face, she struggled with her confusion, "Are you related to Lord Greenwood?"

The man gave her a polite smile, "I apologize. I must have appeared as a doppelgänger. My name is Lord Fox. And yes, Lord Greenwood is my cousin. However, I have been told that we look the same. I also have another cousin."

"Does he look the same as you as well?" Ella said, recovering from her initial surprise and confusion. She could have kicked herself; it was a rookie mistake. She had been too busy worrying and not focusing on things around her.

He gave her an affable grin and shook his head. "No, Thomas looks nothing like his brother," he said, pointing to a rather plump, blond hair gentleman. Then he gestured to his slim figure and russet hair. "Many believe that we were switched at birth."

Could this be the man whom she had fought with? He was affable, but not as much of a jokester as the swordsman was. But then again, neither was Lord Greenwood. And if he was truly clever, why would he name himself Fox? Doubting her instincts and keeping a wary gaze on Lord Fox, she asked, "Do you believe it?"

"No, that would be an insult to his mother." He raised his brow at her, but his face held no anger as he continued, "But I do have an uncle who looks similar. Normally your words would have been considered rude, but considering I gave you quite the scare earlier and you didn't know, I will take it as an equal exchange. Besides, I'm a pacifist. I would rather not get into a fight with anyone. The only fighting I do is in a game of chess. Besides, I'm really more of an observer. I would rather not get caught up in things."

The person she fought was definitely not a pacifist, but then again, he could be lying. "What about your cousin? Is he a pacifist?"

The man held his hands up in surrender, "You wish me to tell on my cousin? I should not, but I will tell you that your husband will be out soon. My cousin is a proper businessman, or so he thinks."

That was a very telling conversation from someone saying that he didn't want to tell on his family. But of course, all of it could be lies. The oddities surrounding this family made her even more sure that something nefarious was happening. She needed to contact Helena, her friend from the Academy, sooner rather than later. "Thank you for telling me so. I was rather nervous about being away from my husband. I'm still rather new at these parties."

"Ah, it seems introductions are in store." His disarming smile was soft compared to his sharp chin that bordered on cheeky. But being the proper gentlemen that he was, stopped just shy of showing too much emotion. Flights of fancy were for commoners. He pointed to the group of ladies who were taking a break on the edge of the dance floor. "The lady with the black feathers in her hair is Lady Astor. She is stern but very kind to children. Over there, in the dress that is heavy from weight of too many jewels, is Lady Montague. She married into money and liked to show everyone that she had it. The lady that is standing over by the room where your husband is now is Lady Stratton."

He had been pointing to Dorothy, who had been doing as Ella had asked and was keeping an ear out for her husband. A warning rang through her. Wanting to distract him from her, Ella pointed to a Lady who seemed to stick to the walls and was doing her best to look like a statue hiding her presence. "Who is that lady over there?"

Lord Fox, who was wiping his wide forehead with his kerchief, turned to where she had been pointing. "That Lady? Oh, she is my cousin's adopted daughter, Agatha. Sorry, I meant Lady Greenwood. Forgive the slip of the tongue; she is family."

Ella raised a brow. Their ages seemed too close for her to be Lord Greenwood's adopted daughter.

Seeing her reaction, he said, "Let's just say there were some odd circumstances in how she came to the family."

Grabbing the nugget of information, she squirreled it away for further use. Just then, Adrian came out of the private room. Her shoulders relaxed as the tension she didn't know she had been holding released as he returned to the room safely. Turning to Lord Fox, she bowed her head good by as she ended the conversation, "Thank you for that insight. It was very helpful. Thank you for your help."

"It has been a pleasure meeting you, Lady Cooper. I will be seeing you again." He bowed his head in respect and then headed away to make his way to the outskirts of the room.

After that conversation, Ella still didn't know what to make of him, but for now, she couldn't do anything about it. Moving toward her husband, she went to see how his meeting went. She moved forward to claim her promised dance.

"My dear wife, would you have this dance?" Adrian asked, reminding her that he was once a prince.

With a smile of relief, she placed her hand in his as he led them to the dance floor.

"How was your business deal?" Ella asked as Adrian twirled her as they danced to the Waltz. The Whispers had done a good job growing the dance's popularity over the years, and Ella was glad for it. It was much easier to gain information from a slower, much more personal dance rather than the energetic group dance of the Quadrille. The only annoying thing was the width of the skirts, which made it feel like she was pushing him away. Maybe she could drop a suggestion to change the shape of the skirts.

Doing a good job of keeping in character, Adrian answered, "It was rather *informative*, but I felt as if he was hiding something. This isn't something that should be talked about while dancing."

He turned her around the dance floor, and Ella interpreted his answer as he gained information, but not a lot. They would need to discuss it at home.

It seemed as if Ella's worries were wrong. Remembering the blood that had run down Fox's face after she cut him with her fan, she tried to remember if either of them had a scar. She didn't notice it. If they did, she would have to keep a closer watch. She could have mistaken their faces for the flickering light and high emotions that were five years ago. For now, she needed to find a person who would be a candidate for a Ghost. The original intention of coming to the ball. And she knew just whom to talk to. Enjoying the rest of the dance, Ella soothed her nerves. When the song ended, Ella motioned for Adrian to mingle while Ella moved closer to where Lady Greenwood was. Might as well see if the information that Lord Fox had given her was correct.

Lady Montague was talking to a group of ladies in front of Lady Greenwood. Ella needed an excuse to talk to Lady Greenwood, and Lady Montague was just the person to talk to. As Lord Fox had said, her jewelry was excessive, with several rings on each finger and several layers of pearls to accent the weighty number of bejeweled feathers that were tucked into her updo. Despite their lack of a high title, Ella understood the Montagues to be of very old, albeit recently recovered, wealth. Now, they are one of the richest families in England from selling paintings.

"Of course, my husband will be taking me to Paris this year as a wedding present. He said he would be replacing these old things," Lady Montague said, gesturing to the pearls dripping from her ears.

A lady dressed in a blue out-of-season dress cooed at the appropriate times, ogling the jewelry the festooned Lady Montague. The twinkle of greed in her eyes as she smiled, endearing herself to the Lady.

"Lady North it is not appropriate to wear that much jewelry. Lady Montague should know better." The one Lord Fox said was Lady Astor to the lady who was ogling the dress. Her sharp features and modest clothing contrasted Lady Montague's lavish clothing.

"Just because it's become more popular to not show your wealth doesn't mean that you shouldn't." The blue-dressed lady North said to Lady Astor. It was about time for Ella to step in, but her entrance faltered as Lady North turned to Lady Montague, "Though wouldn't it be difficult when you went to Paris with your pregnancy?"

Icy fingers wrapped around her heart, clenching as it squeezed out all the air from her lungs. Her hands automatically started to reach toward her stomach, but she instead folded them. No. There was nothing she could do about her lost child. She had to stop thinking about it. She had to stop this conversation.

Panic pushed her forward as she rushed to change the topic. "Pardon me, Ladies, but you are the highlight of the party. I decided I should introduce myself." Ella managed to hold back her tears as she plastered on a polite smile to hide the emptiness she was feeling.

Lady Montague was rather ecstatic to introduce herself, "My name is Myrtle *Montague*. You have taste if you want to be introduced to me."

The woman made sure to emphasize her last name as she showed off her rings with a tilt of her hand.

"My name is Lady Astor, and over there is Lady North," Lady Astor said as she eyed Lady Montague. The pressed lips of Lady Aster showed her distaste for Lady Montague's failure of duty to introduce everyone. Turning to Ella, Lady Astor raised her brow at her to show that she had yet to introduce herself.

Quickly correcting herself, Ella said, "My name is Lady Cooper. It is a pleasure to meet you."

Though Ella had started off awkwardly, she could still salvage the conversation. The goal was to interest Lady Greenwood, and a fumbled greeting would cause interest. Ella opened her mouth to speak when another spoke first.

"You don't want to speak with her, Baroness Montague. She is not born of noble blood." A voice she hadn't heard in a long time appeared from behind her—her stepsister Euphemia. The stepsister who had tormented Ella during her younger years on behalf of her mother. After the sentencing of Ella's stepmother, they had separated. Since Effie had helped provide evidence against her mother, she had bargained and attained a deal that the king would support her as a minor noble. It was odd seeing her again. However, it was unsurprising that she knew of Ella's backstory. She always was a clever one, and Ella had been in society for a few years. She should have been more surprised that she hadn't seen her until now.

Feelings already in an uproar, she swallowed her mixed feelings that had arisen and acted as Ella's backstory dictated. "My father is a nobleman."

The icy stare of her stepsister, which Ella had seen directed at her for half of her life, rekindled feelings that she had thought long gone. What Effie said didn't help matters, either, "Your father just recently gained a title. One that came *after* you were born. And your husband is the one who gave you your title, not your father."

No, Ella couldn't allow herself to get riled. That was what caused so much pain to her loved ones before. With her emotions subdued, Ella prioritized what she needed to do. That was to find a reason to talk to Lady Greenwood. And considering how her eyes rested on Ella, she had accomplished it. Now it was time to leave the conversation. Allowing the pain she had been feeling and conflicting feelings well up, tears came to Ella's eyes as she cried out, "How could you say such things in front of company?"

Ella dashed away to the corner of the room. After letting out her tears for her performance, it was hard trying to shove them back in. Sorrow and guilt that had been eating at her since her mission five years ago tried to strangle her again. A fleeting thought of her lost child flitted through her, and she shied away from it. Swallowing the lump of feelings, Ella tried to ready herself to talk to Lady Greenwood.

She managed to hold them back precariously as Lady Greenwood came up, leaning against the wall beside her. "That is the way of nobility. You should realize this by now."

The way Lady Greenwood talked was nothing like what Ella had expected. Considering how she was constantly on the outskirts, Ella thought she was shy, but that didn't appear to be the case.

"It doesn't make it right. She humiliated me in front of everyone," Ella said with a sniffle. It was a real sniffle. It was difficult to press down her emotions.

Lady Greenwood replied, "The nobility are hypocrites. And by doing so, will destroy everyone." That came off stronger than Ella expected, but Ella understood those feelings. The conversation she just heard was still fresh in her mind. Since becoming a noble, she's realized that their image of purity is a complete fabrication. They carry dirty secrets and lie, just like everyone else. They just do it in a pretty dress. During her missions, she had seen the destruction they had caused around them, but she had to keep her head and had to work slowly to discreetly to put a stop to it.

"What can we do about it?" Regret for the things she failed to stop came to mind. Regret for the things she couldn't change.

"Nothing will change if we don't do anything about it." The anger in Lady Greenwoods's eyes was fierce. Ella was so used to the controlled feelings of the nobility. Taking a good look at Lady Greenwood, she almost reminded her of her mother. With red hair and blue eyes, she looked closer related to Nora than Ella did. They looked similar in age and could have been sisters, though she had less grey hair than her mother. Agatha's straight-back, and steady eyes that Ella so frequently saw in her mother showed her confidence. The only difference was that Lady Greenwood did something about what she believed. Or at least said something about it. Her mother always had a restrained air, just like the rest of the Fan Society. But they had been right in taking it slow back then.

Taking a deep breath to steady her emotions, Ella couldn't let her emotions run away from her again. "I could never do something like that. I'm not as brave as you are," Ella said as she softened her voice and put a quaver in it.

There was a pause. Glancing nervously at Lady Greenwood, she saw her giving Ella a pensive look. Catching Ella's gaze, Lady Greenwood was filled with a look of concern, and some of the confidence she had slipped away as she said, "I'm sorry, I just dropped my feelings on you. I just thought that you would understand. But it's hard under the pressures of your duties, isn't it?"

Ella nodded. It was hard to keep up with her duties, but it must be done. If she did it, then no one else would get hurt. And it was time to do hers, to gain a Ghost in the Greenwood household. Considering her odd impressions of the family. With Lady Greenwood's more outgoing nature and desire to create change, she would be the perfect candidate. She just needed to place the breadcrumbs, "It's just that I'm worried about my husband. He is getting into a business deal with Lord Greenwood, and I've heard he is into shady business. Maybe you could help? I don't know much about him."

The smile faltered on Lady Greenwood's face. If she was truly against the lies of the nobility. If Lord Greenwood was into the shady things that Ella thought he would, she would want to fight back. If not, she was in on it.

"Lord Greenwood, you say? Where did you hear that?" She said, her face turning ashen.

Ella shifted her gaze about as if checking to see if someone was listening, then leaned over and whispered to Lady Greenwood, "My maid heard another maid talk about some whisperings in the basement of the home. Then they kicked her out, saying that she was crazy. She said that she heard the voices talk about some deals being made, and it was in her Lord's voice. It could be nothing, but I don't want my husband dealing with a household like that."

"That sounds a bit like a ghost story," Lady Greenwood said, glancing in her adoptive father's direction, "but I will look into it. I happen to have connections to the Greenwood family."

Ella was unable to read her expression, but it did look like she would look into it. Putting on a look of relief, Ella smiled, "Really, you would do that for me? You have my gratitude. But I have just realized I don't know your name. My name is Lady Cooper. And yours?"

A nervous smile appeared on Lady Greenwood's face as she replied, "Call me Agatha. I know we haven't known each other for very long, but I feel a connection with you."

"Yes, of course . . . Agatha. After all, you are helping ease my sorrows. Call me Priscilla. We must meet again." Ella returned a smile. Now that they had exchanged personal names, they could be considered confidants. A hook had been set, and now she had to see what she reeled in. After her conversation with Agatha, she didn't want to think about her guilt or sorrow for the rest of the night. Instead, she tried to push down the emotions of the previous conversation that kept threatening to overwhelm her.

How could Lord Greenwood keep anything from me? After everything? That girl is very much like me when I was younger. Naïve, earnest, and with a desire to do what is right. She sounds like she wants to do what is right. Maybe I can help her on the right path. There is so much we can do together. I just need to figure out what to do with Lord Greenwood.

Journal of Agatha Greenwood
Year 1837

Chapter Six

The next day, Ella arose at home with Adrian already up. After making her way down for breakfast, she saw Adrian sitting there, waiting for her. It was unusual to see him up this early, as he was used to a noble sleep schedule. Because of this, he often woke up later than her. But seeing the look on his face, she knew why he was up early. Ella knew that look on his face, but she didn't want to have any of it. Feeling horrible that morning with nausea and a headache that she had thought gone away, had come back with a vengeance. That look in his eyes said they needed to have a talk, and they will, but not right now. At this moment, she couldn't handle it.

"Sorry, Adrian, I need to visit Helena as soon as possible," Ella said as she walked past the breakfast nook where Adrian had been sitting patiently.

Eyes bleary from waking earlier than usual, Adrian called to her, "At least have some breakfast."

Eyeing the light breakfast was set before him, the smell of eggs made her want to gag. "No thanks, dear."

Ella was about to flee the room when Adrian quickly stood and grabbed her by the hand. She refused to turn and look at him. Ella could already feel the weight of concern as he watched her. She knew that they did need to talk, but . . . not right now. The very thought of it made her nausea rise again, "I will when we get back, but I need to leave now."

Shaking off his hand, she was about to leave when he captured it again. This time, with a strong grip meant to hold someone and not hurt them. It was a hold that Ella had taught him. Though she knew how to escape, she stopped. The pain inside her grew as she waited for his words. The concern made her pain even more evident as he said, "We *need* to talk. Make sure to take Clementine with you, and please let Flora examine you or at least Abigail."

A lump of emotions caught in her throat, making it difficult to say anything. Instead, Ella just nodded as Adrian released her. She didn't look back as she headed to the front door, and Clementine came forward to help with her hat and a light jacket for the early morning chill.

"You should listen to him, you know," Clementine said, holding the door open.

Ella refrained from glaring at her friend. She was too tired and sick to tease her back. Her friend was only doing her best to help her. She sighed, holding back her urge to look back at Adrian, but she was afraid that all of her emotions would come tumbling out, and he had his own problems he was dealing with. Today, he was going to visit his father. And she had a friend to visit.

As they left the house, Clementine saw who their coachman was and smiled. Ella looked up at William. William, no longer the gangly boy she had known from the academy, had broad shoulders and straw-colored hair. She hadn't known what color of hair he had till recently, when his employer finally forced him to wash it daily since he had moved up from a stable boy to the coachman. Nobility tended to dislike their coachman, if they smelled of horse sweat and looked like he rolled around in the stables. Not that Ella put it past him to do. He tended to be hyper-focused on one thing, and one thing only: horses.

Ella watched as Clementine slipped a note to William, who rolled his eyes but did his job. As they entered the carriage, Ella gave Clementine a sidelong glance. Her friend refused to blush and sat across from Ella in smug defiance.

Trying to bring back levity from her dark mood, Ella raised her brow and said, "A letter to your man?"

"If you must know, yes, it is to Arthur." She pouted with her heart-shaped lips as she tucked her warm brown hair back behind her ear. "Yes, I have been using William to exchange letters with Arthur. And, yes, you can wipe that smug grin from off your face. He is courting me."

Ella felt a smile pull at her cheeks. She knew that they would do well together. During their final year at the Academy, she had met Arthur, who was now helping her Proctor with rooting out black-market slave traders.

"Oh? and how is that going?" Ella asked.

Exasperated, she threw up her hands, "If you must know, he is doing just fine. He writes me letters all the time and sends me flowers even when he is busy running errands for Baroness Smith. He is the perfect gentleman."

Wanting to tease her more, Ella pressed further, "And the family? What do they think of their son marrying a commoner?"

Snorting, Clementine said, "First, they have fallen from nobility, and they weren't nobles for long. Second, his family is happy that I helped rescue their daughter and kept their son out of danger. They adore me." Mentioning the time during her final year at the Academy when she stumbled upon Baroness Smith's mission.

"Good, they better treat you right." By that time, all the tension from that morning had relaxed, and an easy smile had made its home on her face.

"Glad to see my love life makes you smile." Clementine smiled back, all traces of her pout gone as a mischievous glint twinkled in her eyes. The tension eased, and they sat back in companionable silence as the carriage drove off toward the person who may have some answers.

Adrian was sitting next to his father once again, listening to his father's raspy breath. He had come to visit through the secret passages after Ella left to find information. He had hoped to speak to his father about Nora, maybe finding some way to help his wife, but his father had already been asleep. Fidgeting, Adrian's thoughts tumbled about as he tried to think of a way to help his wife with her troubles. Abigail sat next to him, sewing as she kept a keen eye on his father. When she was in charge of keeping watch over the king, Adrian could visit since she was one of the few to know his secret that he was the prince believed to have died five years ago. It was odd seeing his funeral, knowing very well that it could have actually been his funeral if Ella had been too late or if Mathew hadn't found them.

He shivered at the thought. Abigail stopped the stitch she was on. Standing, she grabbed a nearby blanket and covered Adrian. Adrian smiled at her, "Thank you, Abigail."

She nodded back as she picked up her sewing project again, "The king is not my only charge, Adrian."

A warmth filled him as he watched Abigail make practiced stitches in her cotton dress. Though Abigail wasn't that much older than he was, she had been like a mother to him, even though she had recently married Mathew, who was more like an older brother. But she had always been kind to him, pushing the boundaries of what connection a nurse should have in a familial way, giving him the attention he had needed in his darkest days. She also gave him admonishment when he was acting childish. Maybe she could help.

"Abigail?"

"Hmm-mm?" Abigail questioned with a raised brow, continuing her stitches as she fixed the hem of her summer dress.

"What would you do if you knew a person was hurting but didn't want to talk about it? But you knew that if they talked about it, they would feel better."

"Did you tell this person that you want to talk?" Abigail asked as she cut the thread while she finished stitching the hem and pulled out her basket of embroidery floss.

"Yes," Adrian sighed as he ran his fingers through his hair, "but she avoids it and runs away."

"Well, from what I understand, your wife has been through a lot. And most of it she had to deal with on her own. You might want to try talking to Clementine, but the best thing you can do is just be there for her."

Adrian tried unsuccessfully to hide his embarrassment from her. Abigail always knew so much. "How did you find out?"

She looked at Adrian's awestruck face. "Adrian, you didn't think I could guess you were talking about your wife? She is the only female you talk about other than me and Lady Nora."

"Oh, of course," Adrian's face flushed. Clearing his throat, he asked, "Since you know about the situation, what do you think I should do?"

Abigail had already placed her fabric in the wooden hoop, and she had started making a red flower with the embroidery floss. "That girl has been through a lot of emotional upheavals. Her family either died or went missing when she was a child. The one who was supposed to take care of her mistreated her. She then found a place at school."

She raised her brow, letting him know that she meant the Fan Society. It had been quite a shock to find out after he became a friend of the society, that she was a member of the Society herself as a Medic. However, looking back on things, it made a lot of sense.

Adrian nodded his understanding as she continued, "During that time, she found information on her mother, who most thought was dead, then ordered not to look into it and was sent on her mission."

"To marry me."

"Yes."

It still boggled his mind that Ella's mission was to marry him. Before their marriage, Ella explained everything and was surprised that he still wanted to marry her after knowing everything. Adrian could only chuckle at the thought. The heart wants what it wants. Thinking about what Abigail was saying, he picked up the rest, "Then after that and with how the riot went down, losing her child, then her mother coming back, it was a lot for her."

Abigail nodded, then bent down and picked up some green thread. "That girl has barely had enough time to try to deal with everything on her own, then to be forced to confront it all at once, it's overwhelming. I'm not surprised she is sick all the time."

"So, what can I do?" He couldn't change what had happened to her. He wished that he could alleviate some of her worries.

Putting her stitching down, Abigail leaned over, placing her hand on his knee, just as she had done when he was younger. "Keep doing what you are doing. Having someone by her side to listen when she is ready will be enough."

"Is there nothing else?" Adrian said, fingers clenching. Even though so much is going on, is just quietly watching all he can do?

"It will have to be enough." Abigail looked him in the eyes, holding them until he bowed his head in acknowledgment. Sighing, she gave him a final pat. She was about to start working on her stitching again when his father coughed. Abigail put down her sewing and helped his father take a sip of water that Adrian passed to her.

Adrian looked at his ailing father, who had once been a vibrant man. As he helped his father sit up, Adrian only had one thought. *Was waiting the only thing he could do?*

There have been comings and goings through the new hippodrome. The suspect has been meeting with several individuals from the slums. We think exchanges must have been made but are unable to find where they have been meeting. We need more individuals investigating this matter.

Officers Report
To the Metropolitan Police

Chapter Seven

They arrived at Helena's manor in the afternoon, and Ella was now sitting in Helena's parlor. It was bright and cheery, with yellow curtains and furniture made from a honey-colored wood. It matched her friend's personality. She had changed so much since her Academy days. The shy and withdrawn girl who rarely let out a smile was now replaced by a confident, exuberant, and chatty woman.

Breathlessly, Helena apologized for calling her out so far. "I know that you have been in London, but thank you for coming. I was going to lose my mind if I couldn't talk to everyone. It is beautiful in the countryside, but can be dreadfully boring. How is the city? Are the police force doing their job?"

Ella sat sipping her tea as her friend chatted away. During the Academy, one of her missions was to gain a Ghost. Helena's personal maid was Ella's target. Because of how she gained the Ghost, Helena has since become a friend of Priscilla Cook, her undercover name, which has since become her name again after the riot. However, her last name is now Cooper, her own family name. The King arranged for the prince to fake his death and take her family name so that when they married, Ella would be returned to her rightful place in the Cooper household.

"Speaking of the police force, has there been anything big going on?" Ella asked, managing to insert a question between her friend's whirlwind of words. Ella needed to guide Helena to the information she needed, or else Helena would go off on a tangent. Helena was married to the head of the Metropolitan Police Force, which had been recently founded. There was a lot that she picked up from her husband.

Tilting her head, Helena thought about it. "I'm not sure that I would call it dangerous, but the new hippodrome that just was built? The one with the racetrack. My husband has been getting reports about that place. And let me tell you about the mud that officers have tracked in after going to that place."

"What kind of reports?" Ella asked as she pressed for more information. She knew that Helena was massively interested in the police force and would note everything.

"Why do you want to know?" Helena asked, brows furrowed in concern. It was obvious that she was remembering their time in the Academy. According to her, Ella had put her reputation on the line to save her. This made her think that Ella was too altruistic for her own good.

Ella shrugged, hoping to ease her friend's discomfort. "I want to know what to watch out for."

"It is opening near Pottery Lane. Do you know what they call that place? Cut-throat lane. It's dangerous with scoundrels and murderers," Helena said, her voice a warning.

Nodding in acceptance, she took another sip of her tea, letting her friend know she wouldn't press for more information. She had hoped that it would put her friend's mind at ease.

It didn't.

"Don't even think about it. I know that you are all for putting yourself in danger to help others, but don't even think about going there. Do you hear me? Even though I'm eternally grateful for what you did at the Academy, you shouldn't do something like that again." Helena's face flushed at her last words. It was obvious that she was skeptical that Ella would just avoid the danger.

Guilt pricked at Ella, knowing that Helena felt responsible for Ella taking the fall for the rumors of her, even though they were rumors that Ella herself had started. Ella nodded, letting her friend admonish her about the dangers. As she did so, Ella could see her rubbing her stomach in a familiar way. And before Ella could stop herself, she asked, "Are you pregnant?"

Her friend stopped what she was saying as her face glowed with pride, "How did you guess? I was going to surprise you with it later, but that is the reason I was staying away from carriage rides. The vibrations of the carriage are a bit much. I still get queasy. Ella, are you alright?"

Ella's heart dropped. She didn't know what expression she had on at the moment, but she had to put a smile on for her friend. Ella was happy that her friend was pregnant, but that didn't stop the lump in her throat that had grown as she talked about being pregnant. Holding back the urge to touch her own stomach, she swallowed the lump of emotions as she replied, "I'm so happy for you. Congratulations."

"Thank you. Are you sure you are well? You turned as white as a sheet." Helena started to stand, but Ella waved her away.

"I am fine, just a little weary from my carriage ride," Ella said to stave off her friend's questions.

Nodding her head, she reached for the bell that was beside her. "Let us just make sure you are doing well. I did ask you to come here." Helena turned as Ada, her personal maid, entered. "Ahh, Ada, please call in the doctor to check on Priscilla?"

The older woman nodded and then headed out the door. Heart pounding, Ella said, "That isn't necessary. I just need a moment to calm down."

Helena smiled, "It's too late. I have already called the doctor. It is no trouble at all, besides I've already called for him. Ah, look, here he is now."

The doctor made his way in, flustered as he hurried to put his bag down in front of them. He was in his late forties, with his brown hair threaded with grey. Then he stood looking around and patted his clothes and turned as if to leave.

The maid who had led him in leaned over to him and said, "Your bag is on the table."

"Oh, that's right," He turned back around and made his way to Helena to check on her. His rumpled clothing and hair that was sticking out at odd angles made Ella raise her brow.

"I promise, he is the best. Though his quirks can leave much to be desired." Helena said to Ella. The doctor didn't comment on what she said about him. Either he didn't care, or he was too scatterbrained to have her words compute that they were talking about him.

"I'm well, but please, can you check on my friend here?" Helena said to the doctor, stopping his motion towards her. Then, turning to Ella, he said, "I promise, he is the best doctor around. Just let him check to see if something is wrong."

The doctor turned from Helena and then knelt in front of Ella, "Excuse me, my lady. May I take a look at you?"

Ella sighed as the doctor observed her. "Yes." She might as well get this over with, and if he did find nothing wrong with her, then she wouldn't have to talk to Flora.

Pulling out a notebook, he started asking her questions, "What is your age?"

Blushing, Ella said, "Twenty-five."

"Married?"

"Yes, but what are you . . ."

He cut Ella off by asking, "Have you been eating breakfast?"

"No . . . I feel too sick in the morning, but that is normal." Ella said, knowing what his line of thinking was. The blush deepened as he continued.

"What about headaches and your sense of smell?"

"I've been rather sensitive." Ella sighed if anything smells too strong, but that had been happening for a while now.

"Does it happen for specific foods? And are you craving specific foods?"

"I haven't been craving specific foods, but eggs and meat make me sick," Ella said, remembering the eggs that morning.

"Do you get tired more easily?"

"Yes, but I've been having late nights."

He muttered to himself as he wrote some things down. Then, reaching into his pocket, he pulled out a boiled egg. Not knowing why he had a boiled egg in his pocket, Ella gagged at the sudden smell. Helena did at the same time.

Tucking his egg back in his pocket, the doctor continued to write down everything that she had said, but didn't say anything about her condition. Ella shifted nervously in her chair. "Is there something wrong?"

"Humm?" The doctor looked up from his writing. "No, but I believe congratulations are in order. Based on my observations and your answers, I believe you are pregnant."

"Pregnant?" Emotions exploded within Ella. Joy at the thought of being pregnant turned to fear. Fear that she wasn't pregnant, fear that if she were, then she would lose it again.

Bile rose, and it wasn't from the egg. Ella's face felt numb from fear, and she didn't know what expression it held. She felt as if she was no longer connected to her body, as if she was watching everything from afar. Even as she spoke, it didn't quite feel as if it was coming from her, "Doctor, why do you believe I'm pregnant?"

"Humm?" He looked up from his pages. Then he tilted his head, answering. "I have worked with many pregnant women, and I know the signs of it. I have never been wrong about it. You can trust me when I say *you*, my lady, are pregnant."

"Thank you," Ella whispered as fear hung around her like a shroud. "I need to get home then."

Helena motioned the doctor to leave and walked over to Ella, taking Ella's hands in her own. "I'm so happy for you. If you ever need anything, please let me know. You are still looking a little pale. Are you sure you don't want to rest for a bit before you head home? You must take care, for the baby's sake."

Forcing a smile on her frozen lips, she pushed the words out, "I will be well once I go home and tell my husband the news."

Ella could hear the tension in her voice, but thankfully, Helena didn't mention it. Instead, she called for a servant to have her carriage readied. "Take care of yourself. If you can't come, don't push yourself, just send me a letter. And wishing you all the best."

"Thank you." The few moments she waited passed in a daze, and she continued as she made her way to her carriage.

Clementine helped her in, and as the carriage set off, Clementine asked, "Are you alright?"

Looking at her friend, Ella could see that Clementine had information that she needed to share that she had received from Ada, but she was concerned about her friend as well. Shoving her feelings aside for the moment, she ignored her friend's question. She feared if she said anything, then she would break down in tears. That wouldn't help the situation. Ignoring her friend's question, she instead asked, "What do you have for me?"

Raising her brow in concern, she reached out to Ella, but Ella flinched and pushed her away. "Just tell me the information, Clementine."

Clementine hesitated, then sighed. Reaching into the hidden pouch in her skirt, she pulled out a note. "Ada received this when she was in London last week. The person said it was for you."

Holding her hand out, Clementine passed the note to Ella. However, note was rather generous word for the dingy scrap of paper. It smelled horrible as well, causing Ella to gag again. Doing her best not to breathe in the stench, Ella opened the crumpled piece of paper that looked as if it had been torn from a newspaper. Inside was written with charcoal words, *claiming the favor, 3 PM Potters Lane.*

Shock ran through Ella. She had thought that he had forgotten about it, but she should have known better. A man like that would always take what he is owed.

"Is it from who I think it is?" Clementine asked.

Ella nodded, "Viscount, Edmund."

The name rang hollowly in the enclosed carriage. That name held a deep weight for Ella. He was the one who sold her mother to the slave trader. He was the one who was working for the Duchess's financier to poison Adrian. He also was a major influence in the events surrounding the riots. Between the news of her pregnancy and Viscount Edmund, her hand fluttered to her mouth as she called for the carriage to stop.

Fumbling with the door, she hopped out before the carriage came to a complete stop. In a rush, she hurried to a nearby tree and let out the contents of her stomach. Soon, she felt Clementine's hand on her back as Ella let out another round for her practically empty stomach. Once she was done, Clementine held out a handkerchief for her and helped her back to the carriage.

Clementine watched Ella with a concerned look, pressing her lips together. She didn't say anything until the carriage started moving. After they started moving, Clementine opened her mouth to speak, causing Ella to brace herself for the coming question. Yet words different from what she was expecting came from Clementine's mouth. "How dare they move so fast. They are lucky that we were still on the outskirts of the city, or else people would have seen. They better keep it at a moderate pace next time. Don't worry, Ella, everything will be taken care of. You can make it through this wild ride."

Ella knew that those last lines had nothing to do with the carriage and everything to do with the situation. Ella nodded in gratitude to Clementine, who didn't push because if she did, Ella didn't know what would happen. Looking out the window, she didn't say anything as the nasty taste stayed in her mouth, and emotions churned within her like the churning of her stomach.

Chapter Eight

Adrian arrived home to Mathew, hurrying him to the secret door. They heard raised voices through the floorboards as his wife shouted from below. Looking at Mathew with a raised brow, he questioned him.

Throwing his hands up in defense, Mathew shook his head, "I am keeping myself out of it."

Adrian sighed, then made his way down the secret staircase. As he made his way down, he could now clearly hear what his wife was saying.

"...I don't need your help with this. I will take care of my own mistakes." Ella shouted, face flushed as Lady Nora sat exasperated across from her. Adrian had never heard his wife shout like this before. She has always been passionate when she spoke, but never this angry.

Lady Nora sighed, holding her hand to her forehead, "How could you make a promise for a favor from a notorious man? If you are dealing with such people, then you promise monetary things, so you can't be caught in such a thing as you are dealing with now. Did you learn nothing?"

Ella clenched her teeth at Lady Nora's words. Taking a deep breath, she calmed down enough to push out the words in a quieter tone, "Mother, you don't understand. I needed this information to help someone. That is why I made the deal."

"No one is important enough to put the safety of the Fan Society member at risk." Lady Nora said.

"But that . . ."

Cutting her off before Ella could finish, Nora said, "There are no buts. This is for the good of the Fan Society. There are rules for situations such as these, so there wouldn't be mistakes." She sighed, then pressed her fingers on the bridge of her nose. "I should go with you to make sure you don't get into any more trouble."

Not knowing what was going on, he had been hesitant to interrupt, but this argument had gone on for long enough. Adrian was about to step in when Ella spoke up. "No. I am the one in charge here. You are my assistant. You will not go with me. And since you are such a stickler about the rules, you must abide by what I say."

She whirled around, freezing when she saw Adrian.

Adrian saw tears starting to form and threatening to fall. Staring at him in shock, she covered her face and ran out of the room.

"Sorry you had to hear that, Adrian." Lady Nora said as she slumped forward and held her head in her hands. "Yet again, you are stuck in our family business."

Eyeing the way Ella left, he desperately wanted to run after her, but he knew she needed a little time to get control of herself. She wouldn't speak to him if she was in tears. However, he could talk to Nora at this moment.

Walking forward, he said, "You are my mother-in-law, and your daughter is my wife. I *am* your family."

"You know I meant the Fan Society." She gave him a stern look as he came forward and refilled her cup of tea.

"Which I am also a part of, whether you like it or not." He sat down across from her, "Now, what happened?"

"My daughter made a deal with someone who is now calling in the favor and asking her to meet in an unsavory part of town."

Starting to understand the situation, he asked, "Did she tell you who it was?"

Taking a sip of the tea Adrian had poured, she set it back down on the table, "No, even though I asked her multiple times. She would only say that it happened five years ago, and it was the reason that she had been demoted to support." She eyed Adrian. "You know why she didn't say anything, don't you?"

If it was whom he thought it was, Adrian knew very well why Ella didn't tell her who it was. She was trying to keep her mother from any grief and heartache, but Adrian knew full well that when she found out, it would be even worse for her. Knowing how stubborn his wife was, she would never tell Lady Nora, but this needed to stop. "This is going to be difficult to say."

Furrowing her brow, Lady Nora sat up a little straighter, "Go on."

"Five years ago, Ella went against orders and spent most of her time finding information on you. She finally tracked down information on where you had been sold to. But to get the information, she had to make a deal. The only thing he wanted in return was a favor. A favor that would not go against the Fan Society sensibilities."

Lady Nora sat in stunned silence, hand covering her mouth. Then she gasped, "The person she is going to meet must be Viscount Edmund."

He should have known it wouldn't take much for her to understand the situation. Viscount Edmund was the one who planned her capture, and sold her on the black market, and caused her to live a miserable life for years. Adrian nodded, confirming Lady Nora's suspicion. Adrian studied her reaction to see if she could handle the horror of the information that she had just received. The strong emotions played across her face, letting Adrian read them with ease. Shock filled her eyes first as her suspicions proved accurate, then turned to revulsion at who Ella was to meet. Then she became aghast as she realized she had just told her daughter that she shouldn't have made a deal with them. A deal that saved her from the continued life of pain. A tear leaked out of her eye as she realized that her daughter was trying to protect her from meeting with him. Any anger or irritation she had once had vanished.

Adrian smiled. It was the right decision to tell her. Leaning forward closer to her, he said, "Lady Nora, you are her mother. And everything she has done was for you. If you look, you can see how much you influence her. You should talk to her and maybe not be as protective of her. She does know how to do her job. But first, I need to speak to her."

Then he stood to leave her to her thoughts.

"Thank you, Your Highness." Lady Nora said, standing and giving him a curtsy as if he were the crown prince. Normally, something like this would bother Adrian, but he could see hers as a true form of gratitude.

Adrian bowed back and then turned to the stairs. It was time to talk to his wife.

Ella sat in her room, furious at herself for losing control of her emotions but too tired to care anymore. She didn't know how long she was in her room staring out the window when a knock came at the door. Ella didn't answer, and a few seconds later, the door opened. Not acknowledging the person who entered without permission, Ella continued to stare out the window at the people passing outside.

"Are you ready to talk now?" Clementine asked, standing beside her. Ella knew her friend was only looking out for her, but nausea from her emotions, as well as what may be a pregnancy, made her afraid if she opened her mouth, it would all rush out like a dam breaking.

When Ella didn't answer, Clementine continued, "I know that you have a lot of emotions going on right now, but we need to know what we are going to do about Viscount Edmund. I trust you, Ella."

But she couldn't talk to her friend. How could she talk to her about the crushing weight of despair she felt? The fear? All of her past mistakes were being thrown back at her, and now she couldn't make a decision. She couldn't talk to Clementine about that. Clementine may be a friend, but she also relied on Ella's confidence in her decision-making. If Ella turned to look at her, she would be forced to look at the reminder of what bad decision-making could cost.

Clementine sighed, then said, "If you are not going to talk to me, then you need to talk to him."

Ella turned around, startled as she hadn't realized that Clementine had left the door open, leaving it to reveal that Adrian had been standing there.

Clementine stood up to leave.

Ella reached out to stop her.

"I gave you opportunities to talk to me," Clementine said firmly, showing that she was serious. "My job is to make sure you can do what needs to get done. And right now, you can't. *Talk* to Adrian."

Clementine gave her a squeeze on the shoulders and then turned to Adrian, saying, "I'm leaving her to you."

After Clementine left, Adrian came in and sat on the bed next to the chair that Ella had dragged across the floor to sit by the window. Ella hadn't wanted to talk to Clementine, but she certainly didn't want to talk to Adrian. His face was too full of concern and love. He was always one to wear his heart on his sleeve, and that was the thing she loved about him. But she couldn't handle it right now. He had been going through so much recently that she didn't want to dump it on him, even though she yearned to. She was afraid of giving voice to the dark thought that she had avoided for so long.

The silence grew too much for Adrian as he shifted, and his voice came out with an extra wheeze to it that made Ella wince, "Ella, I don't know what to do for you. I just want to say you are allowed to cry. Don't hold yourself on my account."

The break in his voice made a tear roll down her face. Ella struggled against the emotions that clogged her throat; she spoke her dark thoughts. "It's my fault."

"What?" Adrian asked, seeming almost surprised that she spoke. "What's your fault?"

"Everything. It's all my fault." The feelings that she had been suppressing and the dark thought that haunted her in its insanity. "I put you in danger, and it's karma. That is why we can't have a child. It's my fault.

There is no way I can be pregnant. And if I get pregnant again, I will lose it as punishment."

Ella knew that it was insanity to think that it was her fault that they lost the child. It was something that happens sometimes. Yet even with all the time they spent together, they still hadn't gotten pregnant. And she could only feel like it was because she caused harm to the ones she cared about. Now, she was cursed to never have her own child. It seemed inevitable that as soon as she was told that she was pregnant, her dark past would come to haunt her. The dark past would not only harm her, but her mother. Not to mention the slow death of Adrian's father. What would happen next? Or, in the meeting with the Viscount, would Clementine be injured? While she was away, would Adrian get the crushing news that his father had died? Or would her child . . .? She couldn't complete the thought.

As the darkness started to consume her, Adrian crushed her against him. In an instant, her face soaked his shirt as she clung to him. She hadn't even realized she was crying. The words that had been holding back the flood burst. Now that the dam had been broken, the waters couldn't be stopped until they ran out.

She didn't know how long she sat there in Adrian's arms as he stroked her hair, crooning softly to her. Ella had known that her dark thoughts were nothing but an impossible fear, but it had consumed her, only getting worse as time went by. As if a hand was squeezing her, and with each new difficult situation, it tightened its grip, making it impossible to leave as her own emotions slowly suffocated her. The more she tried to get out of it, the further she fell. She spent most of her time trying to show her strength and dependability, knowing that it was only a house of cards, easily collapsed with a puff of air. Her pain, hidden behind a paper door, with its darkness spread behind it, is never-ending.

But even though it felt as if the pain was eternal, eventually, the flood of tears did lessen, and her grip relaxed its death hold, letting the blood return to her fingers. The suffocating darkness that held in its crushing weight now seemed so unimportant. Her knot of emotions had left a blush that spread across her cheeks. She tried to wipe away the tears that had now completely soaked his shirt and flatten the wrinkles that had marked where she gripped his clothes.

"I'm sorry for this shameful display of emotion, especially after everything you have been going through." Embarrassment from the flood of tears made it so Ella hadn't been able to look him in the eye. She wanted to avoid looking at him as her fear came creeping back, held on by a final tendril. What would Adrian think? Would he feel disgusted at the crazy notion she had? Would he feel sorrow that she had kept this in for so long? Or would it be weariness now that he now had to deal with an emotional woman?

He didn't answer right away, and nerves got the better of her. Looking up into his eyes, the emotion that was there was nothing like what she had imagined. Instead, his eyes were full of love. Her eyes started to water again, as she felt wonder how such an amazing man had come to love her.

After he looked Ella in the eyes, he quickly pulled out his handkerchief, which had somehow managed not to get soaked during her emotional upheaval, and passed it to her. She turned to blow her nose that had been running while Adrian pointedly looked away from her. Instead of feeling embarrassed like she would normally be, his presence near her helped stabilize her frenzied emotions as she regained control of herself. The last vestiges of her dark emotions fleeing from Adrian's love for her. A watery smile grew as emotions threatened to overwhelm her again, except this time of warmth.

But it was time to get off this emotional ride. Clearing her throat, she whispered, "Thank you."

Adrian gave her a gentle smile, "Of course. Thank you for telling me what was wrong. I never thought that . . ."

Pressing her hand against his lips, Ella cut him off, "It was an idiotic notion. I know."

Giving her that charming grin of his, he pulled her hand away so he could speak. "I was a horrible thought that festered, making all of your other problems much more difficult to handle."

"How did you know?" Ella asked. In all the time that she had known him, he never once showed that he was having difficulties. Even though she knew that his life had drastically changed since he had met her.

He looked down at her hand that was still clenched in his, "You know that I was deathly ill as a child."

Ella nodded. Because Adrian had been born early, he had many lung issues, and they had grown worse since the fire. Even now, she could still hear a rasp in his voice.

"Though the doctors had always tried to make sure I couldn't hear their concerns, there were times I heard their worries that I would never wake up. After that, I would have nightmares that death would come for me in the night."

Old sorrow filled his face as dark memories resurfaced. Ella wanted to brush away the weighty emotions that had appeared on his face, as he had done for her. But his hand on hers held her back as he continued. "Books were my constant companion at that time. I had read a fairytale about a young boy who had a sick sister. To save his sister, he went on a journey to find a fairy to heal his sister's illness. He ended up finding the fairy and gained a boon from her. He used his boon to ask for a way to heal his sister, the fairy said to keep sage, thyme, and lavender by the bed, and it will scare away death. After reading that story, I would constantly have those herbs by my bed to keep death away from me. I knew it wasn't real, but it kept my dark thoughts away."

"I knew that you had been sick, but I never knew you had nightmares," Ella said, feeling the weight of his emotions. His story brought to mind her own nightmare she had about Adrian, Clementine, and her mother dying as they told her that she failed to reach them in time. One that she still had. "But I don't see you doing that now. How did you get over it?"

The weight went away as if it had never been as he looked her in the eyes. "Because I married a fairy. I didn't need a boon anymore."

A blush came back in a flash as Ella turned away from her husband and wondered how he could say such things with a straight face. But then again, he had always been that way. She couldn't keep back the last piece of information from him. He deserved to know. Taking a deep breath, she forced the words through her lips, "I may be pregnant."

His eyes widened in surprise, then turned to a wide smile, until worry eked across his face once again, "Will you be well to do the meeting? I wouldn't want to. . . "

His words faded away, not wanting to hurt Ella to mention his worry about losing the child again. But there wasn't much Ella could do about the situation. "I have to go. It was a promise. If others found out that a Fan Society member broke a deal, there would be more problems. Besides, he promised that he wouldn't make me do anything that would break my morals. I will do everything to make sure I stay safe."

Ella pressed her hand against her stomach, trying to keep her hands from shaking as her fears returned, threatening to overcome her again. Adrian gripped her hand more tightly, reminding her that he was there, and for the first time in a while, the dark emotions didn't overwhelm her and retreated back from where they came.

"I will come back as soon as possible," Ella said, swearing and ingraining that promise within her. The worry in Adrian's eyes failed to disappear, but he nodded his head in understanding.

Taking a deep breath, she stood on shaky feet to get ready for the mission. As she was about to head out the door to call for Clementine, Adrian grabbed her arm and said, "Please come back safe. I don't know what I would do without you, my love."

Warmth flooded her. She turned back and gave him a kiss on the forehead. "You would thrive like you always do. But I will make it back safe."

With one last smile, she turned away to get ready for a meeting with the head of the black market.

I will take the mission that you asked of me. It is time to right the wrongs of the past. We must not let what happened before happen again, and we must not let the mistake fester. We will find Justice.

To codename: Rose

Assumed to be Madame Briar

From Codename: Phoenix

Chapter Nine

Ella steadied her nerves as they rode in the carriage to the meeting place. The regurgitation of emotions should have made her unbalanced, but she felt relieved. The weight of her emotions that she had been carrying around had been lifted. All would be right in the world except for the child growing inside her. She pressed her hand against her belly as a worried smile grew on her lips. She had been reluctant to admit that she was pregnant because, if she had, then her fears would have increased tenfold. But now, with the release of her fears, she could handle the knowledge that she was indeed pregnant. Now, she just had to make it through this meeting without anything happening to her or her baby.

Clementine, who was sitting across from her, furrowed her brow. Glancing from Ella's hand resting on her stomach to Ella's worried face, she asked, "I know that this is a hard thing to discuss, but . . ." She hesitated.

Not wanting to cause her friend any more torment, Ella answered, "Yes, I'm pregnant."

Her friend's brow furrowed even deeper as she instantly understood the implications of what could happen. But after taking a moment, her worried look turned to one of determination. "What do you need me to do?"

Warmth bloomed within her at Clementine's trust in her. The trust that had allowed her to get injured. Ella's eyes drifted towards Clementine's hidden scar, and worry threatened to return. She wouldn't allow it to return, but she couldn't do what she had done before. She would not allow the darkness to take over her again.

"Clementine, even after putting you in harm's way, why do you still trust me?" Ella asked. Instead of the dark thoughts and guilt assaulting her like they normally would, Ella felt genuine curiosity. Clementine would have had every right to be upset with her. During the time of the riot, she had become overly focused on her mother, which caused Clementine, Harriette, and Adrian to get seriously injured. They could have died. Yet, through all of that, Clementine stayed by her side. All three of them did.

Sitting back as far as the small carriage would allow her, Clementine sighed. "I was wondering what has been going through your mind. Do you really not know?"

Ella kept her gaze on Clementine, unflinching. She had always put off asking Clementine the question for fear of what the answer would bring. But no more.

Clementine sighed again, "Ella, we *both* trained to be part of the Fan Society. I knew it was a dangerous position when I started training for it. I also knew about your desire to find your mother and what it meant to you. Do you really think I would be upset with *you* for something I *knew* could happen? If anything, *you* should be upset at me for getting caught in that trap in the first place. Besides, I could have told the Fan Society what was going on, but I didn't."

"Oh," Ella had never thought of it from that perspective. Not that it changed any of the guilt for her friend's condition because of her actions, but it did give her insight.

"You trusted me," Clementine said, "and I wouldn't have it any other way. Besides, I would have despised it if you tried to be overprotective of me."

The last sentence was said with a twitch of the lips, showing Ella that she was teasing her. What Clementine said reminded her of what she hated when working with her mother. Her mother was always second-guessing her work and hovering like Ella was still a child, and Ella knew just how much she hated that. Clementine must be the same.

Pushing aside her desire to be tentative and protective of Clementine, Ella said, "Do you think you can keep watch for outside dangers?"

Clementine gave her a sidelong glance and a pout, "Did you really just ask that of me? Whom do you think you are talking to?"

"Oh, I forgot I was speaking to the magnanimous Clementine," Ella said with a laugh. It was the first real laugh that she had since the emotional ride she had previously.

"That's right, and don't you forget it!" Clementine replied with a cheeky grin. But then, in a more serious tone, asked, "What about the Viscount? Will you be all right?"

Ella nodded, "Viscount Edmund is a businessman. If he wants his favor, he will have to keep me alive. But it would have been better if we had asked for help ahead of time. I don't want you to be alone this time around."

"Already done. Cloak will be helping us."

"Thank you," Ella said, gratitude filling her words after receiving the note, and with all the emotional turmoil, she hadn't prepared for the meeting as well as she should have. Clementine knew that and took care of everything just as an Assistant should. Just as a friend does.

Brushing her skirts, Clementine's face beamed, "As I said before, who do you think you are talking to?"

"The best Assistant to have ever roamed the lands," Ella said with a chuckle and a smile. Thankful that Clementine had helped prevent a disastrous outcome, she gripped her fan. Rubbing her finger over the lace that had been woven to have the Fan Society emblem on it, Ella looked out the carriage as they drove through a dirtier part of town with people who were far too skinny, and their faces covered with coal dust. Placing her hand protectively over her belly, she prayed that the meeting would go as planned.

They exited the carriage several blocks away from the meeting place. A hooded woman was already there. She was a graduate of the academy, and Ella only knew her by her codename Cloak. They had once worked together on a mission while Ella had been at the academy. She was a matronly woman that had commonplace features, with her hair tucked up under a bonnet, and well-worn clothes, the hem of her skirts stained from tromping through the muddy streets. Her wrinkles of age showed even more, with dust filling the crevices, making her look older than her thirty years.

"Cinders, it's good to see my daughter again," Cloak said as they made their way toward her.

Ella smiled, happy that Cloak had remembered that Ella had played the part of her daughter years ago.

"It is good to have your help, mother," Ella said, playing along. She had to breathe shallowly, or the stench would make her nausea worse. Pulling her cloak around her tighter, she glanced around, "Are there any intruders to our meeting?"

"No, but there are a lot of hiding places around these parts."

Nodding, Ella steeled herself for her meeting, keeping a wary eye on the shadows. Swallowing to keep the contents of her stomach where they were supposed to be, she pulled her bonnet down to cover her face more, but it would only work for a glance. She was as out of place as a peacock in a pigeon's nest. Even though she had on commoners' clothes and had brushed dirt on her cheeks, it did little to hide that she had been living as nobility for a while. Anyone who had lived in this area for a long time would know she didn't belong. Good thing they tended not to ask questions.

"Clementine, help Cloak with lookout. Find me if anything seems wrong."

Clementine nodded, then pressed a small bag into Ella's hand, and said, "Just in case. Throw it behind you, and it should hold off pursuers. Stay safe, Ella."

Nodding to both Cloak and Clementine, she showed that she was ready. They each took to a different side of the street as Ella made her way into Asher St. It lived up to its name, as all the buildings were covered with soot and ash that had fallen from the nearby factory. The buildings, with a porous stone, absorbed all the dirt, making it look like she was in a cave. Even the ground, though it had been paved, was now so full of soot that had never washed away that it was like walking on a dirt path. Even though the sun was still out, the narrow street made it so the sun couldn't reach the street. Ella wondered if the sunlight had ever had a chance to reach the ground, even in the afternoon. She made her way down the street. Since there was no specific address, she walked slowly so that no one could sneak up on her.

Halfway down the street, she saw movement from the corner of her eye. A grungy figure made his way toward her. It wasn't until he was closer to her that she was able to recognize the figure on the gloomy road. He no longer wore his expensive suits and instead wore the rags that were common on this side of the city. Unlike the clothes that Ella was wearing as a disguise, it looked as if he had been wearing his for some time. His usually clean-shaven face was now sporting a wild, unkempt beard. The only recognizable thing was the scar that he had running from brow to cheek and a confident expression. Ella had to refrain from covering her stomach protectively. She wouldn't want him to have any information to hold over her.

"You came." His voice was the same smooth tone, though Ella detected undertones of fear as he shifted from foot to foot and flinched when a bird took off near him. Maybe he wasn't as confident as he seemed.

What had happened to him? After the riot five years ago, he had disappeared. Ella and the Society thought he had gone to the ground, keeping low so that he wouldn't be connected to the mess since it was a well-known secret that he was involved in the black market. Yet, from how he looked, it was more like he was living underground if the grime covering his clothes and skin was any indication.

Even dressed as he was, she couldn't keep her anger from her voice as she said, "What is it that you want, Viscount Ed-"

He cut her off, "Don't say my name."

He glanced around warily, as if someone was haunting him. The Viscount that she knew wasn't one to be scared like this. He could be putting on an act, but the shaking of his fingers didn't look fake. It seems his confidence was a farce. But even though they just started the conversation, the anger burned brighter within her as she remembered that it was his men who kidnapped Clementine and Harriett. Then, her thoughts fluttered to her child. She couldn't let her feelings get the better of her. She had her child to protect. Whatever it was that was scaring him was something she needed to watch out for, even though she was angry at him. "What have you called me for?"

Edmund reached for her, and in an instant, Ella smacked his hand out of the way and held her fan at the ready.

Holding his hands up in surrender, he shifted from side to side as he watched the shadows, "I'm not trying anything. But let us move out of the open. Your fan is a dead giveaway that you are not meant to be here."

Ella glanced at her clean white fan, and though she agreed with his sentiment, she didn't trust him. Her fan stayed where it was.

"You have no idea of what is going on," He paused as he looked behind her, "We need to get out of here right now."

The fear in his eye seemed real enough, and though she hated the man, he had told the truth. But was he still the same man that he was when she last met him? "Why should I trust you?"

Holding his hands out in surrender, he looked ready to bolt as he glanced behind her again. Then, for the first time in their conversation, he looked her in the eyes, "I'm a hunted man, and you are the only one who can save me. Besides, there is a man at the end of the street that I haven't seen before."

He could be lying to her, but if he wasn't, then that means the man at the end of the street was skilled enough to get past Clementine and Cloak. But no matter how he tried to look calm and collected, he was doing a very poor job of it.

"Please."

It was that word of his that made her truly trust him. A man as proud as him would never say please.

But that still didn't change that she had to protect her child. She couldn't be pushed along by his wiles. She stood her ground and said, "If so, then why should I go with you? It will only make me the next one he hunts down. I should just leave right now."

Any pretense that he had had about being calm fell away as he said, "These are the people who hired me to start a riot. Do you really think that you could get away with talking to me and live? Besides, you still owe me a favor."

Bile rose as she realized that he had caught her quite neatly in his trap. Now, if she were going to get out of this situation, she had to help him. Struggling to hold onto her worries, she remembered what Clementine had said. She wouldn't do this alone, not again. "Do you have a place where we can go?"

"Yes."

"How close is he behind me?" Ella asked. She had to time it right if she was going to get out of this alive.

Shifting his eyes to look behind her, he said, "Only a few feet."

Ella could tell that the only thing keeping him from bolting was that he needed Ella's help. Lowering her voice, she asked, "Where is your hiding place?"

"Down this alleyway to the north."

"Then on my signal." He nodded, but obeyed as Ella listened for the hunter. No matter how trained he was, he would be unable to be quiet in mud, so all Ella had to do was listen as the footsteps squelched closer. When he was close enough to grab her, Ella whirled around and screamed, "What are you doing to a lady?"

She caught a glimpse of the hunter. He had the eyes of a killer, though they were now widened in surprise. Taking her chance, she threw the bag that Clementine had given her between them. A massive cloud of powder grew between them, giving them a chance to run away. She could hear two sets of footsteps hurrying down the alleyway.

A sense of relief filled her as she knew that Clementine and Cloak had heard her. But it wasn't over yet, and the hunter was still close. Once they get away, she would be alone with the man who had sold her mother as a slave on the black market.

I have my answer. I will meet with you to figure out our next plan of action. Help is desired; I do not wish for Cinders to be a part of this.

To codename: Rose
From codename: Phoenix

Chapter Ten

Adrian had been pacing the room since Ella had left for the meeting. He couldn't help but worry about her. The news still shocked him, which made his emotions change from joy to worry. Was she pregnant? But what if she falls into danger? She was strong; she could handle it. But what if her emotional breakdown hampered her in some way? She could handle the situations; she was good at that. But what if she lost their child again? Would she still be alright?

He could feel his chest tighten from his walking and stress, and his wheezing was annoying. Stopping mid-pace, he calmed his emotions. Why was he just standing around? He had promised that he would help her and he wouldn't let her down. He just had to do what he could, and the pacing wasn't going to solve anything.

"Mathew," he called, and within moments, his friend's head popped in.

"Yes, sir? What do you need?"

Adrian was already pulling out a fresh shirt and jacket, and upon seeing this, Mathew hurried over to help him change, not commenting on the drying tearstains that marked his clothes. But Adrian shooed him away,

"I need you to send a letter to Lord Greenwood that I will be taking his proposal as long as I can see the goods."

"Yes sir," Mathew said, giving him a worried look, but left to comply.

Buttoning his shirt gave him time to think of a plan, but to be honest, it wasn't much of one. But there was one person he could ask. After he finished getting ready, he headed out to the sitting room, finding Lady Nora looking out the window.

"Lady Nora, may I have a moment of your time?" Adrian asked when she turned in his direction.

"I think since our last conversation, you have earned the right to call me mother. What do you need?" It had only been a few hours, but something had shifted in her view of him. Instead of the disapproving looks he had received since the beginning, she now had a warm countenance when she saw him.

Warmth ran through him. She had finally approved of him, but now was not the time to revel in it. "I was hoping to have a conversation away from prying eyes."

He motioned to the hidden room, and Nora raised her brow inquisitively, but let him lead her down to the stairs. Henrietta appeared as they headed down and stood guard. Adrian hadn't even realized she was there. Ella had trained her well.

When they arrived in the room, Adrian turned to talk to her, but Nora turned and motioned to the chairs, "Even in a rush, we cannot act like savages. If it is important, it will take more than a few seconds to speak of it. Come. Sit."

Adrian acknowledged her insight and did as she asked. After getting settled, he spoke. "Lady Nora -"

"Mother."

"Yes... Mother." Adrian smiled, then clasped his hands together, and looked her in the eyes. "Ella is currently in danger. I cannot stand by and wait for everything. I am going to help her, but I need your advice."

Folding her hand in her lap, she asked, "What do you need my advice on?"

She didn't give anything away about her feelings, but Adrian had watched her and knew that she was testing him.

Adrian was not as good with his wordplay as Lady Nora, so the only thing that he could give her was the truth, "I cannot just stand by and wait for Ella to get the information. I need to help. I have trained to do my part in this, and I will not leave everything up to her. I am planning to visit Lord Greenwood, and I want to get information from him, but I need help. I am weak and naïve and have had little training. What do I need to do?"

He waited with bated breath. Adrian knew he wanted to help Ella, but didn't want to make things worse for her, and the only person who could help with that would be Lady Nora. The same person who despised Adrian even knowing about the Fan Society, let alone participating. He had hoped that his breathing didn't sound as wheezy as he thought it did as Adrian struggled to control it. He didn't know if he could do this. But he had to try.

Lady Nora held his eyes in her own, not saying a word as she studied him. Tension grew as he tried not to twitch as the moment stretched on to minutes. And yet they sat there in silence.

"Henrietta? I need your help," Lady Nora called after what could only have been a short time, yet felt like a lifetime.

Giving a sigh of relief, he slumped in the chair.

"If that is all it takes to give you a sense of relief, I fear for your success in your mission," Lady Nora said with a raise of her brow. Then, seeing Henrietta making her way down the stairs, she motioned her over, "Come here, dear."

Adrian watched as Henrietta made her way through the room. He remembered when he first met her. A gangly waif of a girl who had slipped him Ella's message. Their next encounter was in a burning church, where she was injured and rioters were banging on the door. He had helped her escape, but it had left him in a deadly situation. If Ella hadn't arrived, he would have died. The sense of helplessness in that memory and the fear that this would be the same situation was difficult to shake. He was ever aware of his weakness.

Lost in thought, he almost missed what Lady Nora was saying to Henrietta, "Would you be willing to help Adrian? This may get messy, and you could be put in a dangerous situation. You are usually only an informant but have become a trusted informant for us. I'm sure you already know whom I speak of."

Henrietta nodded. She sneaked a few sidelong glances at Adrian and then turned back to Lady Nora. "What do you need me to do?"

"You understand that this is dangerous?"

"Yes," Henrietta said without hesitation.

"Hmm. I see," Lady Nora said after flicking her gaze in his direction. "Then, my dear, this is what I need you to do. You are to follow Adrian and keep an eye on him. If he falls into any danger, you must get help. You know where to go. If it is a kidnapping, follow where they take him, then get help. Do not show yourself unless you deem it absolutely necessary."

Bowing, Henrietta said, "I understand."

"Good girl, now hurry along and prepare yourself."

With one last bow, the girl scurried away. Leaving the room to Nora and himself. Though he thought he had a better hand on Lady Nora's emotions, it was at times like this when he couldn't reason out her far-off look. The unfathomable expression was now resting on him. He shifted uncomfortably in his chair. As always, he had wanted to earn her respect, but she was a strong woman who had very strong ideals so very much like Ella. He wished that they would have a better relationship, especially now that she was pregnant. Ella had been so cold after the loss, and it was only news that her mother had been found that she returned to her more usual self. No matter what Ella said, she needed her mother just as her mother needed Ella. His weakness was that he needed Ella.

"Would you help me with this endeavor?" He asked, breaking the silence.

Nora shook her head, "No. I wish I could, but I already have an appointment that I cannot miss. Henrietta is the only person I can send at this moment. Though I do believe that my daughter told you to do this through an intermediary, sometimes you must do a job alone."

Adrian hung his head; she was right. Ella had told him to do an intermediary, but from the conversation with Lord Greenwood, he didn't think that he would accept an intermediary. He had hoped for more than what Nora had told him, but what could he do? He was as weak as he normally was, asking for help from everyone else. But he had made his choice, and he had only hoped that it wouldn't end with Ella being hurt.

"Stick with the training that Ella has given you," Nora said. Then, standing, she made her way to the stairs, leaving him with a few words.

"Don't die. That would break my daughter's heart. And... thank you for asking for my advice."

With that, she was gone, leaving Adrian to collect his thoughts as he ran through the plan one last time.

Adrian was staring at his hand as he collected his thoughts on the ride over to Lord Greenwood's manor. Henrietta was sitting solemnly across from him. She was going to hop out once they arrived closer to the manor. Adrian had been imagining the part that he had to play as they drove through the streets of London, but as they approached, Adrian eyed Henrietta. No longer the skinny child that she once was, she was a confident young woman, and from the way she practiced her daggers, quick on the draw. But they had never talked much, even after the events of the fire. He wondered why she would come with him, even though it would be dangerous for her.

His face must have shown his curiosity, because Henrietta asked, "Are you wondering why I decided to come with you?"

"Yes," Adrian furrowed his brow, "We have never been close. Why would you be willing to be in a dangerous situation that you do not need to be in? Having to play babysitter is not in your job description."

Though she usually played the part of a bubbly girl, Adrian had learned that she was very serious when she didn't have a part to play. She folded her hands in her lap and said succinctly, "Your job description never involved saving my life either."

Not wanting to have her feel pressured, he quickly replied, "You don't have to feel the need to repay me for that. I was just doing that for my own satisfaction."

"And I am doing this for the same reason." She turned to look out the window, neatly ending the conversation.

Guilt pulled at him. Was this what Ella felt when she had others to put in danger? His lungs clenched at that thought. He looked at Henrietta, who was resolutely looking out the window, and he remembered his wife's determination. Just as he wished his own determination wouldn't be looked over, he couldn't do it to theirs. He could only hope that his weakness wouldn't put them in harm's way.

His lungs stayed tight as they stopped to let Henrietta out and as he made his way into the Manor.

Lord Greenwood greeted him as he motioned them into the sitting room. A maid brought in tea, and once she left, Lord Greenwood started testing him. "Lord Cooper, have you reconsidered the business proposal?"

"I believe in my letter I stated I would accept once I see the goods." Adrian said, as he sipped his tea. Though he had been running through his part in his mind, it had been difficult to get into character. Adrian continued to sip his tea in hopes that it would calm his wheezes. It did not. But that meant he just had to distract him, just like a new noble would do.

Lord Greenwood eyed him, "Ah yes, of course. I just thought it rather odd that you decided that you wanted to do that now, when you seemed so uninterested during our previous meeting."

"My wife said that it would be better to see it first to make sure you were not swindling me. Not that I believe you are, but the missus can create such a fuss." Adrian tried not to wince as he apologized to Ella in his head for using her as an excuse. Even though Ella had given him permission to, he still didn't like doing it, no matter what she said.

Lord Greenwood rubbed his chin, "Thought you said your wife wouldn't care how you used your money?"

Adrian cursed at himself. Why was he having so much trouble getting into character now when he was alone? Was that just a curse of his weakness? No, he had to regain control of this conversation for Ella, for his unborn child, and for himself. "You are right. She doesn't care about how I spend it, only how it looks to society. It would be remiss if I bought something without seeing it first."

Adrian's uncaring attitude seemed to have worked. Lord Greenwood smiled with a hint of greed behind his eyes, "I thought as much. I have already prepared a carriage that will take us to the Kensington Hippo-drome."

Taking one last sip of his tea to calm his wheezing lungs, he followed after Lord Greenwood.

During the 19th century, due to the massive number of buildings, many of the rivers in London were shunted to subter-
ranean tunnels beneath the city. Now, a vast network of rivers
is underground. What is interesting to note. . .

The Underground History
Written by Professor Carter,
Archeologist of Cambridge University

Chapter Eleven

Exhaustion pulled at Ella. After fleeing from an unknown man, they ran through the narrow alleyways. Edmund knew them well, and he didn't hesitate when he took the many confusing turns that Ella couldn't memorize. Now, she had to rely on him to make her way back home. She could only hope that her instincts were correct. But the run and growing nausea pulled her to a slow walk.

The viscount turned to her, "I know you don't trust me, but we are almost there."

He didn't have that fear on his face that he had in the alleyway; he seemed to have regained his sense. Grateful that the shadowy alleyways hid her expression, Ella picked up her pace, struggling to keep the nauseated look from her face. She couldn't let down her guard with him.

It wasn't much further that he made his way into a dilapidated building. Fingering her fan, Ella listened for signs that their pursuer had followed them. From the sound of water, they must be by the river. They had gone further west than she had originally thought, but there were no sounds of a pursuer. Relaxing a bit, Ella poked her head into the grimy building, not wanting to follow Edmund any farther in. Using the time to catch her breath, Ella watched as Edmund made his way to the back of the ramshackle building. It was full of debris from the crumbling walls. The small building must have once been a stable but was now fallen into disrepair. Ella observed as Edmund pushed aside some broken boards that were scattered across the floor and opened one of the stable doors. Creeping forward, Ella could see that he was brushing away the mildew straw that had been left behind. Curiosity bloomed as he revealed a door set into the floor.

The door creaked ominously as he pulled it open.

"Ladies first," His cheeky grin had returned to his face, showing what he once was.

Dangerous.

"Can we not speak here? I have no desire to go down a dark hole in a dress." Ella said, stalling. He had pulled her away from her team quite effectively. She would have to follow him, but she would not allow him to control the conversation.

"Awe, but there might be rats listening in the walls." He replied, amusement at her concern evident in his voice, "And you know what happens to rats."

He was pushing her; that comment might have angered her if it hadn't been for Adrian. It was as if she could feel his arms around her, giving her time to think and make the best decision. His last request was for her to return home safely. Right now, her mission was to return Edmund's favor so she wouldn't have the debt hanging over her head and keep her child safe. That was the way to return home. "Is that the favor you are asking for? Need me to protect you from *rats*?"

His brow raised in surprise at her comeback. His business face held the smirk that he always had when he had spoken to her as if he knew everything. It was as though their run through the streets never happened. It should have been odd conversing as if they were in a manor rather than covered in dirt and standing in a broken-down stable, but this was a business proposition. His pride wouldn't allow for anything else. "Of course not. I have my own way of dealing with them, but I wouldn't want them to interfere with our conversation. Besides, I have some information that would be of interest to you."

Folding her arms, Ella remembered the last time he traded information. The price is why she was stuck in this situation. But she needed to remove this price and finish this sooner rather than later. "I would rather find that out myself. Your information comes at too high of a cost."

He laughed. It still sent chills down her spine. A reminder that everyone who had crossed him had vanished under mysterious circumstances. "How about we wait until you hear my favor first, then see if you wish for more information."

Clenching her fan in her fist, she refused to be moved by his words and instead raised her brow as her mother would have. Dealing with her stubborn mother had taught her a thing or two.

"I see you are not to be moved," Edmund said. "Then shall we make our way down now? I'm sure you would want to remove the debt, and I will only do it when there is no chance that prying eyes can see. You can hear the deal first before you accept. Would that suffice?"

This was the best she was going to get from him. If she was going to down into the darkness, and Ella wanted him in full view in front of her, "Are you not going to help me down? It would only be proper."

Without comment, he disappeared down the hole. A splash sounded below a moment later. Remembering her promise to her husband and the child growing within her, she took as deep of a breath as her nausea would allow to try to calm her unsettled stomach and prepare. She had learned her lesson; running a deal with Edmund without any preparation was like running into battle naked. Only fools would do it, and how much a fool Ella had been.

Ella took one long look around to see if anyone was following them. Still seeing none, Ella rubbed her foot across the dirt, creating a fan shape in the dirt that was hidden in the corner in hopes that she could find this building later. It was poor preparation, but then again, she hadn't expected an interloper in this conversation. She will take what she could get.

There wasn't much else she could do other than keep her ears open and her fan at the ready. Looking down, she could see that it was only a few hands' widths deeper than Edmund was tall. There was a metal ladder that was attached to the edge of the hole. With careful steps, she tested the rung. It held her weight. Edmund, still playing the part of a gentleman, helped her over the lip of the hole and made sure she didn't fall.

As she made her way to the ground, he said, "Please excuse the water, madame. The water is a hazard that we have to face if it means having privacy."

His words helped the shock as she stepped off the ladder into the water below. It was only ankle-deep and slightly chilly. It pulled at Ella, reminding her of the nearby river. Looking around, Ella couldn't see anything due to the only light source being the open hatch above her. One that Edmund was closing, leaving them in pitch blackness. She was already used to moving in total darkness from her time spent in the hidden hallways of the academy. Ella knew what to do. She controlled her breathing and took in information with her other senses. The smell of wet dirt and river water permeated the moist air. She heard the clatter of Edmund's feet as he climbed down the ladder behind her. Considering the river was so near, the tunnel wouldn't be big. Taking a few steps to the side, she held her hand out until it found the feel of rough bricks and clay, though it was difficult to tell due to the thick moss that covered the surface.

"My lady? You would want to keep close so you do not get lost. These tunnels are vast, and we wouldn't want you getting lost before I have my favor, now would we?"

A chill ran down Ella's spine, but her eyes had started adjusting to the dark, and she could vaguely see his form next to her due to some light entering from small openings in the ceiling. "A favor you promised would not go against my sensibilities, and right now, I can assure you that this is going against my sensibilities."

Edmund moved towards her voice. "I always keep my business deals," he said. He reached for her, and Ella held out her arm to allow him to escort her through the dark, keeping her fan against the wall, to scrape off a path should she need to escape.

The sound of sloshing water accompanied them as she was led through the darkness. The easy confidence as he strode through the water showed how well he knew his way around. It appears that her suspicion was correct. He had been living underground. But if he was this confident underground, then what had him so terrified earlier?

Pulling her to a halt, he pulled open a squealing door. Light flooded the tunnel, and Ella could finally see a few other tunnels forking up ahead.

"Careful on the steps."

Ella nodded to Edmund and took his advice as she looked at the algae-covered steps that led up to dry ground. Cautious, she made her way into a small, well-lit room. There were a few comforts: a blanket covering a straw mound and a rickety wooden chair and table that held the lit lantern. On the table was a mark burned into the table. It was a dagger with two snakes intertwining it.

"This is just one of my many hideouts," Edmond said, closing the door behind him. "Do not think that your little trail will lead you to me later."

She had hoped that he wouldn't have noticed what she had been doing, but he was still as clever as ever. "I have a right to protect myself."

He motioned her to sit in the chair while he leaned on the table. Not wanting him to be above her, she stayed standing.

Eyeing her, he raised his brow, then shrugged. "I would normally prepare you a cup of tea, but alas, there is none available."

This had gone on for long enough; flicking the moss that had covered her fan into the large-covered stairwell, Ella asked, "Viscount Edmund, what favor are you asking of me?"

"Why in such a rush, my lady?" Ella folded her arms. He laughed, then held up his hands in an appeasing manner, "I will tell you. But first, do you remember the Bristol riots five years ago?"

How could she forget? That was the first time they had spoken to each other. It was the time she made that fateful deal. "Yes. I remember. That was when you asked for a favor."

She just barely managed to hold back her anger and not spit out those last words. She had to pay attention to everything and not let her anger get the better of her.

Edmund brushed his hair back, "Because of your actions that night, you interrupted a very important deal that I had."

Biting back a sarcastic remark that Ella would have flung at him, she waited until he finished.

"Now, because of this, I'm in a spot of trouble with my client," Edmund continued. "They want me dead."

"What do you want me to do about it? I am not sorry that I stopped the plans for a riot. Besides, this is a favor. I am not going to bodyguard you until your client gives up their well-deserved desire to kill you."

He let out a laugh. "Thank you for that, Lady Cooper. But no, I am not asking you to bodyguard me. Not even you could do that. "Holding back a sigh, she asked, "Then what do you want?"

"I want you to stop their plans."

That was a surprise. Why would he want to stop the plans that he tried to help enact? If they were clientele of Edmund, they most certainly had dark intent. But was it enough for her to get involved? What would make him so terrified of them that he wanted her to stop them?

Worry for her child made her ask, "Why should I stop these plans? Do you even know what they are?"

Edmund let out another bout of laughter, "Lady Cooper, who do you think hired me to start the riot?"

If she hadn't been as tired as she was, she might have picked up on it sooner. He said he had an important deal. One that was broken because of her actions. Ella knew that he was involved during riots, moving the headquarters around, so it was difficult to gather people to help stop the riots. But the riots had happened, so if that was all they wanted, why did he fail? It must mean that they had wanted something far worse than what had happened. There were several riots during that time, and many people lost their lives, and he is saying that that wasn't enough. That he failed.

"Who are they?"

She hadn't even realized that she had said those words out loud until Edmund answered her.

"They call themselves the Society of Shadows." His eyes glowed in the lamplight as he said those words. "The leader is called Mirror."

Chapter Twelve

The carriage ride felt longer than it should have to Adrian. But thankfully, the long ride gave him time to grapple with his fears. By the time the door opened, he was in character. He was Lord Cooper, a young newly made noble who had received the king's favor with the station and money that went with it. He is full of himself and eager to show off his wealth to prove that he belongs in high society. The place where they arrived was nothing that he would enjoy.

"Where have you taken me? Is this a trash pit?" Adrian wrinkled his nose at the smell. They had passed by a street that bordered the slums, not a good option for a racetrack. Normally; the smell of horses and manure didn't bother him, but this was stronger and mixed with the smell of mildew. Covering his nose with his handkerchief, he turned to Lord Greenwood. "What is this? I demand an explanation!"

"I did tell you that it still isn't open." Lord Greenwood said, looking at the building that was far too beautiful for the surrounding area.

"Yes, but not that it smelled like a pigsty and looked like one," Adrian said, motioning to the mud that covered the area. It was thick, and judging from the footprints, was everywhere.

"I do apologize for that. There was much more clay in the area than expected." He crinkled his nose as he flicked a glob of clay from his shoes. "It has been worse than normal due to construction."

This was not what he expected. Considering how Lord Greenwood was, he hadn't expected it to be perfect, but the man fancied himself a businessman and wouldn't give bad goods. But why would he think that this would be a good idea? "This is what you want me to pay for? Maybe my wife was right to have me see the goods before I bought them. I would hate to have my wife be right."

"Appearances can be deceiving, count," Lord Greenwood said, motioning for Adrian to follow him. "Let us speak in a better environment. I dislike having the riffraff listening in. I promise you will be rewarded greatly if you come."

Putting on a grin that he hoped was greedy enough, Adrian said, "If it's not, I will make you pay for my wasted time."

"I would expect nothing less."

Adrian followed Lord Greenwood through the hippodrome as he described the venue and how it would compete with the more well-established courses. It was difficult to keep up appearances as he walked through the place. He could see some horses being trained in the pasture, which was far too muddy for them. The horses were likely to get hoof problems if they had to continuously train there. The rest of the area was no better. Though the place had just been built; it looked like a child had used it to create mud pies. When they entered a hallway that appeared to be offices, a servant waited to clean their shoes. That was the only reason that this area was cleaner than the rest of the place.

Lord Greenwood led him into one of the rooms on the far side. He locked the door behind them, then moved to the back of the office and started pulling something from the desk.

Hearing the lock click reinforced his fear that there was no backing out now. There was no one standing next to him. His chest clenched, but he forced a relaxed smile on his face, hoping that he wasn't failing miserably. He couldn't allow himself to be in a situation that would get Ella hurt. He wouldn't be her weakness.

"I have yet to see how bringing me here will change my mind," Adrian said, trying to appear as if his lungs weren't being squeezed in a vice. Lord Cooper would not be shaken by this.

"Just one moment. Since I have invested a lot, they have given me my own office to conduct business. That is how much I believe in it, but one can never be too careful when money is involved. There is one thing that I would like for you to take a look at." Lord Greenwood came forward carrying a wooden case. "What do you think people enjoy at racetracks?"

Adrian had never had a chance to visit racetracks due to his health. However, he did have a vague idea about what most people did at the tracks. Gambling. "Betting, but that is a gamble in horseracing."

With a nod, Lord Greenwood continued, "Exactly, but what if the house knows which horses are going to win the race?"

Even though he knew little about racing, Adrian knew a thing or two about horses. "But horse's conditions change depending on a lot of things. It will be very hard to predict which horse is going to win."

"True, but that is why we have this." Lord Greenwood opened the box he had in his hand. It contained a few glass vials. A greedy smile filled his face. "With this, we will know exactly which horses are going to win.

Bile rose in Adrian's throat. He recognized that as a drug given to horses to run faster, but it ended up destroying the horse. Adrian didn't know what to say, but the character he was playing did, "So you fix the race then?"

Adrian felt revulsion as he picked up the vial to check the contents. He could already hear the heavy wheeze in his breathing.

To soften the noise of his wheezing, Adrian asked, "Can you get other drugs?"

A twitch of Lord Greenwood's lips showed his pleasure. "As I said, I have ways to earn money for sure. I know how to procure many things for my clients. I would never do anything to earn the ire of my clients, like a certain someone."

Adrian hadn't expected that question to bear fruit. And as he watched Greenwood's expressions, he hadn't noticed it at first, but he saw jealousy in his eyes. He remembered Ella speaking of Viscount Edmund being the biggest black-market dealer, but since past events, he hasn't been seen. Is Lord Greenwood taking his place? He would let Ella know when they returned, when *she* returned. But first, he needed to leave this enclosed space. "I would like to see the horses. After that, I will see if I make a deal with you. And maybe we might make another deal since I can no longer get in touch with a certain *someone*."

His voice came out with a confidence that he didn't feel.

A smirk grew as Lord Greenwood closed the box, "Of course, I would be happy to."

Returning the box to the desk, he then pulled a rope near the desk. Then moved to unlock the door. Adrian couldn't help but feel some relief when the lock clicked open. Standing in the doorway was a young man with a charming smile. "What can I do for you, my Lord?"

Lord Greenwood motioned to Adrian and said, "Arthur, Count Cooper wishes to see the stables."

Chapter Thirteen

By the time Ella made it back to her carriage, night had shown its face. Slumping on the bench, Clementine threw a shawl over Ella. It was difficult to see in darkness, but streaks of dirt covered her skirts and face. Too tired to sit up but needing the information now that it was fresh in everyone's minds, Ella asked, "What happened to the man?"

"I will write a report for you. It's best if you rest," Clementine said as she looked Ella over. Then, seeing Ella shiver as the night air seeped through the carriage doors, she pulled out a blanket from inside the bench.

Letting her tuck the blanket around her, Ella forced her eyes open, "It's better to do it now."

"Are you going to be able to stay awake?"

Ella glared at her. Throwing her hands up in surrender, she sat across from Ella. Then knocked in sequence on the wall behind the carriage driver, letting him know that he needed to be on the watch for any eavesdroppers. "I will talk as long as it gets you to sleep faster. You have a child to think of."

Ella rubbed her belly, ever aware that pushing herself would be bad for the baby, but the things that Edmund had told her and the expressions on his face made her worried. Memories of the riots spun through her mind as she thought, what could be worse? A storm was coming, and she needed to be ready. "The faster you speak, the faster I can go to sleep."

"Fine." Clementine started brushing the dried mud from her face as she spoke of her encounter with the mysterious man, "He was very strong. The man fought more like a soldier than how we fight. Not to mention, he also managed to avoid our poisons and seemed to know our fighting style. That man was playing with us. He only stopped when you had disappeared."

As Clementine had been talking, Ella remembered a battle of her own that she had amidst burning buildings. "Did you see his face?"

Clementine shook her head, "No. His face was covered. It was obvious that he was up to ill intent. It was a good thing that you escaped when you did. But he did have a message for you. He said he would play again when the little cinder fan girl could play."

A chill ran down Ella's spine as Clementine revealed her fears. It was Fox.

"Ella?" Clementine said, pulling her from her dark thoughts. "What did that bastard want from you?"

Ella relayed what she had learned from Edmund, still lost in thought about Clementine's new information.

"How have we not heard of this secret society?"

"What?" Ella said. "What do you mean?"

Clementine folded her arms as she sat up straighter, "I mean. Wouldn't we have seen signs of another society? We have informants at every level of the government. Why haven't we seen or been told about another secret society? Maybe that man was lying to you."

Ella shook her head, trying to think more clearly, "I don't think he was. He seemed rather terrified, and I think that man you fought was part of that society. Maybe the reason we haven't seen it yet was because we were looking in the wrong place."

Sniffing, Clementine flicked off a clump of mud from her skirts, "But Madame Briar should know about it."

It was like a smack on the wrist, clearing away the fog of tiredness that had filled her. It would be difficult to see a secret organization since many of the agents don't have all of the information. They just have pieces of it. But Madame Briar sees all of the information she should know. Maybe she did, but hadn't told anyone. Odd pieces of information that Madame Briar had said flitted through her mind.

"Ella," Clementine called.

"Yes?" Ella said as her thoughts dashed back and forth.

"I want you to close your eyes for ten seconds for me."

Confusion filled Ella. "Why?"

Clementine gave her the stare that she wasn't going to budge on this issue until she did as was asked. She hadn't done that in a while. Ella sighed and then complied. As her eyes shut, the weight of sleep pressed upon them, and she didn't open them until much later.

Adrian had arrived back at his home earlier than Ella. He had paced back and forth when he arrived, frustrated at the lack of information that he had gathered and worried that his wife hadn't returned home. Lady Nora wasn't home when he arrived, making it even more frustrating that he didn't have someone to relay what little information he had managed to glean from Lord Greenwood. When the carriage came to a stop in front of their door, he rushed out to find his wife curled up in the carriage. Fear filled him as visions of her being hurt flashed through his mind. He hurried to her side. As he opened the door, Clementine gave him a glare that warned him not to wake her. Tension eased from his shoulders when he realized she had just been sleeping. The shadows that were cast under her eyes by the lamplight were not the dark vestiges of death that could be seen about his father but the weariness of exhaustion.

"Let us move her to her bed," Adrian whispered. He refrained from touching her face in case he would awaken her.

Clementine nodded and motioned for William, the carriage driver, to carry her inside. As he followed behind, Adrian winced at his own weakness of being unable to carry his own wife into the house. When they reached his room, William gently laid her on the bed and then made his way out of the house. Adrian watched Ella's slow breath of sleep as his breathing labored. Then, before he could do anything, he was shuttled out of the room as Clementine and Henrietta came in to help Ella get ready to sleep.

The thud of the wooden door shutting behind him reminded him that he, once again, could not help.

The Society of Shadows needs to be investigated. I want you to keep an eye on this. I have a feeling that past mistakes have played a part in creating this dark society. Be wary.

To codename: Phoenix
From codename: Rose

Chapter Fourteen

Ella sat at her desk writing a letter. After waking from her exhausting meeting with Edmund, Ella had spent the next week organizing information and sending messages to Lady Greenwood. Ella had not managed to set up a meeting with Madame Briar. She had been rather closed mouth on the concept of another secret organization, though Ella was not surprised. Madame Briar's message was to continue on the thread of information that had been given. If Ella found information leading to the Society of Shadows, she was supposed to let Madame Briar know. Adrian had also retrieved some interesting information about Lord Greenwood. She disapproved that Adrian had put himself into a very dangerous situation but was very grateful for the information. From how Adrian had described Lord Greenwood's reactions, he is trying to take the place of Viscount Edmund. This made her suspect that her feeling about Lord Greenwood was correct, but he may also be involved with the Society of Shadows.

Ella sighed and absentmindedly placed her hands on her stomach. There was so much she needed to do. She still had to find out what Lord Greenwood was up to. She would not allow another incident like her mother's to take place. And she had to make sure that it was safe for her child. She had to find out about the Society of Shadows. But considering how Edmund is in hiding from the Society, they would need someone else to do their dirty work, and Lord Greenwood is a perfect choice to replace him. She would need more information on him. And she had the perfect way to get it.

"Clementine," Ella called. She folded the letter and slid it into an envelope.

Clementine was immediately by her side. "Yes?"

Ella finished placing a wax seal on the envelope and pressed her seal into it. Passing it to Clementine, she said, "Please send this to Lady Greenwood. After it is sent, it's time to get ready."

Nodding, Clementine took the letter.

Exhaustion pulled at Ella again. Even though for the past week she had been resting, no matter what she did, she still felt tired.

"Are you having a tea party with Miss Greenwood?"

Ella turned to see her mother standing in the doorway. Standing, Ella went to her closet to choose her dress for that afternoon, "Yes, I need to start gaining information from her about Lord Greenwood."

As Ella riffled through the dresses, she struggled with her emotions. Guilt weighed on her. She still hadn't told her mother that she was pregnant yet. She knew she needed to, but after losing her first one, it was still difficult to say it out loud. But she knew she needed to.

Before she could even attempt to say anything, her mother said, "I have my own mission starting today. Madame Briar believes that I have regained enough of my strength to do my own missions."

Irrational irritation shot through Ella. "So now that a big mission is here, have you decided to leave me on my own?"

Her mother raised a brow, "Dear? I thought that this was what you wanted?"

That brow raise infuriated her even more. It reminded her of Madame Briar. The person who was constantly keeping secrets, ones that could now put her and her child in danger. "Yes, of course, that is what I wanted. Now, do I get to know what mission you are going on, or is that another secret to be kept?"

"Are you all right?" Her mother moved in closer to her, and she snapped. "Get out!"

Her mother's eyes widened in surprise. Giving her one last look, she left. Ella wanted to call back to her to tell her story about her outburst, but it was already too late. The door had shut. Ella collapsed on her bed. What was wrong with her? Tears fell down her face, and Adrian entered the room. Tears fell down her face even harder as nausea rose. He sat next to her and tried to hold her in his arms. That caused a violent reaction in her as she smacked him away. "Don't touch me."

Holding his hands up as worry filled his features, and with a calming voice, he asked, "What's wrong?"

Ella couldn't answer. Taking deep breaths, Ella tried to calm her odd emotions. It was nothing like the dark emotions that she had felt previously. But they were sharp and confusing. Taking deep breaths as random tears spilled down her cheeks. Then she remembered her last pregnancy, and the tears became real, "I'm just being emotional."

Adrian nodded, giving her some space, then asked, "Are you going to be alright with the tea party this afternoon?"

Swallowing, Ella wiped away her tears. Letting out a slow breath, she gave him a watery smile, "I'm going to have to be. We need this information. I fear that we will need it sooner than later."

He did not ask why she felt that way. Instead, he just asked, "Is there anything I can do?"

Ella smiled and relaxed. She didn't have to do this alone. The meeting with Edmund weighed on her mind. That could have been dangerous for her child. Even though she disliked Adrian being in danger, she needed his help. She had to move forward from her dark thoughts and trust in Adrian's decision to be in harm's way.

"I need you to talk to Drina to see if she knows anything odd going around society. Maybe we can find out what the Society of Shadows is up to."

"If that is what you need from me." Adrian's answer was firm, but Ella saw a hint of worry in his eyes. Adrian blinked, and it disappeared as he continued, "Her weekly visitation to my father is today; I can slip in then to speak to her."

"Are you well?" Ella asked, concern in her voice.

Adrian's wide smile brushed aside her worries, "I am well. Now, let us get you ready for your tea party. Stay safe, dear."

His hands squeezed hers before stepping out as Clementine returned.

After the ball a few days ago, Ella sent correspondence to Lady Greenwood. Though she had been unwilling to look into her adoptive father at first, she had finally relented. Yesterday, she had asked for a meeting under the disguise of a tea party.

The carriage pulled up to the Greenwood Manor, and Ella was greeted by the butler, who had received her letter about her arrival ahead of time. He escorted her through the manor. Ella scanned the halls and memorized the hallways in case there was a need to break in. The halls were decorated in an ornate style, far more expensive than a baron could afford. The disruption of the horse races wouldn't earn him this much. It seems that he has someone strong backing him in his endeavors. The question is, are they part of the Society of Shadows?

"In here, Countess Cooper." The butler bowed as he opened the door to the veranda, where Lady Greenwood was waiting. She was shifting in her chair and fiddling with her cup as Ella entered.

Looking up, she set her cup down and made her way toward Ella, calling her by her fake name. "Priscilla, it is so good that you could come."

Ella could see the trembling in Agatha's hands as she motioned for Ella to sit. "Send for some tea, Rupert."

The butler bowed and left. Ella wondered what was scaring her so and if it had to do with the Society of Shadows. But for now, she needed to calm her down. Though Agatha was as old as her mother, she had never been trained for situations like this. Ella knew from their last encounter she was brave, but it's different when it's your own family. She wondered what she actually knew to cause her to act like this.

"Agatha," Ella said, hoping to calm her nerves. One never knows what a frightened person would do. "I heard you went to Princess Alexandria's birthday party last month. How was it? I never got the chance to go. Was is as beautiful as everyone says?"

Ella had gone to St. James's Place, but was undercover as a commoner to help Luella with a mission. It was a big, lively celebration.

Mentioning the party seemed like the wrong thing to say as her face paled, and she pressed her lips together. She brushed her red hair back into its bun as if stray hairs had fallen, her fingers shaking.

She jumped as a knock sounded on the door. Collecting herself as a proper noble, she called for the maid to come in. A young footman came in with a cart. He came in a rush, causing the dishes to rattle. Agatha's jaw muscle twitched with each noise. He poured the tea and left as Agatha shooed him away.

Agatha didn't speak until the door was shut, and they were left alone. Ella wanted to speak to ease her tension but worried about making it worse. For now, it would be best to wait until she is ready to speak.

Agatha took a sip of tea and set it down with a clatter. With hesitant breath, she said, "I would like to apologize, Priscilla."

"What do you need to apologize for?" Ella nudged, trying to eke out information without pushing too hard.

Stirring her tea, she hesitated. "I once called out the nobles for being hypocritical, thinking I was different from them. I thought I could teach my junior that some nobles were different. But I was wrong."

Now wanting to guess what she was being hypocritical about, Ell muttered noncommittally, "Oh?"

Setting down her spoon, she looked Ella in the eyes, "I did not think that my adoptive father could do this, but you are right to be wary of him."

Could this be what she had been looking for? Ella held back her excitement. Calming her emotions, she took several breaths, hiding them by acting like she was drinking tea. She didn't want what happened that morning to happen again. She needed to keep calm. Putting on a worried look, Ella asked, "What do you mean?"

Tilting her head, she thought about it. Then that confident look she had during the ball returned, "I don't want a young lady like you to get involved in this. It is too dangerous. This is my problem. Just promise me that your husband won't take a deal with Lord Greenwood."

Ella hadn't expected that. Looking out to the small private garden, Ella let her thoughts rumble around. It wasn't surprising that an older woman would be protective of a younger. She also already had strong opinions about the nobility. What did she need to say to have Agatha tell her what was going on?

Testing the waters, Ella let her lips quiver. "Thank you for letting me know. But I believe you are right about needing to do something about nobility. You were kind enough to talk to me, and I wouldn't want anything to happen to you either."

She bit her lip and locked gazes with Agatha to show that she was determined. Agatha shook her head as she regained her confidence. Ella just wished she hadn't done it at this point.

"No," said Agatha. "You don't know what you are getting into. I will not play the hypocrite and let you enter into this."

Clasping her hands, Ella twisted them together to show that she was nervous and to organize her thoughts. She couldn't rush this.

"Agatha," Ella said slowly, as if she was struggling with the words she needed to say. Which, at that moment, she was. "Do you mind if I speak forthrightly?"

Agatha shook her head, "Please, speak your mind. Heavens know that I very rarely say what is proper."

Pressing her lips and giving pause for effect, Ella continued. Using her memories of when she was on her first mission, she poured the nervousness and determination she had felt into the words she spoke. "I am very new to the world of society. As you heard from Lady Euphemia, I did not come from the best of households. Since I have been a part of it, so much has gone wrong. I have seen people do horrible things, all with a smile on their faces. Your words were the first I've heard spoken that rang true with me."

And they had. Ella hadn't spent most of her time dwelling on the fact that everyone had horrible intentions behind smiling faces. She focused on her mission. But now that she was pregnant, she couldn't help but wish that it wasn't so. How was she supposed to protect her child when the country was controlled by nobles who cared little for everyone else, and the people who could do something about it only worked slowly? Who were they beholden to?

"You shouldn't place too much on my words, dear," Agatha said, shifting uncomfortably in her chair. "As I've already stated, those are the words of a spinster who knew nothing of her own family."

Ella couldn't allow her to pull away, and besides, even though it had been only a week of correspondence, she had enjoyed writing letters to her. It was one of the few things that kept away the weariness lately. "You say those words because you want to protect me even though you haven't known me for very long. But I don't want to hide my eyes from the things that are happening. I believe that you are the one who can change society. If we have more people like you, we can change it just like you said. Please, I need to know what is going on."

Watching her, Agatha regained that spark that Ella had seen at the party. I am not apologetic; I need to protect your stand, but I can change things. "Do you wish to know? This will be the final time I ask."

Leveling her eyes on her, Ella said, "Yes. I want to know."

Nodding, she stood, "Then let us speak where fewer ears can hear."

Ella stood, following her off the veranda to the private gardens.

John Constable, the painter, has died. Many art lovers are having a hard time consoling themselves as he is one of the many painters who have died in the last couple of years. Many believe that this will be the end of an era of art.

Newspaper
Year 1835

Chapter Fifteen

Making his way through the secret passages in the palace, Adrian headed to his father's room. He had wished that he didn't have to see him before an important meeting. It still hurt how every time he had seen him, he withered even further away. Shying away from those thoughts, he peeked through the opening in the wall to his room to see if anyone was in there with him. Abigail was with him. Knocking lightly on the door, Abigail turned in her chair and opened the door, letting him in.

"He is sleeping. He is not doing well. I don't know how much longer he has. Prepare yourself." She whispered in his ear, then moved into the passage to give him privacy with his father.

Adrian didn't know whether to be grateful or sad that she left him alone. But he had to face the reality that his father was dying. Holding back his tears, knowing that if he started crying, he wouldn't be able to stop, he faced his father.

His father was closer to skin and bones rather than the broad-shouldered man he knew. He pulled the chair that Abigail had been sitting in closer to the bed. The rasp of wet breathing reminded him of when he had been sick, and death was hovering over him. Reaching out, he held his father's hand.

It was warm from the raging fever that wouldn't go away. Sweat was already forming on his face. Adrian found a bowl of water on the nightstand beside him, wrung the towel, and wiped his father's forehead.

His eyes opened at the cool touch. They were bleary and unfocused. Adrian was surprised when he spoke with raspy words from his persistent cough, "I must protect my son. I need to stay alive as long as possible."

Adrian's hand froze. Then, closing his eyes with his hand, he said, "Just sleep. You have done your part."

His father relaxed against his fingers and fell back to his fevered sleep. Adrian placed the towel back in the bowl. His father's words rang in his head. Was this what his father felt like watching Adrian as a child suffering from sickness, being unable to do anything? Adrian patted his father's hand and whispered, "I'm sorry I put you through so much."

A knock sounded on the door, causing him to pull back and rub his watery eyes to make sure they hadn't leaked into tears. Agatha came from the hidden passage and went to open the door, making sure that it was opened only enough for them to enter, but not see Adrian in the chair.

Drina entered the room, and Abigail took her place on the opposite side of the bed to keep an eye on his father. When Drina saw Adrian sitting in the chair opposite him, she gave him a bow. "Greetings to your Highness, Prince Adrian."

He wished she wouldn't be this formal, but it was her way of showing respect, as well as her responsibilities. He reciprocated the bow, "Greetings to the heir apparent, Princess Alexandria Victoria."

She turned to his father and bowed, "Greetings to your majesty, King William. May your reign be seen as prosperous."

Adrian was pleased to see a kind smile as she did this. She moved forward and tucked the blanket further under his chin. Then, she sat in the chair next to him. Folding her hands in her lap, she sat straight-backed, "Adrian, I didn't expect to see you here. It is a pleasure to see you."

Drina had grown into a beautiful young woman. No longer the gangly young girl, she had just had her 18th birthday and was now considered an adult. Considering how much her family has been trying to control her, Adrian could see the confidence that defies their control. Smiling at his cousin, he was happy that she was one of the few who knew that he was still alive. "Drina, how have you been?"

"I have been working on bettering myself to become a wonderful queen for the people." Pride showed in her eyes. His decision to step down and fake his death was a good decision. He had worried about the pressure of the role, but seeing her like this, he knew that she would be fine.

"You will be a wonderful queen, Drina," Adrian said, confidence reflected in his voice.

Drina patted his father's hand and, with a hint of sorrow, said, "Though I am sorry that it will come at a cost. King William is a great man and a wonderful king."

"Yes, he is." Emotion filled his voice as he cleared it and continued, "Thank you for coming to visit him, as I am unable to do often."

"It has been an honor to do this duty." She turned to him, "What reason have you come at this time?"

Adrian smiled. Of course, his wise cousin would pick up his need for her assistance. During the last five years, after the attempt on his life by the Duchess, Drina had been key in many Fan Society missions with her information. Though she did it for Adrian, not knowing he had been asking on behalf of the Fan Society. It still made him uncomfortable that she didn't know anything about the Fan Society, but he swore that he wouldn't speak of it. Drina had just assumed that Adrian was helping her from behind the scenes, which he was, just not by himself.

"Have you noticed anything out of the ordinary with the nobility?"

Drina thought about it. She was never one to rush if she didn't need to. "Baron Greenwood has been gaining power recently. He is trying to fill in the hole that Viscount Edmund did before he disappeared. A new hippodrome will be opening soon, which is causing a lot of controversies, considering the stables are set against Potters Lane. Many people believe that ruffians will take over the racetrack. People are worried about a small-pox outbreak. And I know that some businesses are having some troubles since the parliament building was burned, and many files were destroyed. It was a surprisingly quick spreading fire that many believe was caused by arson. And what else? There have also been many deaths in the arts and performing arts this year. It has caused concern about what is going to happen now that John Constable has died. But most of these are common occurrences. Is there something you are looking for?"

Adrian shook his head, "No. Since it seems as if my father won't last much longer," The words stuck in his throat as he said them, but he continued, "I just worry that your mother and Conroy might try something."

She sighed, "I've been playing the part of an obedient daughter. My mother doesn't suspect anything. She still believes that she can control me once I take the throne. Since she very rarely lets me leave her side, it also means that it is easy to keep an eye on her. I am just lucky that she considers looking after Uncle good for public image and lets me visit him alone."

Though her voice never trembled at the horrible things she was saying, Adrian knew it still bothered her. She hated that Conroy got to her mother at a weak time in her life and twisted her. But Drina, even with all of those circumstances, became a fiercely independent woman. Stubborn to the core.

Proud of his younger cousin, Adrian smiled, "Keep a wary eye on things. It would be bad to get this far only to have something come up. If you ever need anything, send me a message."

She nodded and bowed her head in respect, "Thank you for everything, Your Highness."

He bowed back, and they spent the rest of the time together next to his father's bed. Then, as he was leaving, he turned back and asked Drina, "Would you put sage, lavender, and thyme by his bed for me?"

She nodded. Then Adrian left, leaving only a myth to protect his father.

Ella waited until Agatha would talk. They had wandered through the gardens a few times. It wasn't very big, but Ella knew enough not to push at that moment. It was when they were in the gazebo that she glanced one more time around and then had her sit on the benches that were inside. Sitting close to Ella, Agatha whispered, "I want you to know that I am ever grateful for my adoptive father. He took me in when I was a teen. Everyone had abandoned me, but he took me in, even though he wasn't much younger than I was. And he didn't throw me out when no one asked for my hand in marriage. I was nothing. He never asked to have a spinster as an adoptive daughter. I have done everything I could to repay him for what he has given me. But I *cannot* forgive what has been done."

Staring into her eyes, Ella could see sorrow and anger in her eyes as she said those words.

Reaching out, Ella touched her hand, "Agatha, what happened?" She had hoped she said it with enough worry and not desperation to learn about the information. Already exhaustion was pulling at her, but she needed this information.

She hesitated again but then took a deep breath and looked her in the eyes, "I think he killed someone."

That was not what Ella expected. She had expected something about the black market, fraud, or even something about him working with others. Murder was *not* on that list of things expected.

"Ww-ho," Ella stuttered, using her own fears to make it seem like she was terrified. Which, in a way, she was. It's like Viscount Edmund all over again. She thought they knew about him, but yet another secret gets pulled out at the last moment, upping the stakes.

Glancing down at her hands, she muttered, "I don't know."

"What do you mean you don't know?" How can she know that he killed someone but not know who it is?

Agatha looked into Ella's eyes, a tear dripping down her face, "I saw a letter that told him to kill someone in repayment for the funds that have been given him."

That explains the sudden money, but if the letter was repayment, then that person may still be alive. "Agatha, did it mention any clues as to who might be the target?"

Busy dabbing at her eyes with a handkerchief, she shook her head.

Why was it that this woman wouldn't be courageous at the times she needed to be? "Agatha, the target might still be alive. Do you know how who sent the letter?"

"They just signed it as Mirror." Agatha let another tear drip.

From her already emotional day, Agatha's wishy-washy attitude was making her irritation rise, as well as a desire to shake the woman. The many walks through the garden had pulled at her exhaustion and had given her a headache, causing her already touchy emotions to color her thoughts. But now she knew that Lord Greenwood really did have a connection to the Society of Shadows. If Ella could believe Edmund's information, which Ella was leaning towards it as the truth. Or at least as he saw it. But she needed more information.

"Did you keep the letter?"

Agatha shook her head.

"What about how much money they paid him?"

Agatha shook her head again.

Frustration and exhaustion made Ella snap. "Agatha. You said that you would help change the nobility. And if you believe that he is doing something wrong, isn't this the best way to do it? We can't let him get away with it. What if my husband were caught in it? If something happened to him, I wouldn't be able to survive on my own. And besides, there is someone who needs our help. Let's show how nobles can care about others."

She nodded and wiped her face one last time. "He was paid 10,000 pounds."

Ella's eyes widened. That was a lot of money. Who was he supposed to kill if it was worth that much money? "Do you think you can get more information from his office?"

Shaking her head, Agatha gripped her kerchief. "No, I don't think I can. I never done anything like this. Besides, after everything, I can't go against him."

"Then let me help you."

Again, Agatha's eyes showed the brave woman Ella had seen at the party, "I can't get you any more involved than this."

Holding her hands and showing her determination, Ella said, "We can change the nobility."

"And I thought I was supposed to teach you things." Agatha hesitated, searching Ella's face, then said, "Don't regret it later."

Ella held back a sigh and replied, "I won't."

"Then what do you need me to do?" Agatha said, griping Ella's hand.

A smile grew on Ella's face. Now she had an monitor in to Lord Greenwood and was closer to the Society of Shadows.

BP

Assassination order of a noble girl high
profile.

Payment of 10,000 Pounds.

Will send orders if accepted.

Mirror

Message Mirror

Unknown Recipient BP (noble?)

Chapter Sixteen

Ella and Adrian had been invited to a party at the Greenwood Manor, thanks to Agatha. Her mother once again didn't join her, and she had her own mission to do. Ella felt a stab of disappointment that her mother wasn't there but turned her attention to the party. She would need to talk to her mother when they got back. It wouldn't do her or her baby any good if she held in this feeling, but habits were hard to break.

"Are you doing alright?" Adrian whispered to her.

Ella nodded, brushing the wide, heavy skirts of her dress, wishing the dresses were lighter. Already feeling the exhaustion, she brought her focus to the ball. It was going to be difficult for her to last the entire evening, so they would need to get the information quickly. Her eyes wandered over the various guests to see who would be able to give her an excuse to leave the party in a rush. Her eyes wandered over to a few guests who were chatting in the corner. She recognized most of them. But what was Luella doing with her stepsister?

Snapping her fan open to gain her husband's attention to her fan, Adrian looked at her, eyebrow raised. Then, tapping beneath her eye with it open, she eyed the corner that her stepsister was in. Adrian recognized

Effie and gave a slight nod of understanding. Tilting his head to side, he questioned her about what she wanted him to do. Flicking her fan in Lord Greenwood's direction, she fanned away from her. Releasing her arm, he made his way to Lord Greenwood to keep him away from Ella.

Ella made her way towards the corner, trying to forget the last conversation she had with her stepsister at the last party Lord Greenwood had hosted. Luella held her fan in front of her as she listened to Effie talk to Lady Montague. Her eyes flicked in her direction as Ella neared; she tapped her open fan, indicating that she was busy on assignment. Undeterred, Ella tapped her closed fan with a single finger held upside down, indicating that she needed one moment of time. Then, flicking it open, she fanned it in a circle, showing she needed an excuse to leave. Ella could tell she was holding back an eye roll as she turned to Effie and clicked her fan closed to get her attention. She pointed to Ella, twisted her fingers, indicating that Ella was an ally, and flicked it open aggressively. Ella gritted her teeth as she held her polite society smile on her face, recognizing the sign as one to make a scene.

Ella knew how Effie made a scene.

And on cue, Effie turned to Ella, leaned to Lady Montague, and whispered in a not-so-quiet voice, "I didn't realize they invited fake nobility here. The Greenwood's parties have gone downhill, it seems."

Normally, she would have retorted back that she also married into nobility, but this was too important. As Ella watched Effie, she realized that the things that used to matter didn't as much. Her only thoughts were to protect her child. And to do that, she must play a part. She had no anger towards her stepsister; instead, letting her smile waver, Ella played the part of a girl who had been hurt before. "I-I, that's not true. I am real n-n-nobility."

Letting out a snort wouldn't have been best in proper society, but considering how much Lady Montague loved to show off, it was much enjoyed by the group. Effie's polite smile turned to a smug grin; she had always known how to make others happy. Playing off of their reactions, she said, "You should leave. You don't belong here."

Letting her emotions go, she let a tear drip from her eye, then turned in a whirl of skirts and headed down the hallway that Agatha had told her about. From what information she had been told to her from Agatha, as well as Adrian's encounter with a locked door, Lord Greenwood was paranoid. He had his office tucked away in a basement, the most difficult part of the house to get to. It would be noticeable to anyone that she did not belong in these hallways.

She made it easily to the stairs, but that was unsurprising since most of the house servants would be helping with the party. Ear straining for any sounds, Ella made her way down the stairs. The odd thing was the man sitting at the base of the stairs in front of the door. She knew that Lord Greenwood was paranoid, but not this paranoid. The information she wanted must be behind the door. Now, to distract the guard.

Pulling a small canteen of scotch from underneath her skirts was a common tool for this kind of assignment. She pulled a small pin from her updo and threaded it through the lace of her fan so the pointed tip was poking up above the lace. Listening again to make sure that no one had come closer, she smiled as everything was silent. Walking a few steps back down the hallway, she readied herself for her performance.

Flicking her fan open in one hand and holding the open canteen of scotch in the other, she let out a hiccup. Walking forward, she stumbled forward, pretending to trip on the empty air as she staggered near the top of the stairs. She could hear the man at the bottom stand and take a few steps up the stairs.

"Madame, you shouldn't be here." The guard said.

Ella giggled once again. And turned as if noticing him for the first time, "Oh my, I didn't know they kept such a handsome man down here."

The man, who was built more like a wall than a man, was unflustered by her words and instead motioned her away, "You do not belong down here. Head back to the party."

With some difficult maneuvering, she tripped down the stairs. Fear filled her as she slipped when she caught herself, making her trip farther than she intended. A beefy arm caught her. Blinking, she looked up at the man and gave him a sincere, "Thank you, but sorry that I have to do this."

The man reacted too slowly as she pricked him with the pin that had been stuck in her fan. He slid down the narrow hall wall as he collapsed to the ground. Ella checked his breathing to make sure he was asleep and listened to see if anyone had heard his fall. The drug would cause his memories to be fuzzy and knock him out, but considering his size, he wouldn't be down for long. Closing the flask, she tucked it back under her wide skirt. Climbing over his massive form, she headed to the door. With shaky fingers, she pulled the key that Agatha had given her from her sash to unlock the door. Seeing her shaky fingers, she took deep breaths. She didn't fall; her baby was still safe. Pressing her hand against her belly, reminding herself why she was doing this, she turned the key and hurriedly made her way in. Lighting the lamp, she took a look around.

It was a simple office. Only a desk was present, with a table and a few chairs in front of it for receiving his guests. All the papers were stacked perfectly on the desk, and nothing was out of order. It was the most organized office she had snuck into. That worried her. If she didn't replace everything exactly, he would know someone had been there. First, she would need to see what he thought was fine out in the open. That could be just as telling as what he keeps hidden. Keeping her ear out in case the guard woke earlier than intended, she looked over the documents on the table. She didn't touch anything before carefully noting where it had been so she could return it to its exact spot. Most of the documents were for legitimate businesses that Lord Greenwood ran or from the people on his land. They focused mostly on trade. However, they seemed to be written in two different handwritings. But they were both ones she didn't recognize.

Ella sighed, placing the stack she had flipped through back in its place. She was surprised that he kept the trade stuff in the open. Other nobles and merchants would like to use that kind of information to ruin a business or receive better deals. Either he placed those as a plant, or that was considered nothing compared to what he was really hiding. Remembering her previous mission of paranoid people who did dark business dealings, Ella knew that they would hide their important papers, but where? Taking in what she knew of him, she moved to the desk again. He would never let the information be near his guests. He would keep it near him. Moving the desk where his right hand would be, she felt the draws for any hidden compartments as she worried about when the guard would wake up.

She didn't find anything in those drawers, so she took a gamble and studied the drawers on the left. Hidden where he would sit, inside the desk on the left was a hidden compartment. It had been difficult to find since it was under the desk. Her wide skirts did little to help with crawling in small spaces. She made a mental note to tell Madame Briar that they needed to change the fashion again. She pulled out the papers and found them coded.

Normally, she would find a paper to copy the information onto, but the organized desk suggested that he would know if she used the paper. Ella would have to risk taking the papers with her.

She strapped the papers under her skirt, and the image of her mother's papers burning made her double-check the straps. Ever aware of the time, she knew she couldn't spend much more here, so she blew out the lamp. Ella pressed her ear to the door to check if anyone was coming. Her heart fell as the sound of multiple footsteps came towards the stairs. Dressed in wide skirts, there was nowhere wide enough for her to hide as the steps came closer.

Adrian kept an eye on Lord Greenwood as he sipped a drink by the wall. He nearly spat it out when a voice spoke near him.

"If you stare at him like that, he is going to notice."

Adrian blinked in surprise as Effie stood next to him. Though he had seen her during some of the recent balls, he last time he had spoken to her was for a few minutes before Audrey tried to pull him to the dance floor. He didn't know what he thought of Effie. She had tormented his wife for years, all to make her mother happy. Adrian knew better than anyone the desire to please your parents, but to torment others in their name was horrible.

"What are you talking about, my lady?" He asked. Adrian didn't know why she would talk to him. She shouldn't know who he was. Effie was not one of those privy to the knowledge that he was the prince, and his current name was a higher rank than she was. They were from different social circles. She shouldn't have been talking to him. Most people didn't know what he looked like or remember what he looked like. It would be surprising if she could recognize him after only seeing him for a few minutes.

A sly smile grew on her face as she turned to watch the dancers.

Adrian eyed her. She still wore a smug smile, and kept her cold blue eyes firmly away from him. Could she know that he was the prince? Shaking his head, he hunted for Lord Greenwood.

"He has already left for his basement. You should stop him before he catches your beloved wife." Effie said as she turned, leaving him behind.

He wanted to go after her but knew that he couldn't waste time. He would talk to Ella about this meeting later.

As Adrian made his way toward the basement, he saw Agatha leaving the hallway that Lord Fox and Lord Greenwood had just passed. When he passed by her, she had a smile on her face, but Adrian couldn't be concerned about that. He had failed at what Ella had asked him to do, and that was to keep Lord Greenwood away from the basement. The footsteps ahead of him were moving ever closer to the office, and soon, it would be too late to interfere. What could he do? Looking down, he realized that the glass he was drinking from was still in his hand. Instantly, he threw the glass to the floor, shattering it. Then, to make extra sure that they heard it, Adrian cursed and shouted, "How is this such shoddy glass work! Why are there no servants here? I don't want to walk all over this glass!"

The footsteps stopped heading away and came closer. He hoped that that would help. Now, he had to figure out what he was going to say to get out of this situation.

The breath Ella held, released as the footsteps stopped and headed away from her. Waiting a moment for them to move further away from her, she opened the door. As she was stepping over the fallen guard, his hand moved, catching her by the ankle. In horror, she fell towards the stone steps, catching herself before she smashed into the stonework. A sharp pain stabbed through her wrist as she struggled to pull her foot from his grip. His hand engulfed her foot, making it difficult to escape. Holding back a yelp of pain, Ella bit her lip as the guard's hand griped her ankle with such force Ella could feel the grinding of her bones.

Reaching around her mass of skirts, she tried to grab his hand, but with the thick fabric and hoops, she couldn't reach his hand. A groan filled the space between them. Worry pierced through her. If she struggled too much, it might bring him back to full awareness. She couldn't prick him again because it wouldn't make him go back to sleep. If anything, the sharp prick would bring him back faster.

Her mind furiously ran through her options as she tried to ignore the pain. She couldn't wait much longer because either the guard would wake up or whatever had drawn the attention would end. It was difficult to reach her foot to try anything to release his hand, but she could reach him. His glazed-over look and limp body showed her he was still under the effects of her poison, so it meant that it was just his body reacting.

With deep breaths, she relaxed her foot. It was difficult, considering how painful it was, but after a few moments of not resisting, his grip relaxed. Ella almost let out a sigh of relief as she didn't have a painful grinding in her foot. But now she had a new problem. She couldn't pull away because he would just tighten his grip again. Voices rose behind her again, and she tried to ignore them. Focusing on the task at hand, she opened the hidden compartment in her necklace. The white powder was light enough that with a puff of her breath, it blew into the face of the guard. His nose twitched. Ella held still, trying not to tense, as he finally released her and brushed his nose. As soon as his hand was off her foot, Ella pulled it far from his reach. Scrambling up the stairs, Ella tried to hear the argument above the beat of the heavy pounding of her heart.

Her ears picked up a few pieces of jumbled words.

"What are you . . ."

". . . Greenwood what do you think you are . . .unhand me."

"You seem to be . . ."

". . . glass . . . not drunk. . ."

". . . move away. . ."

"NOT MOVING—"

Ella had heard enough. She stood, nearly falling from her lightheaded-ness and the pain in her foot. But she stood firm. She couldn't show any pain when she moved, or they would get suspicious. Taking a look down the hallway, Ella could see three men talking: Lord Greenwood, Lord Fox, and her husband. Warmth filled her at her husband helping her. He saved her, but now it was her turn to save him.

Pushing down the pain and the dizziness, Ella strode forward, saying, "There you are. I was looking everywhere for you."

Adrian looked up, and a bright smile fell across his face, but he quickly fell back into character. A sense of pride filled Ella, pushing back her pain. Though he broke character for a moment, he regained it within moments.

"Stop nattering, woman," Adrian said in character, though Ella could see him wince as he said those words. He turned to the other men, "I do not want to dance with you."

Ella gave a long-suffering sigh, as she had seen many women make, and gently took Adrian by the arm, "Yes, yes, you don't want to dance with me. Now, let's make our way away from this glass."

Adrian grumbled but allowed Ella to hold his arm. Speaking to the other men, Ella said, "My apologies for this disgraceful sight. I believe it is time for us to leave. Please keep this between us. I don't want others to know of this. You know how gossip spreads."

Lord Fox gave a bow and, with a beaming smile, replied, "Of course not. I would never leave a damsel in distress."

Lord Greenwood was rather irritated but waved them away. Ella bowed her head and led the mumbling Adrian away.

When they were out of earshot, Adrian asked, "Did you get what you needed?"

Ella nodded but didn't say anything out loud. It was still too public. As they continued out of the hallway into the ballroom, the pain in Ella's ankle started flaring. Noticing her discomfort, Adrian grabbed her hand, causing her to wince since it was the same one she had caught her fall with.

Worry filled his eyes. He opened his mouth to ask but glanced at the crowd. Instead, he held some of her weight as he tucked her arm under his. Gratefully, Ella let Adrian take some of the weight. She was sweating by the time she left the manor. Now, all she wanted to do was have Clementine have the carriage ready for them, but she was nowhere to be seen.

"I will find her. Will you be all right?" Adrian asked as Ella desperately sought her friend.

She didn't know if she would make it, but Ella caught a glance of Clementine really close to a gentleman. "There she is."

Now, she just needed to get her attention. It would be in ill form for her to call for her, and she feared that if Adrian weren't holding on to her, she would fall over. Seeing her distress, Adrian took the initiative and told the footman to call for our carriage. Love for her husband warmed her for his small actions. He was very astute at noticing those types of things. It was one of his great strengths.

The footman called for Clementine, and when she turned, she noticed who she had been talking to. It was Arthur. She didn't know that he had been working here. And if he had been, why didn't he tell Clementine earlier?

The wait for the carriage to come was nightmarish, and she was barely concentrating when Clementine opened the carriage door for her. Ella managed to keep up the act until the carriage started moving, and she slumped in her seat.

"What happened?" Clementine asked, concerned as she looked Ella over for problems. She immediately noted Ella's hand. Squeezing beside her, she gently took her hand and pulled off her glove. It was difficult to see anything in the night light, but from the streetlamps, a bruise was starting to show on her wrist where she landed.

"It's not broken."

Clementine raised her brow and said, "I will let Flora be the judge of that."

Her gaze fell to Ella's stomach as she tilted her head questioningly, not wanting to speak out her concern of what a fall would do to her unborn child.

Ella shook her head, "No, I caught myself, hence the wrist. But I just want to go home."

Pursuing her lips, Clementine gave Ella her stubborn look. "Fine, then I will send for Flora to come visit you. No arguments."

Ella nodded. Normally, she would have fussed about it, but this was for her child, and besides, her foot was now spasming in pain. Then, to distract herself from the pain. "I see you saw Arthur. What was he doing here?"

"He had a mission here. And are you sure that is all that is hurting?"

Not mentioning her foot because if she did, Clementine would take off her shoe, and Ella would rather have that done at home. "I retrieved some papers. They seem to be in some kind of code. Do you think you can translate them?"

With a sigh, Clementine rolled her eyes, "Of course, I can. But don't change the subject. Are you hurt anywhere else?"

Glad that Adrian was in the carriage behind them, if not he would have told Clementine about her foot. But exhaustion pulled at her, and the pain was just too much. She fell asleep to Clementine's worrying.

Assistance will be given to you. Warrior and her ghost will help you in your endeavor to find Justice.

Note to codename: Phoenix
From codename: Rose

Chapter Seventeen

It took Ella a few days before she was up to anything. Flora had come earlier, and though she didn't break a bone in her foot or wrist, both wrist and ankle were badly bruised, and she would have to stay in bed to recuperate. Not that she stayed in bed. They had moved several cushions down to the secret basement so that she could work on spy work while keeping off her foot.

Adrian sat at the end of her mound of cushions, helping her with the papers spread across the bed. He was reading the newspapers as always, as he tried to see if there was any information that would be of help, but he couldn't concentrate. Anxiousness bubbled within him as his worries cast doubt in his mind. If he had been stronger than his weak self, he could have supported her more, and maybe her foot wouldn't be so bad as it was. "I'm sorry I can't be of more help."

Ella looked up from the papers that had been pilfered from Lord Greenwood's hidden room. "You are helping me, Adrian. I wouldn't be able to reach anything if you weren't here."

"No, that's not what I mean. I—"

He was interrupted by Clementine coming down the stairs. "Ella, I just received a message that Agatha will be here any minute."

"Thank you," Ella said, turning to Adrian. "Do you mind helping me?"

Remembering the time he had wanted to carry her inside but not being strong enough. He looked up the stairs and worried about being strong enough to help her up. "I don't think I'm strong enough to—"

Ella laughed, "I meant to put away the papers."

A blush spread across his cheeks, "Of course, I knew that. I would be happy to, my lady."

"And would you call for William to come to help me up the stairs? I should have asked Clementine when she was down here, but this code has me going crazy."

Adrian glanced at the pages that were spread between them. It was hard to make heads or tails of it. Not that it would help, even if he were looking at the papers right side up. Gathering the pages, he was about to head up the stairs to call for William when he descended.

"Looks like you don't need to call him after all. Clementine must have asked him," Ella said. "Would you mind still putting away the papers?"

"Of course."

Ella smiled, then reached out her arms for William to pick her up and carry her upstairs. Holding back his grimace, he turned to the pages in his hands. These pages had stumped both Clementine and Ella. They hadn't been able to talk to Nora yet, but so far, they had been unable to get anywhere with the code.

Maybe he could. Sitting down in front of the lamp, he studied the papers, hoping that he could help Ella just a little more.

Soon after William had managed to get her settled, Agatha arrived. Ella had her wrapped foot hidden beneath her skirts, hiding her bare feet. Shifting her gaze around the room, Agatha came in clutching her fan as if it were a lifeline.

Holding back her sigh, Ella watched as Agatha shifted near the entrance. It seems Agatha was getting skittish again. "Agatha! Welcome, forgive the impropriety of me not standing. And thank you for coming to meet me. Please have a seat."

Giving her a shaky smile, Agatha nodded and then took her seat across from Ella. The sitting room was on the main floor near the front of the house, with a window looking out onto the street. It let in the afternoon light as Agatha attempted to sit comfortably yet failed miserably as her back stayed stiff and her hands trembled as she held her fan. "It is quite all right, Priscilla. I was the one who sent you on the more dangerous part of the mission. I just couldn't."

Nodding her head in a soothing manner, Ella kept a smile on her face for the older woman. "Risk is for the young."

The woman's expression froze, then a genuine smile grew on her face, "Quite right. However, the older generation, get set in our ways sometimes. It is good that I have met you."

Ella worried that her comment would have hurt her, but it seemed to give Agatha the push she needed to regain her confidence. "Agatha, you must be parched in your rush to get here. I will send for some tea."

Turning to the door, Ella motioned for Clementine to bring in the afternoon tea.

"Thank you, dear," Agatha said. After Clementine left the room, she asked Ella, "Did you find everything you needed?"

Remembering the guard that hadn't been in the information that Agatha had given her, as well as her questions about her, Ella asked, "I'm not sure what I received. Though when I received the information, I was surprised by the guard at the entrance."

Covering her mouth, Agatha's eyes widened in surprise. "Oh my, how did you get past him?"

"He was passed out. He may have been drunk." *Or I drugged him*, Ella thought. But she wasn't going to say *that* out loud.

Agatha gripped her hands together, "I'm sorry it must have been my fault that happened. He must have gotten suspicious from when I sneaked in earlier."

Ah, Ella thought, *this was the perfect chance to ask her how she managed to steal the information.* "Speaking of suspicions. How did you manage to sneak in the first time?"

Tilting her head, Agatha started, "Well, I—"

She stopped when Clementine knocked and opened the door with a cart for tea and a tray covered by cloth.

Though it had only been a few minutes, Adrian was already getting frustrated. He could not make head or tales of what the papers were trying to say. He leaned closer to the lamp as he leaned as close as he could to the page in hopes that he might miraculously understand what was on the page. Instead, the pages lit on fire as the heat from the lamp caught the dry pages on fire, causing the flames to start spreading. Adrian immediately started patting out the flames. He sighed with relief as only the edge got singed.

Adrian leaned back in the chair. His attempt at being useful had nearly lost them the pages that his wife had worked so hard to get. It was obvious that he wouldn't get anything from these pages, and he didn't want to damage them any more than they already were. His lungs felt like they were in a vise grip as he gingerly started stacking the pages again. As he placed the now burnt page on top of the stack, he noticed something odd about it. Other than the obvious burn on the corner, some faded brown words appeared between the lines of text. He held it up to the lamp to see, being careful *not* to let it touch the lamp, and words began to appear. Checking the other pages, he found that all of them had hidden lines of text.

He had to let Ella know, but how? The sound of a cart being wheeled across the floor above him gave him an idea. In a rush, he grabbed the papers and made his way up to Clementine before she could give them the tea.

Ella had been confused when Clementine came up to her with the tray, but with whispered words and a glance at the papers, Ella's eyes widened in surprise. Adrian had solved the code. Warmth spread within her. Of course, her husband had always managed to do just the right thing to help her.

"What is it?" Agatha asked, pulling Ella out of her thoughts.

What could Ella say? Should she show the pages to Agatha before she even sees them herself? But would Agatha work with her if she refused?

Agatha does know the people connected to her adoptive father. But how well could she know them if she didn't know he had been doing underhand dealings for years? Those questions raced through her head as she worried what the right decision would be. Looking at Clementine, she knew she had to take that chance.

Waving Clementine out the door, Agatha would have been suspicious if she allowed her servants to hear. She waited until the door was closed and said, "I figured that it would be best to look through the information that I had found together since I can't make heads or tails of it."

Agatha picked up the papers that Clementine had given her. She held them in such a way that Ella couldn't see what the papers said, so she watched her expressions instead.

Curiosity filled Agatha's face as she read the pages, but anger filled it as she read something. Ella wished she could see what she was reading, but Agatha didn't say anything, and the anger was fleeting, changing to concern.

"Do you know what this says?" Agatha asked as she finished reading them.

Ella shook her head. "I showed them to you as soon as I knew about them."

"This is horrible. I can't . . . I just can't." Agatha covered her mouth as she passed the papers to Ella.

At first, she didn't know what she was looking at. Most of it was times and dates. The final page was the most revealing. It looked like random lines, and it took her a moment to realize that it was a map. The words written on it froze her blood.

Sickness spread here 6/8

Route for escape

Do not spread here

Queens route

Medic meet up

As those words, along with the dates and times, connected, Ella remembered what Flora had told her not that long ago. That sickness was spreading oddly. It was too fast. And here was the reason: it wasn't happening naturally. It was being done on purpose. Not only that, but this showed what the assassination plot was for.

Queens route

That would be the route that Drina would take to the palace once the king had passed. If they had a medic on their side, they would know exactly when she would be there.

The Society of Shadows was trying to kill the queen.

Chapter Eighteen

It had been a week after Agatha's visit. They decided not to wait anymore. Nora still hadn't returned, and Ella had been getting antsy. Madame Briar hadn't replied with anything about Drina other than she would send other agents to keep an eye on her. At least her foot had healed well. Adrian could see how she absent-mindedly held her stomach protectively when worst-case scenarios were brought up. He was relieved when Ella gave him a mission. Something that he could do, and since Ella would not be involved in this mission, his actions shouldn't hurt her. They had decided that since they didn't know if they could trust Lord Fox, they would gather financial information through the hippodrome. That meant that Adrian would have to go visit again.

"Don't worry, my lord, Arthur will help us," Clementine said.

Adrian nodded to Clementine. Ella wanted to make sure that Adrian had the proper backup and he was glad of it. He didn't want to ruin the mission, but he couldn't help but feel a twinge of anger at his own weakness. One that he had felt his whole life.

"Thank you, Clementine, I appreciate your help." Adrian turned his attention out the carriage window. He ran through the character that he needed to play. It should have been easier to fall into character since he had played it so often, but he knew by now that the stress of the missions could make even the most well-trained person falter.

He was a new lord. New money. Not someone worried about someone trying to assassinate his cousin. Right now, Lord Greenwood is presenting him with a lucrative deal. But he shouldn't be too trusting since he had already been bitten once. He also needed to find more information about the financial backer. Clementine would check with Arthur and see what he had managed to pick up and for him to gain information for them. He closed his eyes, thinking about how a person like this character would live, think, and feel. When he opened them again, he was at the hippodrome that buttressed up against Potters Lane, nicknamed Cutthroat Lane due to the nature of what happened on those streets. A pointed nickname that fit the situation. Clementine stepped out, opening the door for Adrian.

Lord Greenwood was waiting for him. His disgust for the clay that decorated the entryway was hidden well. However, Adrian could catch the twitch of disgust that was present on his lips. It was very much like the one present on his own. "Lord Greenwood, can we move to better accommodations?"

"It would be my pleasure, Lord Cooper." He led the way to his office. As they walked to the building that housed the office, Clementine disappeared. Holding back his fear, he had his boots wiped off by a servant, and he entered the building. The days had grown warmer as July had arrived, and he was grateful to be inside the cool stone building.

Once again, he was locked inside the office once they arrived. But this time, he motioned for Adrian to sit across from him. Resting his chin on his interlaced fingers, he asked, "Are you ready to join? You said that you would make a deal last time, but you never came back."

He hadn't meant to do that but had been distracted by Ella's injury, but now that was going to come into use. Playing the part of a burned contact, but interested buyer Adrian sat back and gave a smug grin, "You have lied to me about what this place truly is. I know you do more than fix races. You also deal in drugs. Now, I'm a generous man, and it doesn't bother me that you are dealing drugs, but I need information in exchange. And considering you intended on cheating your way into money. One would still need money to set this whole thing up. Who are the other investors?"

Lord Greenwood's lips twitch in understanding, "For this endeavor, we have another investor who will fully fund this. You don't need to worry about the initial investment of such things. Though if you invest in this, we will push our plans further for more returns."

Adrian refused to be budged, "I need to know the name of the backer. Then I can place my trust back in you."

"You will sign the deal here and now if I tell you this?"

Adrian nodded.

Adrian had a higher position in this bargain. Even though his father was overprotective of him and refused to allow him into politics, he still allowed him to watch in a hidden room whenever it was something other than politics. He had studied his father's work as king and learned much. This bargain needed to go well. He needed that name.

"Lord Cooper, you know how nobility is. If word came out that our little business was cheating, and his name associated with it would mean societal doom. I wouldn't be able to tell you unless I'm sure that you are going to sign the bargain." He leaned forward, trying to pressure Adrian to leave it alone.

If Adrian didn't have so much hanging on this, he might have. Considering he is connected to the Society of Shadows, which even the Fan Society had never heard of. If he annoyed him too much, who knows what they would do? But neither he nor the character he was playing would stop with just this much. "Lord Greenwood, you forget that you were willing to attach my name to this mess without telling me everything. Think of this as a safety measure. Besides, since I plan on joining, why would I reveal the name?"

He rubbed his chin, the russet hairs smoothing between his fingers as he thought. Adrian knew that he would give up the name, but it didn't make it any more nerve-wracking as Lord Greenwood made a show of thinking about it. A man like him couldn't fold too easily.

"Alright, Lord Cooper, I will agree to it. Now let us talk about the business formalities."

"The name?" Adrian asked pointedly, reminding him that he had never spoken it.

"Ah, I was just testing." Lord Greenwood smiled. Then, shifting his look around the room, as if anyone could hear them, he said, "Lord Montague is joining us in our endeavor. Is he wealthy enough of a backer? Now, shall we continue?"

He motioned to the papers that he had already prepared before him. Adrian sighed. Now, he just had to escape safely.

Surprisingly, it didn't take long to do the paperwork. Most of it was done over drinks while he did the talking, and Adrian did his best to follow along with all the technical things. Those boring lessons that his father had foisted upon him about legalities really came in handy. Now, he wished he hadn't skipped as many of them as he had. If only his father had taught him about nobility and politics, he wouldn't have had such a gaping hole in his lessons. He tried not to wince at that thought as his thoughts turned to his father's sickbed. Shaking his head, he focused on the papers, trying to catch anything that seemed suspicious.

A line did jump out at him, but it had been difficult to catch. If anyone speaks of Lord Fox's affairs, they'll forfeit everything to Lord Greenwood. "What is this?"

Lord Greenwood looked at the indicated line, his features not giving away anything. "Ah, I put things under my cousin's name so nothing can be traced back to us. Don't worry about such things."

Adrian eyed him. His instincts were telling him that Lord Greenwood was not worried about this sentence at all and believed in what he was telling Adrian. Considering what he was up to, it was unsurprising that he would do things to protect himself. He just hoped that Lord Fox wouldn't get hurt in this endeavor. He signed the papers as Lord Greenwood placed his wax seal on it.

"It was a pleasure doing business with you, Lord Cooper," Lord Greenwood said, standing and shaking his hand.

Adrian gave his greedy smile, "And a profitable one as well."

With a greedy smile that matched his own, Adrian was led from the office. As the afternoon light hit his face, he turned to Lord Greenwood. "I have an eye for horses, and as I was looking over the last time you showed me the stables, I saw a few horses that would be best for our little endeavor. May I take a look again?"

"Of course. I would be happy for your advice. I know little about horse-flesh myself." Adrian could tell that he was being indulged, but he would accept it. It was time to pick up Clementine, and he hoped he had given her enough time. He called a servant to lead him through the least muddy way to the stables.

The smell of horses hit his nostrils before he saw the stables. The familiarity and the joy he received from the stables made it difficult to stay in character. This was the place that he had linked in his mind to freedom. Once he had been well enough, he was able to raise his own horse, who is currently retired and in a pasture. Breathing in the scent, he stepped into the stables, which were full of stable boys hustling about and groomers trying to get the mud from off the horses before putting them in the clean stalls. As he looked around the stalls, he hunted for Arthur, who he now knew was a Ghost, and Clementine. He came to the stall in the back corner, and it was there that he found them rather close to each other behind a large stallion. Adrian tried not to blush as Arthur held Clementine's cheek, and she laughed back. He could see the charming smile he flashed in her direction and the alluring smile she gave him in return.

Then she saw him.

She immediately became the proper maid again, making him almost believe she'd done nothing inappropriate. Sorry that he had to disrupt the mood, he came forward, "The stables house some magnificent beasts, groomsman."

Arthur flashed a charming smile in his direction, "Yes, sir. We have some great thoroughbreds, sir."

"Indeed," Adrian said, trusting that Clementine had told him the plan, he continued with the prearranged role. "Tell the head groomsman what horses are the best for me."

"Yes, sir." He gave him a small bow, and out of the corner of his eye, Adrian could see the flirty smile he gave to Clementine. Clementine's face flushed, but she kept her expression the stoic maid.

They left the hippodrome without incident. Tension eased from his shoulders as buildings grew farther away, though his ears were still red from interrupting Arthur and Clementine's personal moment. Adrian turned to Clementine, "May I know what he said?"

"Though you did invade my personal time, I will forgive you since you didn't mean to. Besides, it's not like we were doing anything improper. He is a perfect gentleman and is waiting to ask for my hand until he can speak to Ella first." She smiled at Adrian's obvious embarrassment before finally stopping her torment of him. "I think you need to know. It's been good that Ella has relied on you lately."

A sense of pride ran through him. Now, he had to be up to the task she set before him. He couldn't ruin it. It would hurt to lose her faith in him. He didn't know what he could do by hearing this information, but he could try.

Seeing that he was ready, Clementine continued, "Baroness Smith sent Arthur here because of illegal trade coming out of the stables. He knows that they have been trading and they are using that place, but it's been difficult to find where or when they have been trading. He had thought that it would be near the stables since it was set up by Potters Lane, but so far, he has seen nothing out of the ordinary. He knows that they are drugging the horses but still cannot find their stash or where they set up trade. But considering the map you showed, there must be an entrance into the tunnels somewhere underneath the stables."

Adrian listened intently, not wanting to interrupt. He stared at his clay-ridden boots as he tried to memorize the words that Clementine was telling him. "Thank you, Clementine."

Her lips quirked into a smile, "You are my lord, husband of Ella. I would do anything to help her."

The steel in her blue eyes showed how much Clementine trusted Ella. Looking out the carriage, his mind drifted to all the information that Ella had told him, and a thought nagged at him, but as he was about to open his mouth, he noticed a carriage leaving their house.

Chapter Nineteen

Ella had just returned from visiting Flora. She had used the excuse that she needed to see how her pregnancy was going to give Flora a heads up on what was going on with the sickness. The anger that had shown in her eyes made her happy that Flora was on their side.

Already exhausted from the ride and the lack of information, Ella made her way into the house. Relief spread through her when she saw who was in the sitting room.

"Mother? Where have you been?" Ella exclaimed. No matter what irritation she had when she worked with her mother, she could only be happy that her mother was here now.

Lady Nora turned at the sound of her voice, yet she didn't smile at seeing her daughter. Instead, she had a no-nonsense look on her face, as she normally did during missions, and motioned her daughter to head down the stairs to the secret basement.

Curious, Ella did as was asked. She had hoped that her mother would give her information on what to do about the assassination attempt. Since she was so close to Madame Briar, maybe she could shed some light on the Society of Shadows.

They sat across from each other in the chairs as Henrietta came down with some tea. Ella waited, knowing her mother would start when she was ready. As she was waiting, Ella gathered the courage to finally tell her that she was pregnant.

"What have you found out about the assassination attempt on the Princess?" Lady Nora asked.

That was not what she thought her mother was going to ask about, but she answered the question. "Not much. The message wasn't very explicit, but considering the wording, they are planning on using the underground tunnels to at least escape after killing her. My guess is that they are going to kill her when she is sent to Buckingham Palace after the death of King William. Since they will know her route, and they mentioned a Medic, though it is difficult to say if they are involved in the plot to push forward the sickness or if they are close enough to the king to know if he has died or not."

"Do not make assumptions. Make sure you get evidence." Her mother said absentmindedly.

Yet again, it's the same old story: "That is why I am telling you my suspicions so that we can find evidence. What are you going to do about the sickness?"

"What do you mean what are we going to do about the sickness?"

Ella furrowed her brow as she felt a sinking feeling in her heart. "That is very explicitly stated in the message. They are somehow spreading the sickness. How are we going to stop that?"

Waving her hand dismissively, she took the tea that Henrietta had given her, "Thank you, my dear. Madame Briar has someone working on that.

You don't need to worry about it. Your mission is just to find out information."

Frustration filled her. This was part of the reason that had always bothered her about the society. There is so much wrong out there amongst the nobility that as long as they were doing something about it, it wouldn't have bothered her so much. How did Ella know that Madame Briar was taking care of anything? But Madame Briar does not *have* to do anything. The Fan Society was a secret society beholden to no one. Besides, if someone did find out, it would soon turn into the ravings of a madman as they slipped things into their drinks. Madame Briar once told her she could leave back when she was training, but now that it had been a few years, she had seen what society does to those who find out their secret. Yet Ella did know that they tried their best to take care of problems and protect everyone. But they could only do so much. Taking a deep breath, she looked at her mother, "But what if the person who gets the information doesn't understand the information?"

Taking a sip of tea, she furrowed her brow, "Madame Briar knows all of the information. She has been in the Fan Society for years. She is very good at what she does. Don't worry about it."

"Then what about the Society of Shadows?"

"They were very well hidden."

Ella shook her head. Her mother was answering with information that the Fan Society teaches. The same way they have been teaching for centuries. But the world has been changing, while they have been stuck in their ways. "I have only started looking for them, but there has been evidence all over the place that they have been working for a while. So why didn't she hear about it?"

"She doesn't have to tell us about it."

"She doesn't have to tell us about another secret society that is working in opposition to what we are doing? That were willing to start a riot to accomplish their means?"

"We don't know what their mission or goals are." Ella could tell her mother was getting nervous and that she didn't even believe the words herself. She was just saying what she thought she should say. Ella had a sinking feeling that this conversation wasn't going to go anywhere.

Ella sighed. "She didn't tell us about a very dangerous or at least potentially dangerous organization, so we could at least keep an eye on them?"

"We are all part of this organization. We all know what we signed up for." Though Ella did get frustrated with the organization, she had also seen all the good it had done. If it wasn't for them, her mother wouldn't have come home, and Adrian would have been poisoned. "It's better to keep you protected."

Her mother whispered the last sentence.

"Even you?" Ella held back another sigh as she saw her mother flinch at those words. Ella knew that she hadn't been told about the Society of Shadows until Ella told her.

"Madame Briar would have told me when I needed to know." It was as if Lady Nora had said those words to convince herself.

"When?"

"Hum? Speak up, dear."

Ella knew that her mother was just saying those words to cover her confusion. It is just as they learned in class. Ask a question or pretend that you didn't hear them to give yourself time to answer. Undeterred, Ella questioned, "I asked, when would she have told you? Would it be when you start working on a mission that involves them? It couldn't be that since I told Madame Briar about them and she still didn't say anything. Or is it when they are planning to kill someone? It's not that we already have a good idea that they are planning on killing someone. So when would she tell us then?"

Her mother stayed silent.

Things that had bothered her started coming out. She hadn't intended to say these things, but now she had a child to think about. A child she had to protect. She couldn't protect the child if she didn't know things. Ella had stayed within the bounds of the Society after what happened five years ago, but she could no longer do that. This wasn't just an emotional response. She had people she needed to protect, and for that to happen, she needed this information. If it is as her mother states that Madame Briar was keeping things to protect the group, Ella didn't want that. She was no longer a child to be hidden away. She was a mother protecting her child. Ella pressed further, "If you can't answer that, then who is keeping an eye on things?"

"What, Ella?" Lady Nora said. "Speaking clearly is a virtue of a lady."

Ella held her mother's gaze, which was one of confusion. "I asked, who is keeping an eye on things? Who is watching over Drina? Who is keeping watch over the underground rivers, Mother? Besides, with Madame Briar keeping things from us, how do we know she is even doing the right thing?"

Lady Nora's face flushed as anger and a touch of fear crept into her eyes. "That is dangerous ground you stand on, dear. It is not our place to say. Just do as you are asked, and it will all be taken care of."

It will all be taken care of? The Fan Society always moved slowly, much too slowly for Ella's taste. It always chafed at her at how much damage was allowed to happen in the name of secrecy. What would have happened if Ella hadn't taken the initiative and retrieved the information? And if they go through with their plan, what would happened to Drina? What would England be like then? What about the Society of Shadows? Did Madame Briar really not know about them? She didn't really think that Madame Briar was a traitor, but having that much on one person never helped anyone. She understood that better than anyone. They needed to ask for help. "Mother, if I hadn't skirted the line that the Fan Society had given me, I would not have known about the attempt on the Drina."

"*May* attempt on her. It's still unknown."

Ella rolled her eyes at her mother's interruptions. She had sincerely wished for her mother's help, and yet she just spoke what the Fan Society had taught. "If someone was planning to assassinate me, would you tell me about it? I'm sorry, I meant *if* there was a high likelihood of someone making an attempt on my life, would you tell me?"

Brow furrowing, Lady Nora deflected, "Is this about Adrian? Though he has been helpful, I still believe that he should not have been told."

By this time, Ella would have been furious and ready to shout, but after speaking with Adrian, she didn't need to. Instead of feeling furious, she felt sad. "What if they take too long to find out who is trying to assassinate her? Unlike you, who just had to do extra work, Drina would be dead. There will be no going back to what it was. We should tell her so she can protect herself."

Lady Nora set her tea down. Though it didn't clatter, now that Ella was in a calmer state, she could feel her mother's emotions radiating from her. "We need to follow the rules. We should not question what information is given us."

Remembering how Adrian had told her she needed her mother, Ella thought about it. Ella did need her mother, but the person in front of her wasn't her mother. She was Agent Phoenix, one of the best Guardians of the Fan Society. "Lady Nora, it is good to do what is needed. The Fan Society has done a lot to help England get to where it is now, but is it enough? Why not tell Drina about her assassination plot? I would want to know. Now that I think about it, why don't we tell the Royal line that we are protecting them? Don't you think we could do so much more with us working together? Isn't it through us society members working together that we can do so much? After the incident five years ago, I learned that I couldn't do things on my own. This is getting too big for us on our own. I wouldn't want this Society of Shadows to destroy our country before my child has had a chance to grow up!"

As Ella spoke, her mother's face turned a darker shade of red until she said her final line. She opened her mouth to speak but only closed it. When she finally managed to speak, it came out in a whisper, "You are pregnant?"

"Yes," Ella said, glad she finally told her mother. Though she had hoped it wouldn't have been like this. Ella was about to continue when Henrietta came down.

"There is someone here for Ella."

Ella nodded in Henritta's direction, then turned back to her mother, "I have a mission to continue, mother. I assume you have yours as well?"

Then, unable to look at her mother without tears gathering in her eyes, Ella made her way up the stairs.

Adrian watched as Nora headed to her carriage. From her posture, he knew something was wrong. As soon as the carriage stopped, he hopped out, coughing from the dust irritating his lungs. But he had no time to lose as he hurried to her carriage before it could take off. Knocking on the carriage door, he asked, "Lady Nora, may I speak to you?"

The silence weighed heavily around him until Lady Nora spoke, "You may enter."

Opening the door quickly, Adrian entered. After shutting the door, she called for the driver to continue. She didn't speak as she watched him. Adrian was already wheezing from that short, dusty run, and a blush rose from his cheeks. He couldn't help how weak his body was. If anything, he should be proud of how well it had kept together, but it still hit home that he was holding others back. But he never wanted to look weak in front of the person he admired.

Once his wheezing had calmed, he looked out of the carriage and asked, "Where are we going?"

"Don't you think you should have asked that before you entered the carriage?" Lady Nora said, brow raised.

Adrian could see a small smile of amusement pull at her lips, and he smiled, "But sometimes a man must do what he must, to help a beautiful lady smile."

"Oh. And why do you think I need to smile?"

Adrian couldn't help but sigh. She was so much like Ella, always keeping everything in a bottle, always trying to stay strong. "I think everyone needs to smile."

She gave a soft chuckle. Turning to look out the window, her eyes look deep in thought. "You once said to me that Ella needed her mother. But every time I've tried to be a mother, it only makes her angry. You also said to not be overprotective, but now I don't know."

Furrowing his brow, he thought about what best to tell her. He didn't know the situation, but he could guess. "What do you think being a mother is?"

"Protecting my child."

The answer was instantaneous. The steel in her words showed that she would put herself in front of a sword if it meant protecting Ella. And Adrian knew that she would do it if it came down to that. It brought to mind all the times that his father did things in the name of protecting him. "Is that what she wants from you?"

"What? Why wouldn't it be?" Adrian could see the confusion in her eyes as she asked those things. But as Adrian held her gaze, she paused and then said with sadness in her voice, "That is all I can do anyway."

Her words were resigned. But Adrian could feel the weight of sorrow behind those words.

"Is that all you think a mother is good for? Protecting? I thought a mother was supposed to be there for her child so she could grow into a fine individual. Which considering how short a time you have had, you have done very well." Adrian's face pulled into a smile as he thought of his wife.

Nora was pensive after his words, then knocked in sequence on the carriage wall. "If I'm not supposed to just protect her, what can I do? I have missed so much of her life. The only thing I can teach her is about Society, and I can't even help her be a mother. I have been gone too long for that."

Oh, how wrong she was. With everything that had happened to her and all of her experiences, how could she not know things? It was not a teacher that Ella needed; what Ella needed was someone to go to in times of trouble, someone who had experience but who was not a teacher. "Have you asked her what she needed?"

She shook her head. Then, holding his gaze with hers, she asked, "Even though you were put in danger, and you had to go through the fear of knowing that your life was in danger, do you regret knowing?"

"Never." His answer was instant. He could never go back into that china cabinet to be protected. His worth was more than his title. After all of his work that he had done, he wanted his worth to be about his capabilities, not a title that was dictated by his birth. Not when he finally gained his freedom.

"Even if you could live your life without the stress of knowing?"

Adrian shrugged, "It would still exist. But if I knew about it, then I could do something about it."

"You remind me of my daughter," Nora said as the edges of her lips twitched up into an amused smile.

"I take that as a compliment."

"I once had a companion who said we need to make the change now to help those who are around us, or for what else are we doing this work? My daughter just reminded me of her words." Nora reached over and took his hands in hers. Adrian could feel the calluses that still remained from her hard labor as her elegant fingers held his in her solid grip. "I am going to trust your decision then."

Adrian furrowed his bow. What was she asking of him? Whatever it was, he could feel her desperation and indecision in her hands as they held his. "What do you need from me?"

She hesitated. He had never really seen her hesitate before. But he understood when she spoke these words, "If you believe, you should tell Drina that there may be an attempt on her life. You can tell her about us."

The carriage pulled to a stop, and Nora pulled away from him and turned to open the door.

"What happened to your companion?" Adrian called, stopping her.

Turning back to him, she said, "I never heard from her again."

A chill ran down Adrian's spine as she stepped out of the carriage. She had placed a huge burden on his shoulders. Now, it would be his words that could ruin everything.

I made a choice. I can only hope that this might keep another mistake from happening, like what happened to Justice.

Note from Codename: Phoenix
To Codename: Rose

Chapter Twenty

Ella was sitting across from Lord Fox. She hadn't expected that he would come. Agatha had been adamant that he would help, but Ella had an odd feeling whenever she spoke to Lord Fox. Besides, she still didn't even know if she could trust Agatha, let alone Lord Fox. But it was too late now; he was already here.

"Lord Fox, why are you here?"

Rubbing his chin, he glanced at Agatha. There was something going on between them. The look he gave her held weight, but she couldn't quite read his expression. She didn't have enough time to observe it when he turned to her and spoke, "Lady Cooper, my niece seems to have gotten you into terrible danger. I would like to apologize for this, but I can take it from here."

It was odd to hear him call Agatha his niece when they were so close in age. And that look that Agatha gave him was more than what she would call "familial" love; that was the look you gave to someone you fell in love with. Maybe that was why she was a spinster for all these years, "Lord Fox, I am already involved, and even if you push me away, I will still be involved since I know things."

He gave a sheepish grin, "Yes, of course, my lady. That is correct."

It should have been odd to see such a childish reaction from him, but considering how Agatha was, it shouldn't be surprising. He seems to enjoy games.

He cleared his throat, "I still don't want to see you in danger, though. You should leave it to me."

Giving him a sly smile, Ella said, "Even though you do the finances for Lord Greenwood and never figured out what he was up to?"

Lord Fox laughed, looking much like a child as he did that. However, it was still difficult to remove the blurry memory of her fight. She flicked her closed fan up, striking close to his neck.

Holding his hands up, he laughed again, "I surrender, dear lady. I can't win against a lovely lady such as yourself."

Lord Fox hadn't moved away from her fan like she had expected someone who knew that her fan hid sharp blades beneath the lace. A fact that her opponent should remember from the cut she had given her opponent. Lord Fox also didn't act like a soldier who would have reacted to movement coming within range, like the guard at the bottom of the stairs. Maybe she was wrong about him. Ella sat back down, her senses still heightened.

"I should show you these then. I wouldn't want to get beheaded by a lady. I would never live that down."

Pulling the case from beside him and setting it on the table between them, he popped the clasps open. Then, with a flourish, he pulled out some papers. He was about to hand them to her but stopped, "Now, I give you these because you threatened me. I did *not* betray my family, and you did *not* get these from me."

"You were never here."

He smiled at her answer and then passed Ella the pages. They were financial documents. Something that Ella never really understood. Luckily, she learned enough from the academy and from Adrian that she could understand what was written on the document. From her minimal knowledge, she knew that it was an odd document.

Usually, on documents like this, they would have from whom the money is coming and how much. This was nothing more than initials or symbols along with money amounts. Furrowing her brow, she looked closer at the initials and saw one appear often with large amounts of money being sent. "Do you know who these people are?"

"If I did, which I'm not saying that I do since I'm not here, I would only know a few of them. Like that BP may be Baron Pole, but it's only a guess," Lord Fox said as he watched her with amusement.

Ella pointed to the initial that she had noted, "Do you know who this is?"

He took the papers from her and studied them, then passed them back, "I suspect that it would be from Lord Montague. He would be the only one I know with those initials and that amount of money."

Ella studied it some more. There was something nagging at her from these pages, but she didn't know what. She scanned through the pages more carefully this time, and she found it there. One of the lines had a symbol on it instead of letters. It was written rather crudely, looking like an upside-down t with two s's entangled around it. A symbol that looked familiar to her. She knew that symbol, but she couldn't place it. The answer was sitting there on the tip of her tongue, but it was like a curtain that refused to part, and she couldn't reach the answer.

"What about this person?" Ella said, needing the answer that seemed so far away.

Lord Fox looked at the symbol she was pointing to, then flinched. "You shouldn't touch those people."

"What's wrong, Gale?" Agatha said, touching his hand. It was a motion that Ella couldn't fail to recognize. Agatha likes Lord Fox.

Pulling the papers from her grasp, he tried to stuff them back into his case, "I shouldn't have shown you these. It was a bad decision."

His face held fear. He hadn't shown it during the rest of the conversation, but once she showed him the symbol, he was terrified. Putting out her hand, she stopped his movement, though the normally genial face was still contorted.

"The person who uses this symbol won't know that I'm seeing this. You can calm down." Ella said, trying to defuse his fear so she could gain more information. He obviously knew about that symbol, and from his fear, she knew that it must be the symbol of the Society of Shadows. Two s's. She needed his information.

"You never know, Lady Cooper. They might be seeing this right now." Lord Fox looked around like they were going to jump out of the shadows. "They always seem to have too much information."

He gave a sideways grin, but his face betrayed his feelings. It reminded her of her meeting with Edmund, and the table that had been there. When he had brought her to the room in the underground tunnels, the table had a dagger with snakes intertwining. The symbol on the paper was a simplified version of it. She gasped. Everything was coming together. The underground passageways, the racetrack, Lord Greenwood, the money, and finally, the Society of Shadows. But something was missing. If the

Society of Shadows' plan was to kill the queen, why were they planning riots and poisoning the water? And what did that have to do with the drugs that were being sold? It was like she had most of the pieces but no way to stick them together. She needed the missing piece. And maybe the one spending the money might know about it.

"Do you know if the Montagues are having a party soon?" Ella asked.

"There is one tonight," Agatha chimed in. "We were planning on heading out after speaking to get ready for it."

Ella gritted her teeth. High society didn't appreciate people randomly showing up at a party, and Ella didn't remember receiving an invitation. She couldn't just show up. Besides, Adrian had yet to come home.

"Why do you want to know?" Lord Fox asked, pulling her from her thoughts.

Debating how much she should tell them and how much she could push the persona she was portraying, Ella shifted in her chair, "Well, if we know that the Montagues are paying for everything, maybe we can see who they talk to in private during the party."

She lowered her chin and looked up at them through her lashes. This time, as she shifted uncomfortably, it was real since she didn't know how they would react.

With a pause that was far too long for Ella, Lord Fox rubbed his chin in thought. "There might be a way to get you in."

Eyes widening, Ella was shocked that he took to it so quickly. It seems like Agatha learned her switching of emotions from him. But she wasn't going to look a gift horse in the mouth, "How?"

He turned to look at Agatha, "Doesn't your invitation say plus one?"

"Yes, only because they wish I would bring someone I want to marry. They needn't have bothered." Agatha flushed as she avoided Lord Fox's eyes.

"Then it's settled, Agatha can get you in. Can you be ready in time?" His eyes focused on her.

Ella nodded.

"Perfect, then we will pick you up in a few hours." Lord Fox took her hand and gave her a kiss. "It really has been a pleasure to meet you."

That unreadable expression crossed his face again as he gave her a quick peck on the back of her hand and stood, letting Ella lead them to the door. As they were leaving, Ella caught a glimpse of Clementine. As soon as they were gone, she made her way down to the secret basement with her.

"Where is Adrian?" Ella asked since they had left together, but she hadn't seen him yet.

"I'm sorry, he jumped out of the carriage. But he seemed fine as he went with Lady Nora."

Ella nodded her head, relieved. Adrian was very good with her mother, though she wished that she could see him before leaving. "Did he tell you what he learned?"

Nodding, Clementine replied, "He found out who the financial backer was."

"Is it the Montagues?" Ella asked on a hunch.

Clementine blinked, hesitating only a moment before answering. "Yes, it is. Arthur also knows that they are selling drugs, and I gave him the information about the tunnels to see if he could find the entrance."

A smile pulled at Ella's lips, as she could see Clementine's ears turn red as she mentioned Arthur. "I'm sure you did more than talk about that."

Clementine nudged Ella with her elbow, "I was serious when I told him."

"Guess I will have to ask Adrian how serious you were when he gets back."

It felt good to tease her friend. She wished she had a chance to talk to Adrian before she left, but there wasn't time.

She passed Clementine the financial documents she received from Lord Fox, "Keep these with the other documents. We will need to look these over. I assume you already sent Harriette to give the information to the Fan Society?"

Clementine nodded, "Why the rush?"

"We don't have much time. I need you to help me get ready for a party."

"When?"

"Tonight."

Clementine widened her eyes and pushed Ella back up the stairs. "Then we must get ready, or we will be late. I will send a message to the Society."

Ella nodded, knowing that even with the speed the Society passed that information, it would still take time for them to send support. She could only hope they would arrive in time. This was a chance that she couldn't pass up.

They hurried to get ready, and Ella had little time to think about the conversation with Lord Fox in her rush.

Chapter Twenty One

They just barely managed to get ready in time. Thankfully, Henrietta came back right on time to help. She managed to make it down the stairs in an off-the-shoulders pale yellow ballgown. Exhausted, she refrained from touching her stomach. She already had guests, and it didn't feel right to let them know that she was pregnant.

"Where is Lord Fox?" Ella asked when she made her way down.

Agatha, wearing a dark red dress, shrugged, "He had other business to attend to. He will be arriving later than us."

They rode the carriage to the Montague Manor. The building was massive, much larger than the Greenwood's estate. It had a large ornamental garden out front to greet the guests. The chandelier over the dance floor hurt her eyes as exhaustion pulled at her. But she needed to do this, and this was the closest she had been to the Society of Shadows. They need information. And she needed to make it through the night.

Like good hosts, the Montagues were there to greet the guests in full ostentation. Even though the style trend was now leaning toward the prude, they still liked to show their riches. They were greeting some of the higher-ranked guests. Ella watched as Lady Montague constantly touched her stomach, beaming with joy.

Ella wanted to show with pride her pregnancy, but if anyone found out, that would be her weakness. She had to stay strong for her child. She would make sure this Society of Shadows was rooted out before her child was born into this world.

Leaning over to Agatha, she flicked out her fan, covering her mouth as she whispered to her, "Who are they talking to?"

Agatha leaned over, "Lord Grey, though he is not usually someone that he should talk to first. Lord Grey is of low standing."

Ella had only asked to keep her cover. She knew Lord Grey well since it was at his party that she found the note that led her to Lord Greenwood. But even though she knew who he was, Lady Priscilla wouldn't contact him. But her instincts were burning. This is one more connection that connects the Montagues to the Society of Shadows.

"What do you know of the Greys?"

"Not much," Agatha whispered back. "The only thing I know is that they are connected to the hippodrome. But it's odd."

The Hippodrome. It comes back around to that place. The map with the tunnels went directly underneath the hippodrome, and Ella knew that it was where they were dumping something into the water to make people sick. Could those have been drugs that were seen by the police force? Where those the drugs they they were receiving for the horses, or something else? And what did fixing horse races have to do with it?

"What is so odd about him being involved with the hippodrome?" Ella asked, with only half a mind on the question asked, as the rest of her head was trying to put the pieces together.

"Because he doesn't even like horses and hates being near them. Besides, he deals in pharmaceuticals and spices. He ships in plants and herbs from other countries."

The creation of the drugs. Lord Greenwood needed Lord Grey's connections to the drugs. That answered the how but not the why. Why are they selling drugs and dumping things into the river, and what does this have to do with Drina? Maybe she was wrong and jumped to conclusions. They may have just been mentioning a street and it was not about Drina.

Shaking herself, Ella refocused her attention. She may have been wrong about Drina, but there *was* something going on here. "We need to get closer to hear their conversation."

Agatha nodded. "I would like to know about this myself."

Ella thought furiously about how to get closer while still staying in character. "What if we chat and move closer? They wouldn't think anything of us coming closer."

Eyes brightening, she said, "That's right, but what sort of things are we supposed to talk about?"

Searching for the right words, Ella's eyes fell on Lady North and smiled, "What would Lady North talk about?"

Agatha returned that smile as they chatted and made their way towards the Montagues.

Adrian returned home far later than he had wanted. When Lady Nora had exited, they were near the river close to the academy. He had a strong desire to visit the school his wife had attended and trained to be a spy, but he knew he shouldn't. He had no reason to be there. Sighing at a missed opportunity, he headed inside the house, fully expecting his wife to be there, eager to listen to the information he had brought home. Instead, Mathew was the only one there.

"Mathew, where is my wife?" Adrian asked, still looking around, expecting her to be somewhere resting.

"She went to a party. You just missed her." Mathew said.

At the odd tone in his friend's voice, he turned to him. "What is wrong?"

He shifted once and gave his joking smile, "How could anything be wrong?"

Adrian knew that there was something wrong. They had been together since they were children, and he could tell that the smile didn't reach his eyes. He was hiding something from him. But he didn't know what it could be. Thinking about it, he realized he barely saw Mathew since he had been so busy helping Ella. "I am sorry that I haven't spoken to you for a while. Things have been very serious."

"I know," Mathew said, stopping his apologies. "I know that things have been serious. I also know that I am the one who didn't want to know what was going on. But I have a feeling that this is far more dangerous than the other times have been. The last time it was this serious, you came home badly injured."

"What do you want me to do?" Mathew had been his companion through everything, and though his friend was worrying about him, he couldn't stop what he was doing. It was too important.

Rubbing the back of his neck, Mathew sighed, "I am not going to stop you. And it is my fault for this predicament. But can I ask you one question?"

Adrian nodded, confused about what he would want to ask him.

Shifting, Mathew took his time to ask, but when he finally did, there was no hesitation in his voice. "Do you believe that you are doing the right thing?"

Even though he knew how serious of a question this was for Mathew, Adrian had already thought about this long and hard. His answer was instantaneous. "Yes."

Mathew nodded, then went into professional servant mode. "Then there is something you should know."

Motioning for him to speak, Mathew continued, "Just before getting ready for the party, Lord Fox and Lady Greenwood came over for a meeting. Right after that, she started preparing for the party. He gave her some documents before leaving."

That wasn't necessarily surprising. He knew that Ella had been talking with Agatha about getting Lord Fox involved. But seeing Mathew hesitate once more made him realize that it wasn't the thing he wanted to talk to him about. "Go on."

"There are no rumors about Lord Fox."

Adrian furrowed his brow. Mathew had been giving him gossip since he was young so that he could be connected to the outside world when he was stuck inside. And no matter who he asked about, there were always rumors to be had. "I think I need to see those documents."

Phoenix has found information related to Justice. There was some contention about what to do with Pawn now that it was going to become Queen. Phoenix asks for authorization as well as information on BP.

Note to Codename: Rose
Unknown sender

Chapter Twenty Two

Ella and Agatha chatted quietly near Lord Montague. They hadn't arrived in time to hear what was said to Lord Grey, but they kept nearby in case they could hear anything else.

"Do you think he keeps his information in his office?" Agatha whispered to her.

"Maybe. How would I know?" Ella had to still play the part of someone who was not an actual spy. This was more difficult than she thought it would be. She didn't want to make novice mistakes because that would be what would be expected of her, but she also needed that information without implicating herself or giving up anything to others.

"Do you think you could get in like you did at my adoptive father's place?" Agatha asked innocently.

Ella's eyes widened. She hadn't expected her to mention that, but using the opportunity, she might be able to use this. "Maybe," she said absent-mindedly as she looked around to see if she could find any members of society. Her eyes fell on two familiar faces, Luella and Euphemia. They seemed to be showing up at every place she was. But they could help her. She could ask them for help, but she didn't necessarily want Agatha to know about them. She was not a member of the Fan Society, nor was she considered a friend of the Fan Society. Though she didn't necessarily like how it was run, she did agree that not everyone should know everything. As she learned in her second year at the academy, it's harder to keep a secret the more people who know.

"How about you? Can you think of any way to get into the office?" Ella asked, grasping at anything that would help her get the information needed without blowing the other member's identity, as well as her own cover.

Agatha thought furiously beside her as Ella glanced over at her stepsister and Luella.

"What if you said you feel faint and that you need to use the waiting room to take a break?" Agatha said.

Shrugging her shoulder, Ella replied, "We haven't been here long enough to use it. Unless you can think up an excuse?"

"What about those girls over there?" Agatha pointed toward her step-sister.

A shiver ran through Ella as she wondered why Agatha chose them. Had she seen Ella's glances? "What about those girls?"

"See the drinks they are carrying?" Ella nodded as she realized where Agatha was taking this. "Do you think you can bump into them to see if their drinks can spill on you?"

Fearing fading a bit, Ella swallowed and focused on the task at hand, trying to calm the butterflies in her stomach. "That could work. Is the office that way?"

"Yes," Agatha said, then hesitated. "Do you need my help?"

Watching Agatha's fingers tighten on her fan and her shifting gaze made Ella sigh. "Would you be willing to keep an eye on things?"

Her nervous ticks softened as she smiled, relief was evident on her face. "I can most assuredly do that."

Not bothering to comment on Agatha's wishy-washy nature, Ella focused her thoughts. This was going to be tricky. This was her chance to pass on information that she was on a mission, but she also needed to do it in a way that didn't seem odd to Agatha and still accomplished her goal of getting wine poured on her.

As she caught the eyes of Effie, a servant pushed past her, spilling a drink on her. Stunned that the servant was able to get past her without her noticing, as well as all of her plans now useless, it took her a moment to realize that the servant was trying to pass her a note. Taking it, she excused herself from the party and made her way to the room that was set aside for the ladies to rest. With the slip of paper held between her fingers and her fan to keep it hidden, she was lucky to find that the room was empty. Turning her back to the door so that if someone entered, they wouldn't see, she looked at the scrap of paper.

Dancer. Tunnels. NH. Now. Danger H.

Ella translated the message, and her fear grew, and nausea bubbled in her stomach. Dancer, Arthur's codename. Tunnels, the place he was headed, the underground tunnels that he was keeping an eye on. NH needs help. He is calling for backup. Danger H, danger high, meaning that he was in immediate danger and feared for his life. He was in danger, but this was her chance to sneak into the offices of the Montagues, and considering the stain she still had on her dress from the beginning of the party, getting back into another party here would be difficult, to say the least. This would slow down her chances of finding the Society of Shadows, and time was running out on the King. When he died, she knew that Drina could be next. She couldn't save everyone on her own; she needed help. But who could she ask?

The door opened as Ella whirled around, hiding the paper in her gloves. Even though the person who entered was considered an ally, she still didn't relax.

"Lady Euphemia, I didn't realize you needed to rest," Ella said as she pulled a kerchief that was tucked into her other glove and started dabbing at the drink that had poured down her dress. She still didn't know what to think of her stepsister. All of her reactions so far had done nothing to change her opinion of that matter. She knew that if her stepsister truly wanted to, she could destroy everything.

Effie flicked her fan open, covering her face. "I was just checking to see how you were doing. Is that so wrong?"

It was difficult to see her features, and Effie had gotten much better at hiding her actual feelings. Her fears started welling up again, but Ella knew she was a Friend of the Society now. She should be able to trust her. At least, that was what Madame Briar thought. But then again, who knew what Madam Briar thought in the first place? Ella needed to send a message, and Effie was in the perfect place to help her. Dare she trust her?

She shouldn't rush this. Even though people's lives are on the line, Ella knew that sometimes it was more dangerous to rush. Ella had to test to see if she could trust Effie. Flicking her own fan out, she covered her face like Effie had. "I'm surprised you feel that way, considering everything."

Effie shrugged, "Everything? What are you speaking of?"

Ella wasn't going to play the game. She had a child to think of, a friend to save, and an evil organization that she still didn't know the full plan.

Ella didn't know how much time was left to stop it all.

The heavy silence must have gotten to Effie as she rolled her icy blue eyes and flicked her fan closed, "I made a bargain, and part of it was to help. And I always keep a bargain."

That struck a cord in Ella. She always kept her bargain. even if it went against her mother's wishes. But things have changed. Effie's mother is now a commoner, and it was because of Ella. The one person whose opinion Effie cared about. Would she be willing to break a bargain with the person who did that? Ella would have to take that chance. Ella couldn't do this alone. She couldn't leave without telling someone.

Trusting her instincts, she pulled the paper from her glove and passed it to Effie. As she passed her, Ella whispered, "Pass this to Luella."

Effie nodded.

Holding back her fear that she had made a terrible mistake, she left the room to find the office and hoped that Effie would pass on the note as soon as possible.

As she looked down the hallway, she noted Lord Fox pacing not far away, hesitant to enter the ladies' waiting room. "Lord Fox, what seems to be the matter?"

He looked up as relief filled his features. "Lady Cooper, I'm so sorry for the spill that happened, and I'm sorry to ask for your help on something."

Furrowing her brows, she asked, "What do you need?"

"I've heard some disturbing news," He fiddled with his cufflinks as he looked around the empty halls.

Keeping her voice soft, she asked, "What sort of information?"

He leaned in close and whispered, "A deal is happening right now under the hippodrome."

The hippodrome where Arthur sent his note. A dangerous place. Ella couldn't help but hesitate. It would put her child in danger, and Effie should be getting her note to Luella. She should be making her way to the tunnels.

"We should let the authorities take care of it. I have heard the police have been doing a great job with that sort of thing, no matter what the nobility say about them." Ella said, holding in her fear. "You are going to be missed. You should head back before people suspect you of something. I need to find his office."

As she turned to head back down the hallway, nausea built and worry filling her. Her emotions were out of control, and she needed to bring them back. At the moment, her duty is to find information about the Society of Shadows. She had to hope that Luella sent for help in time. If only her cover would allow for her to leave.

A hand grabbing her arm stopped her as Lord Fox hissed in her ear, "I heard mention of the Society of Shadows."

It was as if she was struck by lightning. The group she was searching for. She wanted to run for the meeting place once she heard those words, but she held herself still.

"I know I shouldn't be doing this at all." Lord Fox looked around as if looking to see if they were keeping an eye on him for saying those words. "But I need your help. If the authorities get there now, then I may be implicated since I do all the financing."

Ella nodded, trying to understand what he was getting at. Why would he be telling her about this? And what did he want from her? She desperately wanted to go to the meeting since it would be better information rather than the financial papers, but she was suspicious of Lord Fox.

He shifted uncomfortably as she said nothing. "My Lady, I heard from Agatha that you successfully stole papers from my cousin's office. I need. . . I worry. . ."

"My Lord, what are you needing from me?"

Her words stopped his stuttering as he answered her. "I fear that they will find out my connection to them should we call the police on them."

That made sense if the police found information that connected Lord Fox to drug dealers, that would destroy his family's reputation as well as his title. But what was he expecting from *her*? "Stopping those ruffians was the main point of all the work we have done. If you won't allow me to send for the Bobbies, then what are we doing here?"

He hastily held up his hand in surrender. "No, no, no. We should definitely call the authorities. I was just hoping, since you managed to relieve my information from my brother's office, maybe you can relieve information from them that connects them to me before we send for the authorities." He asked, answering her question.

"Where is this information?" Ella's intuition was screaming at her to be suspicious, but what part was suspicious? His reasoning is? The meeting? Or was it something else?

"It's at the hippodrome."

The same place that the supposed meeting was taking place. As well as where Ella had suspicions that an entrance to the tunnel was located. It was also where the drug deal was most likely taking place. If his information is found, then they would lose someone who had information. Information that would lead her to the Society of Shadows. Glancing down the hall-way, she debated which information was more important. Though it was probably a trap, Ella needed to get the information. But she didn't need to get it herself.

"My apologies, but that is far too dangerous for me. But if you hurry, you may be able to obtain the information. I will give you time to retrieve the information, and if all goes well tonight, we may not even need to call the authorities."

Ella thought she saw a flash of anger in his before it was covered by sorrow, "I understand, Lady. It is my fault in the first place. I sincerely hope that your exploits will prove fruitful."

He gave her a bow and then left.

She waited until he made his way back to the ballroom before making her way back herself. Ella stood at the entryway, knowing her dress would make it difficult to enter the room. No proper lady would stay with an unsightly stain. She hunted for Clementine. Something was wrong with Lord Fox; it was bothering her, but to maintain cover, she couldn't go after him herself. She needed help.

Spotting Clementine on the far side of the room, she flicked her fan open to get her attention. Using her closed fan, she tapped under her eye. Then, flicking it away from her eye, she pointed to Lord Fox, indicating that Clementine should follow him. Ella hesitated, debating on whether she should tell Clementine or not, but decided that she needed the information. Getting Clementine's attention again, she twisted her fingers in front of her fan, pointing to Effie, letting her know that she was an ally. Or at least she hoped she was one. She hoped that she wouldn't make another wrong decision by trusting her to pass on the message.

Turning back to the hallway, she made her way further into the manor, hunting for the study.

Chapter Twenty Three

Adrian was looking through the pages of documents that Lord Fox had left, and there was something in the documents that bothered him. However, he didn't have long to look at the documents before Mathew interrupted him as he came down the steps. Dread filled him. It would take something direly wrong for Mathew to set foot down those steps. He hurried to Mathew. The sorrowful expression told him what had happened. "Who is it? Is it my father?"

Mathew nodded, "I'm sorry, Adrian."

Swallowing the lump that had formed in his throat, he pushed down the grief. If what Ella was thinking about was true, then Drina was in danger. "Get the carriage ready. We need to go to Buckingham Palace."

"Are you sure? You can take your time to grieve," Mathew said, reaching out to him.

Facing his friend, he looked him straight in the eyes. "There are things going on that you don't understand. I need the carriage ready as soon as possible."

"Yes, Your Highness." He turned quickly, hurrying up the stairs. Adrian followed him more slowly due to him not wanting to strain his lungs. By the time he made it up, the carriage was already ready. It didn't take long since the messenger had stayed. Adrian nodded to William as he entered the carriage.

It was then that he realized that he had the papers still clutched in his hands. It was too late to return them to the basement. He had to make sure that his cousin was safe. He couldn't let the Society of Shadows' plans continue. Noticing his shaky hands, he smoothed the crumpled papers. As he did, he noticed the handwriting. Furrowing his brow, he studied the pages, focusing on the handwriting. Thoughts swarmed his mind as fear for Ella grew.

Pounding on the carriage, he shouted, "Hurry!"

With a snap of the reins, the carriage picked up speed as it drove through the night and mostly empty streets. He had to tell Ella that she couldn't trust—

His thoughts came to a screeching halt as the pop of a gun and a scream of a woman rang out in the night. The carriage picked up speed as he came upon a carriage bearing the mark of the royal family. It slowed to a halt as Adrian saw his fears unfold in front of him. It had been surrounded by men dressed in black. The horse was on the ground, though Adrian didn't know why. The only thing holding off the men from entering the carriage was a hand sticking out of the window holding a small gun.

A familiar gun.

His cousin always did carry around a gun for safety, but now wasn't the time to reminisce. She couldn't hold off that many men. There were too many people. She would either run out of bullets or they would get behind her. He had hoped to arrive before this situation. He wasn't built for this sort of situation. What would his wife do?

Pounding once more on the side of the carriage, he called, "Charge them."

The carriage picked up speed as it sped through the people who were crowding the carriage. It drove up next to the carriage. Pushing the door open, he called, "Drina, come on."

He could see her determined face through the curtained window. Upon recognizing his voice, she shot one more time through the window and then opened her carriage door. Then, her head disappeared.

Adrian waited nervously as the scattered men started picking themselves up and shrugging off their surprise. Adrian could smell the stench of the sewers from them. The muggy summer evening caused sweat to drip down his face as Drina popped her head back up and dragged her terrified maid into his carriage. Grabbing her hat from the seat, she noticed a man creeping between the carriages and tried to shoot him. The gun just clicked, empty of its bullets.

Adrian kicked the man before he could do anything else, and he slumped to the ground. Not wasting any more time, he pulled Drina into the carriage. As soon as the door was closed, it took off, scattering the men again.

Adrian didn't breathe a sigh of relief until he couldn't see the men anymore. Sighing, he leaned back, sagging against the bench. Though it still didn't give him breathing room with the maid huddled on the floor and Drina sitting next to him in a carriage meant for two. Turning to her, he looked her over to see if she was injured.

He needn't have worried. She was already tucking a stray hair that had been dislodged from her bun during the tussle. She was just as composed as when they were in the middle of the riot a few years ago.

"Are you doing all right, Lord Cooper? I do apologize for my appearance... and for my maid." Drina asked as she eyed the sobbing mess of her maid on the floor. "It was a bit much for her."

Of course, Drina would ask about him and even remember that he was Lord Cooper outside of the Palace, "I'm fine. I'm just glad I could make it in time to help. Do you know a safe place we can talk?"

Tilting her head to the side, her brow furrowed a little as she replied, "Buckingham Place. Is there any place more safe? Besides, I still need to get there as soon as possible. I can't have anything else interrupt the process of becoming queen."

Adrian couldn't help but flinch. He still couldn't quite believe his father was dead. The sorrow that he had pushed down came back up.

"I'm sorry for my words. Are you truly doing all right?" Drina said, placing her hand in his.

She was worried about him even though she had just gone through an ordeal. A smile started to form, releasing some of his sorrow. He already knew that his father was going to die, and he even had a chance to speak with him before he passed. Many never had the chance. The built-up sorrow slowly leaked away during the ride to the palace.

"Do you trust the coachman?" Drina asked as she eyed the maid, who had since passed out.

"Implicitly."

"Good." She motioned for William to pick up the fallen maid, and she led the way into the palace from a hidden doorway. Leading the way through the twisting corridors, they ended up in the servant quarters. They laid her in an empty room. "She will wake up later. You are dismissed. Just follow that corridor there. It will lead you out. Do not speak of what has happened here."

William looked at Adrian as she said this. At this, Adrian nodded and tapped his hand, a signal Adrian learned to have William send for help.

With a bow, William said, "My Lady." Then headed down the corridor indicated.

After he had gone away down the corridor, Drina led him in the opposite direction, leading him through several hallways until she took him to a massive portrait at the end of a hall. A quick motion of her finger along the frame opened it into a dark hole.

Adrian had known that there were a lot of hidden passageways. He used them to make his way to his father's room in the palace, but he had never seen this one before. Though he shouldn't have been surprised that she knew different passages than he did, but he was. He followed her through the passage until they reached a small, plainly decorated room with no windows.

"What is this place?" Adrian asked as he looked around the wood-paneled room.

Drina sat down, adjusting her skirts and brushing some of the dirt that had accumulated during their escapades and couldn't be seen in the shadows of the carriage. Once they were settled and out of danger for the moment, Adrian remembered that he still had the papers. The papers that held information that Ella needed to know and anxiety pulled at him. He had to get a message out to Ella. But who knows if she was still at the party, and even if she was, if someone went looking for her and she was found in a place that she wasn't supposed to be, things could go horribly wrong for her. Running his fingers through his hair, he scanned the pages, hoping that in the light of the room, the information he saw was wrong.

"I need to know what is going on."

Adrian raised his head. Pulled out of his thoughts, he turned to look at Drina. She was sitting, head held high. The rightful Queen Regnant, now that his father had passed. He swallowed the thought before his sorrow could build, "What do you mean?"

"Who are you working for?"

"I'm not working for anyone." Adrian shifted uncomfortably in his chair. It was true he wasn't working for anyone. He *was* helping the Fan Society but not working for them.

Her steely gaze pinned him to his chair as she smiled knowingly and raised her brow. A gaze that held more weight than her young years should have held.

Adrian swallowed. Should he tell her? He did have Lady Nora's permission, but did he want to put more weight on Drina? "Why do you assume that I work for someone?"

"Then why do you always ask for information from me? How did you know that I was going to be attacked today? How do messages get passed to me? I don't think your tutors trained you in espionage, considering your father's views on you." Adrian tried to interject, but Drina continued, "Not to mention all the odd things surrounding your "death." I went along with it because those intentions seemed to follow with my views on protecting Britain. And I was also powerless against my mother's control. But now I need to know. I am going to be crowned Queen Regnant. I need to know if I'm going to protect my people."

Her words struck him with a force. Bringing to mind a similar plea he once made to Ella in a side room. When he pleaded to know what was going on, though his was more of a plea to help Ella. Drina's was of concern for her fellow countryman. Could he really deny everything she has done? Could he keep things from her just from his desire to not have her carry the hardships? She already carries them and does it with the grace and nobility of her station. Something he could never do.

And if he told her, he could save Ella from Lord Fox.

Chapter Twenty Four

Ella crept through the hallways, trying to avoid any confrontation. Though considering the household, that didn't last long. A group of servants was coming through bearing drinks for the party. Thinking fast, she pulled on her necklace, one designed to break easily, and tossed it behind her into the corner of one of the doorways. Bending down, she put on a worried expression that she hid behind her fan. One of the men carrying bottles of wine stopped by her with a flushed and hurried look on his face.

"My Lady, is there anything I can do for you?"

It was obvious that he wanted to be on his way, but his training dictated that he should help a guest in distress.

"Have you seen my necklace? It must have fallen." Ella feigned distress as she pretended to look.

Ella could see the servant's troubling thoughts as he tried to keep his expression passive. But she could see as he cast glances at the bottle of wine and looked towards the ballroom. Making up his mind, he passed off the wine to some of the other already overburdened servants. Turning towards her, "My lady, what does your necklace look like?"

"How do you not know? It was the pride of the ball."

The poor servant was doing a great job restraining himself from stating the obvious of not knowing what it looked like and refrained from saying anything about the stained dress. Instead, he bowed, "Of course, it was the star of the ball."

His eyes fell onto the necklace that she had kicked into the corner, the necklace that she had kicked into the corner. Retrieving it, he asked. "Madame, is this your necklace?"

Holding up the sting of pearls to her, Ella let her face turn red with embarrassment. It wasn't hard with her emotions running high. "How dare you presume that a cheap string of pearls is mine."

The servant held his hands up in a disarming manner, "I am sorry for offending you, madame, but are you sure?"

"I know what my necklace look like and if you don't help me find it, I will search for it myself. I will be telling the Montagues about this!"

Ella turned away before she could see his expression and hurried down the hallway. Now, with an excuse, as well as a reason for servants to avoid her, it was easy to make her way through the manor and find the office. It was by far the easiest one to find. Good thing Lord Montague likes to show off just as much as his wife.

Using the lockpicks that she had tucked in her wig this time, she easily entered the office.

It was just as ostentatious as the rest of the house.

Gilded picture frames lined the walls, and statues were stuck between every shelf and wall space that wasn't covered by paintings. Hurrying to the desk so she could get this done as quickly as possible, she shuffled through the papers that were stacked on the desk. Most of the documents were financial documents, and Ella cursed herself for not spending more time learning about them. With what little knowledge she knew, she looked through the documents, not gaining much ground until she found some documents from a few years ago.

It seems like they weren't in good standing financially at all until a few years ago. It was then that they gained enormous amounts of money. Most of them looked like from sales of paintings. If she is correct that he is related to the Society of Shadows, how would they have made those art pieces sell for more money? There was something here, something that Adrian told her from his conversation with Drina. Her emotions were overloaded with worry for everyone, and she tried to soothe her concerns by rubbing her belly.

What would make an artist's work more valuable? Unlike most jobs, there is a reason the idiom starving artist became the norm. Most paintings don't become famous until after the artist is already dead.

Dead artist. There were several in the art community who had died in the last couple of years, upsetting the art community. If Lord Montague knew that the artist was going to die, he could buy it cheaper and then sell those pieces at an extravagant price after the artist's death.

But how much did he know? How close is he to the organization?

Panic shot through her as she thought the door opened. Spinning around, Ella franticly tried to think of a reason why she would be there. But the panic froze in her veins when she saw who it was, and her suspicions rose. "Lord Fox, I thought you would be trying to find your papers."

He shuffled about nervously and gave his sideways grin, "I thought about it, and you were right. It is too dangerous. So, in order to save my skin, I decided that it would be best to help you."

His joking manner was unnerving. The only relief she had was that Clementine should be following him. Maybe this was her chance to find out what secrets he was hiding. With Clementine to back her up and the out-of-the-way room, she could corner him while he thought she was innocent. "Lord Fox, how did you know about the meeting?"

Cocking his head to the side, he furrowed his brow, "How did I know about the meeting? I don't know what you mean. Are you all right, Lady Cooper?"

Still paying the part of a fool, but Ella trusted her instincts. There was something off about him. Clementine would be right behind her. Ella could see movement from behind the door. Should anything go wrong, Clementine would come. "I just wanted to know how you knew about the meeting. Maybe from how you learned of it, we can find out what the meeting was about."

He gave a wan smile and shifted, "How do you think I found out about it?"

It seems he still didn't want to give up playing his part, but if she could get him to break character, she could find out more. But how to do that? He most likely has been lying to her this entire time. Who was he? Watching him, his eyes caught her attention. Instead of the fear that she expected him to portray, his eyes were glittering with excitement. Eyes that haunted her smoke-filled memories. She heard another shuffle behind her. With Clementine at her back, she took a chance with her gut impression. With a polite smile and sharp gaze, Ella replied, "I bet you were clever like a Fox."

Fox. The name the swordsman gave to her. He reacted to the name. His face lost its joking manner as he forced a smile. "What do you mean?"

She pulled her fan out, flicking it open. Holding out her fan in an aggressive stance, she held it close enough for him to see the sharp points hidden beneath the lace. "I'm sure you know exactly what I mean. Now quit stalling. Where is the Society of Shadows?"

With a greedy grin, he broke the persona he had been holding. "And what do you think you are going to do, little fan girl? You are all alone."

With a smile, Ella held her position, "Who said I was alone?"

Confusion and wariness filled her as he burst into laughter, "Oh, my dear. You are so wrong. The person you are hoping for isn't here."

Fear ran like ice through her veins as Agatha opened the door and stepped through.

"Hello, Lady Cooper."

Chapter Twenty Five

Adrian explained the Fan Society as he knew it. Even though he wanted to hurry and help Ella, Drina held him back as she questioned him methodically about everything he could possibly know. Adrian tapped his fingers as he tried to sit still, though his breathing had become raspier as he talked to his cousin.

"Final Question."

Relief caused him to sag in his chair. Finally, he can go help his wife. With only half a mind on the question, he asked, "Yes, Drina?"

"Why is the Society of Shadows after me?"

Shaking his head, he replied, "I don't know. We still haven't figured out the reason."

Her brow furrowed, "Then how did you know they would be after me?"

Thinking about how to answer her, he realized that he had the papers in his hands. Shuffling through the finance documents, he found the pages he had nearly burned and showed her the one with the map on it. He showed it to her, pointing to the notation that mentioned the queen's route. The spot where she had been ambushed.

Drina studied the document. Feeling the weight of time slipping by, Adrian shifted in his seat. Holding back a sigh, he had hoped this last question, which was now turning into a series of questions, would soon be over, and they could send for help.

He jumped to attention when she asked a question, "Is this all that made them think that I would be in danger?"

"Well, not exactly," Adrian said, remembering the tension between Ella and Nora. "Ella thought that it would be an attack, and based on it mentioning Queen's route, she assumed that it would happen when . . . when my father passed."

Drina tacitly ignored his emotional moment and instead asked, "Why were you so sure that Ella was right?"

"Because she usually is," Adrian said with a shrug.

"I see." Drina eyed Adrian as she looked between him and the papers. "Then what has got you in a tiff? You have been anxious about something since you arrived, and it had nothing to do with the misadventure outside."

Worry twisted his lips as he wondered if he had good reason for concern. This was only his untrained eye and his idea that this *might* be true. He had minimal training and only a few years outside of his own house. What did he know? "It's nothing, just something that bothered me. That's all."

Giving him a flat stare, she said, "Though we haven't known each other for very long, I have learned enough things about you. You do not worry about nothing. What is wrong?"

With only a moment's hesitation, he passed over the other papers. "If you look at the handwriting . . ."

Eyes widening with understanding, she held the note from Mirror and the finance documents together. "They are the same handwriting."

Adrian leaned back as his worst fears were confirmed, "I fear as much."

Pressing her lips in a disappointed frown, Drina asked, "Does the Society not know about this?"

He shook his head and glanced back at the pages in her hand. "Due to Ella's past, she wasn't trained in this sort of thing. I doubt she would have noticed before she left. And I'm still not sure exactly everything this could mean."

Shuffling the papers into a neat pile, Drina held them out to Adrian. "There could be several things. One, he was writing on behalf of the Society of Shadows without knowing anything at all. Two, he is a person who is close enough to Mirror. Or three, he is Mirror himself."

That was even more than he thought of. All he knew was that the person who wrote the financial papers was connected to the Society of Shadows since the handwriting was the same as the note. Running his hand through his hair, he sighed.

"My arm is getting weary, Adrian," Drina said, still holding out the papers. Adrian quickly took them back as she continued, "We don't really know much at this point. But I assume that you took this information to the Fan Society?"

He shook his head, "I realized this as soon as I received news about my father's death." He managed too not to stutter on those words and finished his thought. "I didn't fully understand what I was seeing until in the carriage to help you. And you know what happened after that."

She gave him the "look" that only women can do when men state the obvious. "Do you know a way to get in contact with them?"

"The coachman knows."

"Ah. Then I guess we will just have to wait."

The very thing that Adrian hated to do. Sit and pray that his wife is safe.

There have been several attempts at arson, including the actual burning of
the Parliament building. After the riots, there has still been civil unrest.
What is the government going to do
about it? The new sickness that is going around is causing people's anger
to rise, like the growing fevers. Is this
going to end soon, or will it come to a
flaming end?

Newspaper 1835
Author unknown

Chapter Twenty Six

Ella was cold and wet, and it took her a moment to realize her eyes were open due to the darkness. The cold of damp stones pressed against her cheek as she groaned and tried to sit up. In an instant, the desire to puke mingled with the ringing in her head. Nearly falling back again, she held on with sheer willpower until the wave of nausea settled.

She held her stomach as she tried to stave off her worry that something happened to her child. Tugging on the threads of memory, she struggled to remember what had happened. She had been talking to Lord Fox, and Agatha had come up. What was Agatha doing there, and was she the reason there was a throbbing in the back of her head? Ella gingerly touched the back of her head, and it felt damp. She pressed a few more times to realize it wasn't blood but the dampness of the stones she was laying on. Not wanting to test her nausea, she crawled with her hands out, feeling the roughness of the stones and getting a rough estimate of the size of her cell. Not that it took long, considering how small it was. With the smell of the river in the air, she knew that she was in a cell somewhere in the tunnels. She could feel bars near the front of her cage, but no matter how much she felt along the bars she couldn't feel the lock.

There was no way to get out unless she had a chance to see how the door was locked. Curling into a ball around her stomach, she tried to keep her warmth and not let her fears take over. She had let Clementine know where she was, and Effie must have given the letter to the Fan Society. She had to hope that her messages had gotten out. That Effie had passed along the note. This time, she wasn't alone; there were people who knew where she was. She would just have to hope they find her in time. Her thoughts turned to how she got into this predicament. Was it really Agatha that she saw? Was she just following what Lord Fox was doing, or was she in charge of it? Were they part of the Society of Shadows? These thoughts haunted her as she bided her time in her cell, unable to do anything about it.

As was normal within the darkness, she had no idea how long she had been stuck in the cell when a light shone through the bars. Ella turned away from the sudden light, blinking as her eyes adjusted to the light. A figure was moving towards her. As the light blindness faded, the figure was revealed to be Agatha.

Rather than giving up more than she should until she knew what was going on, Ella continued to play her part, "What is going on? Agatha? Get me out of here."

She laughed.

"Agatha, why are you laughing? Get me out of here at once!" Ella cried as her suspicion grew along with a deep foreboding.

"Oh, my sweet, sweet Ella. Do you still not realize where you are? You can drop the act now." Agatha's words were far more aggressive and teasing than she had ever been. It surprised Ella so much that she almost missed that Agatha had said her real name.

Ella forced a confused look onto her face. Keeping in character to allow her thoughts time to scramble with this new information. "What are you talking about?"

"Still playing this game?" Agatha asked, a smug look on her face. No longer was there the weak woman who wished to do what was best. This was a woman who enjoyed playing with her enemy. And right now, the enemy was her. "Alright, I will pacify you. . . I'm so worried about this dark tunnel. How are we ever supposed to escape?"

It seems like her attitude of changing her mind all the time was her actual personality. But if that is how she was willing to do it, Ella would take the chance. "Do you see the lock? Or keys anywhere?"

Agatha gave an obviously fake nervous look on her face and shifted to the side, "I don't know. Maybe the lock might be up there."

She pointed to the top of the cage.

Now that Ella had the glow of the lamplight, she could see that the door to her cell looked like it had been put on upside down, making the lock above her head. Any average-sized woman would have issues unlocking it, especially if they were trying to pick the lock from the inside. It was odd, to say the least. "Can you reach the lock?"

"Now, why would I want to do that? You are my prisoner!" As she said those words, her false pretense fell completely, and anger filled her face.

Holding back her emotions, she tried to think calmly about why this was happening. Why would she try to capture her? It was obvious that she was involved with the Society of Shadows, but how?

"You are a part of the Society of Shadows," Ella said, hoping that this would make Agatha shed some light on what was going on.

A smile grew on her lips as she laughed, "You still don't know who I am. After everything?"

One more push, and she could get the information she needed. "Then why don't you tell me?"

Her laugh echoed again through the empty tunnels, "I know what you are doing, but I'll give you the answer you are fishing for. I believe you have already heard my codename. Mirror."

It was as if thunder had run through her. Mirror. The one that she suspected ran the Society of Shadows. She was head of the very organization that she had been searching for.

"Now, that is the expression I was looking for." A smug grin spread across Agatha's face as horror filled Ella.

Ella had been working with them. That meant that the entire time, they could keep an eye on her and know her movements. How long had they known?

No longer playing her part, she tried to hold back her expressions, not wanting to show weakness, "When did you find out?"

"When?" Agatha was toying with her, "Since the very beginning, my dear."

Ella struggled to keep from letting her dismay overwhelm her, and she couldn't fall apart now. People were depending on her. Her child, no she couldn't think about that right now or she would burst into tears. She just had to get as much information as possible. "How did you know?"

"How could I not know," she scoffed. "You Fan Society members are all the same. Hypocrites down to your very core and never doing a lick of good."

Ella could see the look of disgust and anger shimmering in her eyes. This was personal. But how did she know about the Fan Society well enough to have that much hatred? "Yes, we may be a bit slow when we try to make a change, but at least we try. What have you been doing? What are you even trying to accomplish?"

Agatha burst into laughter.

"How stupid are you?" She wiped the tears that eked out from her laugher. "I'm going to change this country by ridding it of its corrupt nobility."

"Is that why you are poisoning the water supply to kill those in the poor sectors of town? To get rid of corrupt *nobility*?" Anger laced her words. She had heard how many had died due to sickness this year. They were pouring things into the water, causing people to get sick, and yet she was spouting about the hypocrisy of the Fan Society.

As she held back angry tears, she stared down Agatha, if that was even her real name. It was because of this that she managed to catch a look of confusion across Agatha's face.

"Yet even as people are getting sick, the nobility still does nothing to help. They think that as long as they sit up in their manors, they will be fine." Her words didn't hold the same self-assuredness that they held a moment ago.

A crack.

Ella pushed further, "What about killing artists so you can make money? They aren't nobility. And why kill Drina? The people love her, and she is just a young girl."

Her face grew red as Ella spoke, until she finally burst out, slamming her fists onto the cage bars. "You know nothing! Even young girls can be corrupt. You are just like your mother, so full of self-righteousness. Well, it's too late! You may have missed the news. The king is dead, and your little precious Drina shall soon be joining him. With the recent riots and sickness, and with the nobility only caring about dead artists, they are ready for a revolt."

The horror rose within her as things clicked into place. The turmoil still persisted even though the law was passed. Deaths of important individuals. All done without anyone being any wiser.

A light and footsteps came from down the tunnels as the anger on Agatha's face turned to a sneer. "It looks like the rat was found."

Fear pierced her heart as Ella turned towards the newcomers. It was Lord Fox, leading two men with a third being dragged between them, blood covering his face. That man was tossed to the floor before Ella. Ella gasped in horror as she recognized him.

Arthur.

"What have you done to him?" Ella gasped. The horror that she had been holding back filled her as she watched Arthur's unmoving body.

"Why should you care what I do with someone sneaking into my things? Fox, get rid of him. I wouldn't want him stinking up the place more than it already does."

"Of course. We should continue with our plan, Mirror." Lord Fox said, no longer sounding jovial, and wearing the same grin that Agatha wore. It was only extenuated by the light of the lantern gleaming in his eyes as he rested his gaze on Ella. "What are you going to do with her?"

"Leave her here to rot, as she knows she will be unable to do anything about what is to come."

Then as she left, Fox and the two men who then picked up Arthur and dragged him away.

"Goodbye, fan girl. It was fun playing with you." Lord Fox said as he walked away, footsteps echoing through tunnels as the light and her hope disappeared.

Chapter Twenty Seven

Adrain was pacing the small room as Drina was calmly sipping tea. The time spent waiting was excruciating. There were a few times he planned on running out to find Ella, but Drina stopped him and said that he had no idea where she was. And it was true.

After watching him pace, Drina set down her cup of tea and continued writing the document that she had been working on.

In frustration, he asked, "What are you working on?"

"Something you will need," was her vague answer.

Confused, he leaned over her shoulder to read it when a noise came from the "door" to the room.

Drina pulled her gun from wherever she had hidden it, and since there wasn't much in the room, Adrian held his hand up in a fighting position. Not that it would do much, but it made him feel better.

"Your Majesty, I would prefer it if you did not shoot me. I come from the Fan Society to talk to you." The voice was easily recognizable as Lady Nora.

Looking at Adrian, Drina raised her bow in question. He nodded as he lowered his hands. She lowered her weapon, but he could tell that she could easily raise it should they prove a threat. "You may enter."

Lady Nora entered further into the room, letting them see her with her hand raised to show she didn't have a weapon in hand. Not that she needed one. Upon entering Drina's presence, she curtsied, "Your Majesty, may your reign be long and prosperous."

Drina nodded in return.

Unable to take it anymore, Adrian turned to Lady Nora, "Please tell me what is going on. What is happening to Ella? Where is she?"

Though Nora's face was passive, her lips were tense. Adrian could tell that she was worried. "When Cinders went to the party, she received a call for help. She sent the message to another member as well as a message to follow Lord Fox. No one has seen either Cinders or the Assistant since. I worry that the operative has gone to rescue the Friend before help could arrive."

"No, she wouldn't do that," Adrian answered instantly. Ella has changed. She wouldn't put their child in danger if she could help it. "Something must have happened to her. We need to send someone after her."

Her lips twitched, "Do you know where she is to rescue her?"

It came out closer to a growl, but she took a breath and regained her composer, "Your Majesty, there are assassins coming for you. It was a good thing you didn't go directly to where they would swear you in. So, for now, you should sit tight here until they are taken care of."

Drina shook her head. "Now that I know what is going on, it is time for me to take action. I will not be cowed by those over me anymore. I am to be the Queen Regnant of Great Britain. Can I trust you to take care of the situation while I take care of mine?"

"Yes, your Majesty."

Nodding, Drina turned back to her paper and stamped her seal on it. After rolling it and tying it, she passed it to Adrian. "This is my authority. Use it when needed."

"Why are you passing it to him? We are about to take on a dangerous group, and Lord Cooper should not be involved. It is too dangerous for him." Lady Nora asked in confusion.

"I don't trust you. I trust him. And even though it is dangerous, I believe that he has the capability to do what needs to be done. He will be the bridge," Drina said. The aura around her brooked no opposition. Her head was held high, uncowed by the situation.

She sincerely believed in him, but could he believe in himself? Adrian stopped himself before his thought could go down that path. Just as she trusted him, he needed to trust her. "I will do as you ask. What do we need to do, Lady Nora?"

Eyes shifting between the Queen and Adrian, Nora gauged their reactions. Sighing in defeat, she turned to Adrian, "You must stay out of the fighting then. I can't have you dead when Cinders comes back."

"Agreed."

Nora sighed again. Then, regaining her composer, she curtsied once more to Drina, 'By your leave, your majesty."

"Go."

And with that, Nora turned and headed out the door, and Adrian trotted after her. He followed her through the darkened hallways until they were in a more familiar place within the palace. "Where are we going?"

"If you were going to assassinate the queen, thinking she would be shaken after an attack, where would you go?"

Adrian thought about it, "To her room."

She nodded, not slowing even though his breath was starting to turn to a wheeze again. Ignoring the strain in his lungs, he continued after her. He would not let his weak body stop him from helping. Drina gave him the paper, and he needed to be sure that it was used when it was needed.

As they entered the wing that held the sleeping quarters, she halted and held him back. "Stay out of the way, and don't get hurt."

Nodding, he watched as she glided down the hallway, as moonlight filtered through the windows, reflecting on the gilded furniture. Giving the room a glow, with plenty of shadows to hide in. Nora glided down the rest of the way down the hall. Adrian knew how heavy those skirts were since Ella had shown him her garments that had hidden pockets in them. As she moved, he couldn't even hear the rustle of a skirt. Looks like she lost none of her skills when she was away. Adrian's heart pounded as she moved farther away, and he had to clamp his hand over his mouth to keep his wheezing under control.

She disappeared through a door, and still, he couldn't see any assassins. Not that he thought he was good enough to find any assassins hidden in the shadows. As time ticked by, Adrian could feel stress building. Already, he had to wait for Ella, but now Nora was putting herself into a dangerous situation, and yet again, he could do nothing.

He was startled out of his self-misery by the sound of a vase crashing down and the scuffling sounds of hurried footsteps. Adrian flinched as a loud thud came from the room. Knowing that he should stay out of the way, but unable to keep still, he rushed to the room.

After opening the door, he found that Nora was holding down a man in dark clothes, keeping him pinned to the ground. As he came in, Nora looked up and said, "I thought I told you to wait."

"I just wanted to. . ." He stopped and sighed, "Sorry."

"I'm just glad you weren't hurt, but . . . watch out," Nora called, looking behind him.

Adrian turned, just managing to avoid getting sliced by the dagger that came whizzing by his head. Backing away to put some distance from his assailant, he nearly tripped on the half-broken vase that had been smashed on the floor. It was his saving grace, allowing him to avoid yet another swipe. Now that he was closer to where Nora was, she pushed him to the floor to make him avoid another attack. Adrian winced in pain as his hand landed on a broken piece of porcelain as he struggled to crawl away from his attacker. His wheezing rose to a crescendo as his attacker stood over him. Covering his head, Nora stopped the attack by smashing her fan against his knee.

"Get out of here."

Struggling to do as Nora asked, he rose to his feet. He stood in stunned silence as he watched what was happening. Using the fan efficiently, she disarmed the attacker who had been after Adrian. She was distracted by the other assassin, the one she had originally pinned, who reached for the dagger that his partner had dropped and was going after Nora. Adrian instantly went over and grabbed his arm, just like Ella had taught him.

Nora turned and, noticing Adrian's struggle with the armed opponent, smacked the assailant across the face, and he collapsed on the floor. "If you had stayed out like I had told you, this mess wouldn't have happened."

Hanging his head, Adrian nodded and shuffled in place. Nora gave him an eyebrow raise, then pinned the one who had attacked Adrian as he was crawling away. Ripping off the mask, Adrian didn't recognize the assailant, but she did. Holding her fan, pointed first towards his face, making sure she could see the pointed tips beneath the lace. The man gulped as he stopped trying to escape. "Ah, Baron Pole, it is a pleasure to see you. I didn't realize you have taken up the art of assassination. Perhaps you would be so kind as to tell me who sent you?"

The assassin held his tongue.

Nora tried again. "Do you know who I am?"

He spat at her, refusing to answer. Tutting, Nora pulled a hairpin from her updo while still holding her fan at his face, ready to slice him should he move. With the pin, she pricked his skin, then put it back up into her hair. "Let's see if you refuse to talk now. I will ask you again, who sent you?"

The man's eyes glazed over as he burst into laughter, "The Society of Shadows will not answer to the Fan Society. You are going to lose, just like you filthy women should."

"I didn't realize someone who considers himself a gentleman would use such foul language. Where do they stick the prisoners?"

His laughter echoes at her question, sending a chill down Adrian's spine. The manic sound made him wonder what Nora pricked him with as the man continued to look at her with a glazed look. "Do you really think you will find your little friends in the tunnels? HA! Try again; you will fail, and we will rule just as we should. A girl shouldn't be on the throne."

His words turned nonsensical as he laughed manically. Nora pressed the handle of her fan on a point in his neck, causing the man to pass out.

The man's laughter continued to echo in his ears, "What did you do to him?"

Nora stood, leaving the bodies on the floor, and turned to Adrian. "Do you really want to know?"

Shaking away the haunting laughter, he nodded. Remembering the paper that Drina gave him, he said, "I need to know."

"I'm sure that you already know that we do not kill people." Adrian nodded, confused. "If a girl was seen, to protect her, the society would make it so the person is seen as insane."

Adrian's confusion turned to horrified understanding. He also understood that there wasn't much that they could do otherwise. If the girls were found out, it would be dangerous for them, as well as harmful to the Fan Society. Now, he understood more of Ella's misgivings about the Fan Society. If they made a mistake, they could destroy someone's life. The paper that he held felt heavy as the responsibility that he bore became heavier with greater understanding. "I see."

She started to leave when Adrian stopped her, "Where are we going?"

"To save my daughter." She said, a fierce glint in her eye.

"What about them?" Adrian pointed to the bodies on the floor.

She waved his concerns away. "The maids will take care of them."

Adrian followed after her, glad to be on their way but realizing that if the maid was taking care of it, they must be part of the Fan Society as well. If having this many assassins could come through without anyone knowing, how much power did the Fan Society carry? And yet, why could they only accomplish so much?

Chapter Twenty Eight

Ella lay curled up on the floor, trying to keep warm in the coolness of the tunnels, sorrow engulfing her. It was as if she had fallen right back into the darkness that had shadowed her as if it had never left her. A single tear rolled down her cheek and fell to the hard stone floor. Was this what things have come to? Lying on the floor, helpless to do anything? No, she couldn't. Though she was too late for Arthur, she wouldn't be too late for her child. She had to stop this from getting any worse. She had promised herself she would not return to what she was. Grunting, she moved her frozen legs into a standing position and made her way towards the bars.

Grasping the bars, she leaned her head against them as she struggled to figure out how she was going to escape. Her shoes were missing, as well as her jewelry. Her overskirts were taken away, as well as some of her petticoats. She had been stripped of most of her things, which had made it cold in the damp tunnels beneath London. However, they hadn't removed her crinoline, which was tied over her chemise. This was most likely because it was annoying to remove or put on, and heavy to boot. Thanks to Eleanor's help, the Fan Society turned it into the newest fashion statement. This helped make the skirts wider while reducing many, many layers of petticoats. It also gave the Fan Society more space under the skirts to hide things. All of which had been removed, But the crinoline was made of wood, and wood can splinter. Placing one of the hoops between the bars, she leveraged the hoop until a loud crack could be heard ringing through her cage. Heart thudding in her chest, she listened for the sounds of anyone coming to check on her.

It was hard to tell if it was footsteps or her heart beating in her chest. She thought she heard an echo, but she didn't see anyone. Taking a deep breath, she pulled the broken hoop from the fabric loops, giving her half a hoop with some splintered ends that seemed long enough for the lock. Now, to find the lock that was above her head and pick a lock with a long curved piece of wood without it splintering in the lock, making it then impossible to pick. Her hands had started to shake at the enormity of the mission, but she had people counting on her. The shakes stilled. Remembering how the lock was when Agatha had appeared and using her skill of moving through the dark, Ella positioned the hoop. Slowly, she tried to use the top of the wood to reach above her head and curve into the lock. Using the feel of the wood, she slid it across the metal until she felt a flat piece of metal. The lock. Hands sweaty, she tried to wipe her hands on the chemise while keeping the wood steady. Grasping the wood again with both hands, she slid the end against the lock, hoping to find the opening for the key. It rasped against the metal as she heard a crack of wood.

She froze, breathing in the mildew smell as she hoped it hadn't gotten stuck in the lock. Fear made a tear leak from her eye as she realized it couldn't be stuck in the lock since she had felt the broken piece fly by. Taking calming breaths, she closed her eyes, refraining from wiping them. It's not like her eyes could help her at this moment anyway. With steady hands, she slid the end gently into the lock. Feeling the softer vibrations of the lock, Ella strained to remember if the lock was completely upside down or not. If it was, she would have to think of the lock as upside down, curved, and backward. Ella had always had an instinct for locks, but now was the time for her to trust her instincts. Slowly, she lightly guided the splinter into the lock using the tension of the wood she held in her hands and sound. A light metallic click could be heard as the wood pressed further into the lock. Stress caused sweat to bead on her forehead, trying to make her break concentration as it slid down her face, cooling her further. Her entire focus was on the wood and the lock, and with one last press, she could feel it click into place.

The tension that she had been holding released as she took the time to wipe her brow. Taking a deep breath, she sniffed as she felt a cold coming on. She needed to turn the lock, but it would be easy for the thin sliver of wood to break, leaving her trapped. Feeling time spilling away from her, she turned the wood. As she did so, she could hear the sound of cracking wood. She stopped realizing that she had turned it the wrong way since it was upside down. Frustrated at herself, she tried again as the wood, now barely clinging to the larger piece, managed to hold on until the lock creaked open.

Freedom. She sagged against the bars as all the tension was released from her. But then she remembered the reason she needed to escape. She had to tell them what was going on. Pushing the bars open, she left her cell. Then she looked in the two directions. She didn't know where she was, and the tunnels were complex and vast. Taking a deep breath, she headed in the direction the Agatha had left. Hands feeling the damp brick and clay walls, she tried to hurry, but tiredness pulled at her legs, making it a struggle to lift them. The sound of running water could be heard up ahead, and a flash of hope that she might be able to use the flow of water to find her way pushed her forward until she heard voices.

Freezing, she noticed up ahead was a T, and a faint light could be seen. On shaky legs, she inched forward as the distant voices became clearer.

"... Mirror wanted this done. Make sure all the drugs are poured at the locations."

Another voice grunted as splashing sounds moved further away.

Ella recognized the first voice as Fox. He was saying that Mirror wanted the drugs to be poured, but from the expression on her face before, she had no part in it. What was going on between them? She needed to let people know what she knew, but if she was caught again, they wouldn't know anything. Pressing her hand to her belly, she tried to turn back when a sneeze burst from her like a booming drum. The light started moving toward her, and Ella took off at a run, hoping her wobbly legs wouldn't fail her now.

Chapter Twenty Nine

As they rode in the carriage to one of the known entrances to the tunnels, Adrian showed one of the papers he had accidentally grabbed. Nora studied the map of the tunnels in the dimly lit carriage.

"This is most likely where she might be kept." Lady Nora said, pointing to a spot on the map. The tunnels were wider there, and they didn't have any messages like in some of the other corridors.

"Why do you think that?" Adrian asked, looking for something that mentions dungeons or prisons.

"This map shows actions that they are taking with the drugs. Why would they pour drugs where their base is?"

Adrian nodded in understanding, but he could see several spots that didn't have places to pour the concoction into the water system. "What about the other places?"

She noted him looking at the other blank spaces, then smiled, "Those aren't in an easily defensible position. And considering that they know about the Fan Society, they know enough that they would need a secure place to hold her."

Nodding, Adrian could see what she was talking about. Ella was one of the best at lockpicking since her childhood and had been reliant on it to survive her stepmother.

"What about backup?" Adrian asked. If they had made a mistake and chosen the wrong place, they may not have gotten to her in time.

"I told the fan society, but there aren't many who are decent fighters in the area. You talked to the Queen, and she was planning on sending some of the soldiers, but they will take some time to gather and respond. The new police force is also in the same predicament."

"So, we don't know when backup is coming or even if we will get it in time," Adrian sighed, knowing the reality of the situation. He looked up into Nora's face, which had now turned to face outside the carriage. Her face was shadowed by more than just the lighting; something was weighing on her mind. "She will be fine."

Her worried look softened as she turned to face him again, "That is only one reason why I am worried."

Thinking about her words, he asked, "Does this have to do with the mission you are on?"

Nora raised her brows in surprise, "Why do you think so?"

"You have been very harsh on Ella, as if you knew someone like her. You have been very interested in Ella's missions, more so than usual. May I know more about what your mission was? I believe that it will help with what is going on now. I don't want Ella to get hurt because information was not shared." Adrian was breathing hard with the passion of his words. It surprised him.

It must have also surprised Nora since she sat there in silence until it became uncomfortable.

"If you can't, I underst-"

"I will tell you what I can." Nora cut off his words and spoke, surprising him again. She normally wouldn't tell him anything. She was very strict with herself and others.

Hesitating before she forced the words from her mouth, Nora said, "Before I let you know, this must be kept a secret. This is not to be spread around."

"On my honor."

"I trust you." Warmth blossomed within him at her words. She had never liked him learning about the Fan Society before. Nora continued, "When I was a student, there was an incident where another student went against orders and against the Fan Society code and killed a noble. Due to this incident, she was kicked out of the Society."

Adrian nodded. Considering the long history, he wasn't surprised that something like that would have happened. He was going to ask how this was connected when Adrian saw the sorrow on her face. If she had been a student at the same time as her, they would have known each other, and from the look on her face, they knew each other very well. "Who was she?"

Her fingers twisted in her lap, though her face held no expression as she spoke her next words. "As I said, she was a student with me. A very talented student who would have become great if she didn't let her emotions get in the way of the bigger picture."

Though her eyes were on him, he could feel that her thoughts were far away. "Why did she kill the noble?"

Nora shook her head. "She thought she was protecting someone and then only got them both hurt in the end."

This situation felt very similar to what had happened five years ago with Ella. No wonder Nora had been hard on her. Adrian opened his mouth to question her further, but Nora shook her head, "I will speak no more on this. I need to plan on what we need to do."

Accepting her words, he sat in silence as she looked out the window, lost in thought.

Ella tried to keep her breathing under control, and her footsteps light as she ran through the dark tunnels. But exhaustion pulled at her. She stumbled, crashing to her knees, rough brick scratching at her skin, causing blood to drip down and tearing off another strap from the hoop. The sound of Fox's footsteps pulled her back onto her shaky feet, and she once again stumbled onward. He had sent his men down some of the other tunnels to block off her escape. Ella had to find her way out before her time ran out.

A prayer formed in her mind that became a chant pushing her onward. Don't let my baby get hurt, don't let my family get hurt, don't let England be destroyed.

Those words were the only thing that kept her going as her mind numbed from exhaustion, and the never-ending darkness made it difficult to know where she was. Her hand was already rubbed raw from using the wall to guide herself, but she had to stop using the wall because he could follow her bloody handprint along the wall. Now, she was blindly running into the emptiness.

Her foot missed the ledge that she had been running on and fell into the river, causing her to roll into the water with a splash.

"Are we done with this little game of cat and mouse?" Fox asked, amusement evident in his voice. He could have caught her ages ago, but he seemed to enjoy her weak attempts to escape. "I had hoped that you would have made this more entertaining, but alas, you are just as weak as Agatha."

Ella had been crawling in the dirty water in hopes that he wouldn't hear her as much, but the words froze her in place. Her mind tried to connect that piece of information to what she had, but her sluggish mind couldn't grasp what his words hinted at, and she forced her freezing hand to move forward. Her numbed hands bumped into something that her frozen nerves couldn't feel.

She moved her hand up along the surface until she realized that it was steps. Crawling out of the water, she moved up, desperate to hide from Fox. Fumbling around, she found a door in front of her as she tried to find the handle.

"I am the one in control, Fan Girl. It will be a pleasure to catch you." Fox's words echoed through the tunnel, reminding her that he was coming ever closer. She found the handle and shoved her way inside, closing the door behind her. Fear thudded through her heart as she slid to the floor, unable to move anymore. She stayed frozen on the floor, shivering. She tried curling around herself to return warmth back.

As she did, the sound of voices came from up ahead, causing tears to drip down her face. Not having the energy to move.

Chapter Thirty

They arrived at the entrance that was marked on the map. It was a door hidden under a bridge near the river. Adrian looked around into the moonlit night, casting a haunted glow around them.

"If you are coming with me, you must stay behind me at all times."

Adrian nodded and then followed her into the gaping maw that led into the depths. Thankfully, Nora brought a lantern with them, or Adrian would have spent the time stumbling in the dark. Nora led them through the twisting tunnels. Adrian was glad about it. He had no idea where they were but trusted that Nora would get them to where they needed to go. They moved swiftly and quietly as Adrian tried to be as sneaky as he could. He couldn't see Nora's face, but she didn't seem worried that they would be found; it was almost like she was hoping to find someone. Her fan was clenched in her white-knuckled hand, ready for anything.

The room they had been heading to was not the prison that they were expecting. When they arrived, the door was locked, and with a pair of lockpicks that were hidden in Nora's shoes, she made quick work of the lock. Listening before entering, she opened the door. It was an office of some sort. The papers on the desk curled from the humidity in the air.

The room linked to another. Nora surprised him when she did not do more than a cursory glance at the papers. She must be truly worried about Ella. They pressed forward, moving along the connecting path to the other room. As they moved closer, he heard steps pacing across the floor. It stopped when they reached the doorway. "Hello, Justice."

Adrian couldn't see who Nora was talking to and peeked around her. Standing in front of them was Agatha, with Clementine tied to a chair beside her.

"Justice?" Agatha snarled. "I haven't heard that name in a while, Cinders. I no longer go by Justice. I go by Mirror to show the Society the hypocrisy of what they do."

The words were spat out of her mouth as she glared daggers at Nora. Nora's face was passive and a little sad as she said, "I am no longer Cinders. I am now referred to as Phoenix."

"Oh, a mythological creature who rises from the dead; how pretentious of you," Agatha sneered. Adrian turned his attention to her. She was a few feet away from Clementine, who had her head hanging to her chest. Worry rose as he saw her there, but Adrian could only assume that she was still alive. Otherwise, why would they tie her up? Adrian wanted to check on Clementine, but he knew better than to interrupt the conversation. However, she shifted, showing that she was alive. Unable to do anything to help her, he eyed Nora. He could tell this was the girl she was talking about in the story, and there was a lot not mentioned.

Nora sighed, "You do realize that I don't choose my codename. I thought that you would remember that from your days at the Academy. Though it seems that you have forgotten much more than that."

Face turning red, Agatha took a few steps forward, "How *dare* you? You always were so full of yourself. I remember everything about the hypocritical Society. I remember how we were supposed to save England. It only meant the nobility."

"That is the only inspiration you have received from the incident? I have heard of the exploits of the Society of Secrets, which Mirror runs. It seems you are still as immature as you were back then."

"You call what happened an incident?!" Agatha burst into laughter as if everything that was holding her back was cut with that one sentence. "My friend was being beaten to death by the young lord, and I defended her. You call defending a friend immature?"

Adrian could feel Agatha's frustration radiating from her body as she still shook with emotion. Nora was unreadable. But considering her lack of aggression, she had no intention of fighting Agatha.

"You defended her to his death, which undid years of work." Nora still hasn't taken a step forward, but Agatha has.

"Should I have let her die?"

Nora didn't answer. Only a sad smile that touched her lips.

"You think I should have! It was a good thing they kicked me out. I could never accept being forced to let my friend die." The bitterness in Agatha's voice made it all the clearer how she felt about the Society and Nora. But Nora wasn't saying anything. It was the same thing that happened with Ella. They were not communicating with each other. And if this continued, Ella would be in danger longer.

Stepping forward, he said, "It is horrible to see your friend get injured, and it shouldn't happen, but what happened when the noble died?"

Startled at his interruption, Agatha took a step back, finally looking him in the face, "Who are you to interrupt?"

From what he had picked up during the conversation, he could tell that something was wrong. Agatha didn't seem like someone who would attack the commoners, considering how she felt about her friend. It seemed off. There were oddities in the papers that he saw and his conversation with Drina.

"You don't know anything." His words came out as a whisper, surprised at the thought.

She took it as an attack, "I know more than you, child. What does a sickly prince know? You spent your whole life inside your palace."

This was just making her agitated; he needed her to calm down and see reason. If he could, maybe Agatha would let Ella and Clementine go. Nora wasn't the person who could do that. He would have to calm her down. But could he do it? He was just a prince who spent his life in a sickbed. It was only recently that he left. What did he know? Even after all this time, he is still worried about it. Was it his place to help here? He knew that there had been times when his interference caused more trouble for them. But the same thing happened to Ella, and things worked out. He just had to overcome his fear. He also knew that Ella and Nora had both been scared, but they found the courage to do what was needed, just as he could.

"Madame Agatha, I'm sure you know more than me about the world. Though I don't know how you know about my identity, you are correct. I have lived most of my life away from people. But that is not so now."

Agatha scoffed at his words but didn't retaliate. It was a good start, though his next words will cause some aggression. But if she doesn't hear those words, she will fall. And from the look in Nora's eyes, she didn't want Agatha to fall.

"Madame, you have said multiple times that you didn't wish to hurt the commoners, but from our information, Mirror has done many things that harm the citizens, such as dumping drugs into the water channels near the slums, as well as killing artists to earn money from them. Also, from the documents I have received, the burning of the Parliament building and the mine incident may have also been caused by Mirror." He held her disbelieving eyes, "What do you have to say, Madame Agatha?"

"You too? How dare you say such a thing?" Agatha's face had turned a vibrant shade of red that was visible even in the darkness of the tunnels. "What do you know?"

He had already known that she wouldn't readily accept it, though he hadn't expected someone else to tell her as well. But words weren't the only things he had. Adrian came forward slowly and held out the papers, "Why don't you have a look yourself?"

Agatha glanced at the papers in his hands, a touch of fear in her eyes. She didn't take the papers that he held before her. "Those could be fake. I don't trust the Fan Society."

"You are still such a child." Nora interrupted. "You haven't changed since you were kicked out. Still rash and not able to think about the bigger picture."

Opening her mouth to shout, it snapped shut as footsteps came from behind them, "Let us calm down."

Adrian couldn't help but feel a chill creep down his spine as Agatha beamed at the new arrival, "Lord Fox, what a welcome surprise."

Chapter Thirty One

Ella crouched in her corner, distracted enough by the conversation ahead that she didn't notice her shivering. When she first arrived, she saw Agatha dragging Clementine and tying her to a chair. Ella had to hold herself back from running to her friend. She was too weak to do anything for her other than get herself captured. It seemed that Effie had told the Fan Society about the note. Hopefully, Clementine had sent for help before she got herself captured as well. Holding herself back, she hoped to get the chance to untie her once Agatha left, but soon after she had tied Clementine, Adrian and her mother arrived. As she listened to Nora and Agatha explain their connection, Ella was lit with understanding. Her mother was harsh because she didn't want Ella to turn out like Agatha. She had to hold back her tears when Adrian spoke and calmed the situation. Or at least he was going to if Lord Fox hadn't arrived.

A chill ran down her spine that was more than the cold. Ella froze in place as she listened in on the conversation.

"Should we send for the men to capture the intruders, Madame?" Lord Fox asked Agatha. Ella listened with bated breath for Agatha's answer.

"What are we going to do with them?" Agatha replied. She could hear her voice warm to Lord Fox, reminding her of the look Agatha had given him.

Agatha has truly fallen in love with Lord Fox.

"Check the pages. I don't think you should trust him." Ella could hear Adrian say as he moved closer to Agatha. Ella had to hold herself back. He was moving closer to danger, but the timing was still wrong. If she acted too quickly, it would turn into a fight instead of a conversation. She had to wait for the perfect time, or someone would be sacrificed before this was over.

"You have no idea of what you are talking about," Agatha yelled. Ella watched as Lord Fox held her back.

Nora stepped forward and gently nudged Adrian behind her, "Agatha, you should know that in your line of work, there is always room for betrayal. You should take a look at the papers before it's too late."

It was deathly silent. Ella could feel the intense atmosphere even though it wasn't directed at her. Agatha's next words were said in a scary, calm voice, "I don't trust you."

The conversation was on the edge of a knife; only the tension kept them from falling to either side. But who knew what side it would fall to? Ella held her breath, readying herself to move, and waited to see who would break the tension. Struggling to bring to mind anything that would help in the situation as she fought through her exhaustion. When this standoff broke, it would end in a fight.

But her fears became unfounded as Adrian spoke up. "You may not trust her, but are you willing to accept my information?" His voice came out steady and calm, just like he had always spoken to Ella when she was having a hard time. "You have worked hard to try to save everyone, but are you willing to sacrifice so many people because you were unwilling to look at information?"

The tension eased, though she still gave a sharp look to Nora. She finally took the papers in Adrian's hands and started to look through them.

"Are you thinking I betrayed you?" Lord Fox said. He was calm and controlled, even though Ella knew that he had been going behind Agatha's back. "After all we have been through together?"

Agatha faltered as Lord Fox took the papers from her limp fingers.

Flipping through the pages, he scoffed, "There is no direct evidence of anything. This just shows that I work with my cousin Lord Greenwood, as well as with Mirror."

Though it was difficult to see, Ella could tell that there was confusion on her face as she glimpsed the papers in Lord Fox's hands. "Those aren't my orders, though."

"Oh my, they aren't? Are you sure?" His flustered look seemed genuine, but from what Ella heard earlier in the tunnels, it was all a lie.

With a shake of her head, Agatha said, "Of course, I wouldn't put all the people in danger like this."

"I was positive that you did call for the assassination of Lady Alexandria before she could become queen."

Ella watched as Adrian stiffened at the mention of his cousin. Her heart yearned to reach for his hand that was clenched by his side as he held his tongue. He knew enough by now that if he spoke now, it would only be emotional.

"Yes, but that was one noble member. I would not have called for the deaths of so many commoners. This seems to be the cause of the plague

that had been going around the slums. Why would I put them in danger?"
Agatha still seemed to be resistant to Fox's words at what she saw, but she was crumbling.

"You also told me to use the sickness to set them to riot."

"Yes, but-"

She was cut off as Fox moved closer to her, almost as if he was a hunter stalking its prey, "After everything that I have done for you and how much we have gone through together, why would you believe their words?"

"Well, I," she stuttered out as he put his arm around her shoulders, seeing her abashed by her thoughts. Her confident stance was now one of shame as she turned away from Lord Fox. He was the reason why there were so many incongruities with her personality. The confident woman, then the child the next.

"Haven't I given you leadership? Why would I do things against your orders? I have always sat behind you, letting you shine. After all, who picked you up from the streets after you had been thrown away?" His voice dripped like honey, speaking in a sweet tone that hid the dagger of his words. "After all I have done for you, you want to turn your back on me? How could you?"

His words turned from honey to ice as he leaned close to Agatha. Dropping her head, she turned away. Adrian looked like he wanted to speak up, but whatever he was going to say now that Fox was done, Agatha wouldn't listen anymore. Her mother's brows were crinkled together, letting Ella know that she was getting frustrated and that there was nothing she could say. The time for her to appear was now.

Ella tried to stand, but her feet were numb, and instead, she only flopped forward. She barely managed to catch herself before she landed on her stomach. They all turned to her. Adrian tried to rush over to her, but Ella held up her hand. The information she had to deliver couldn't be done by someone who wasn't strong. Adrian stopped where he was and fidgeted as he trusted Ella to do what she needed to do.

Taking a deep breath, she pulled on the dregs of her energy to try to stand. With weak knees and her body wracked with chills, she moved step by step towards Agatha. Though she wasn't far away, the few steps she had to take were painful. Each step she took with her numb feet shot pain up her legs like she was stepping on knives. But she took another step, focusing on putting one foot in front of the other.

It was agonizing, but it felt like everyone was holding their breath. Though for different reasons.

"Agatha, why are we going to listen to this girl? She is part of the Fan Society as well." Lord Fox's words tore Agatha's eyes from her as he forced her to look back at him. "Remember, I am the only one you can trust."

Fear shot through Ella as she tried to shuffle forward faster. "He is lying to you. You already know that. The papers you see before you are no different from the ones you've seen with me. I already saw your doubt, then."

Agatha's eyes turned towards her, but her face was still in Lord Fox's hand. Her eyes flicked back and forth between them, her brow furrowing.

How could Ella make Agatha believe her? Her only information was hearsay, and considering how much control Lord Fox had over her, who knows if she would believe her? But memories of their conversations ran through her mind as she desperately searched through them to find anything that she could say.

"Nothing will change if we don't do anything about it." Those words slipped from Ella's mouth before she even knew that she was saying them.

Agatha pulled her chin away from Lord Fox and turned to face Ella, "Why are you saying that?"

The confidence had come back into her eyes. The confidence that Lord Fox had suppressed. It was just a spark, but Ella knew that Lord Fox had a lot of control over Agatha. Though Ella had been annoyed at Agatha's wishy-washy nature, now that Ella understood, she couldn't stand by and let her be destroyed. Besides, it was the only way she could fix everything. If she had Agatha's help, she could stop what Lord Fox was doing.

"You have always been passionate about your beliefs. Especially about helping the weak."

"Yes, but how does it pertain to changing things?" Agatha questioned, her arms folded.

"Is not an eighteen-year-old girl part of those who are weak? Are the people in the slums also not part of the weak?" Ella pressed, trying to bring back the compassion that she knew Agatha had, which had been buried under her quest for revenge.

Pressing her lips tightly, Agatha said, "Of course, I already told you I had nothing to do with the sickness."

"Yes, but instead of helping those that are sick, you used them. Right now, I know that there is much unrest due to the sickness. Not to mention causing riots which many people died, most of them commoners. How is using people any better than what you are accusing the Fan Society of doing?"

Ella's words made Agatha pause. She was no longer aggressive in her defensive stance, but now had confusion in her eyes. Ella had to press her advantage before Lord Fox got his greedy claws back in her.

"If you think that using people who could use your help goes against what you believe, then you should stop listening to Lord Fox, who is using you and has been for a very long time."

"That is absurd," Lord Fox interjected.

But this time instead of leaning into him, Agatha stopped him, "Let her speak. What are you talking about, Ella?"

Taking a deep breath, Ella locked eyes with Agatha, showing her sincerity. "As I was escaping, Lord Fox was telling some of your men that, under your orders, they should pour the drugs into the water."

"Why are you-"

Agatha held up her hand to silence Lord Fox before he could continue. Ella felt warmth run through her as Agatha glanced back at the papers and eyed Ella and her allies. Did she get Agatha to change her mind and go against Lord Fox?

"Lord Fox, you have yet to deny what they have said. Are they telling me lies?" Agatha turned to him, and instead of leaning away from him, she was standing tall, though she still had longing in her eyes.

The shock on his face at her question only appeared for a moment before his face turned pleasant again. He grasped her hand and gave it a gentle kiss. "Lies, why would I lie to you? You know I only have the greatest respect for you."

Her countenance faltered. Ella couldn't allow Agatha to fall again for Lord Fox. But what to say?

It was Adrian who spoke, "Sometimes even those we trust hold secrets."

Those words pierced her heart as she knew that he was speaking of her. And yet his words held no anger. If they did, it would have caused Agatha to be on the defensive, and the talk would have failed. Adrian's words helped Agatha regain the strength she needed. Having once been a member of the Fan Society, Agatha wasn't a stupid person. She must have suspected that Lord Fox was suspicious. But from the conversation, Agatha had been in a vulnerable position, and Lord Fox had saved her. That savior became a feeling of love that Lord Fox must have manipulated. A calculated move. The emotion of betraying someone who saved her with her doubts must have torn at Agatha.

"I agree with Lord Cooper. I was just trying my best to help." Lord Fox said, still holding on to Agatha's hand and giving her a sweet smile. Yet again, she didn't feel anything shining in his eyes as he looked at Agatha.

Adrian interrupted, "Not all secrets are bad, but many are. And considering he hasn't really answered your question, I would be suspicious, Lady Agatha. But considering you know him best, I leave judgment to you."

It was as if a door had been opened for Agatha. Considering how Lord Fox had been treating her, Adrian's trust in her was something that she didn't realize she was wanting. Though Lord Fox said that he gave her responsibilities, it doesn't mean that he trusted her. And from Agatha's stance, she could tell that it was so. With backbone straightened and gaze clear, she turned to ask Lord Fox, "What he said was true. Why have you danced around my questions?"

"I have answered your questions."

Agatha cut him off, "No, you dance around the question. It's the same thing I used to avoid answering the question. Something I learned from you. Now, have you been poisoning the commoners?"

"Yes," he said, a crack forming in his mask as Agatha truly questioned him. "But it is for the good of your cause."

"Then I will put a stop to it." Agatha turned as if to call someone as the mask that Lord Fox had shattered.

"You have no right to interfere with my plans."

Dragging her closer, he pulled out a dagger that had been hidden in his coat sleeve and stabbed Agatha.

Chapter Thirty Two

Ella could only gasp in horror as her tired body failed to move, and Agatha fell to the ground in a heap. Agatha's eyes widened as a single tear ran down her face as she lay bleeding on the ground.

"You should *not* have questioned me. I can't have you getting in the way of my plans." He pulled out his kerchief and wiped his dagger before throwing the dirtied kerchief on top of Agatha. Turning to them, he asked, "Now, where were we?"

"She trusted you!" Adrian's words echoed Ella's thoughts as Nora held him back. "Why did you do that to her?"

Lord Fox shrugged, "She questioned me. Though of course, you are next. Can't have you causing problems."

"There are three of us and one of you. Why are you so certain you will win?" Nora asked, holding her fan at the ready, and set the lamp on the ground so that it wouldn't interfere with her fighting.

Clapping at her words and giving her a sly smile, Lord Fox continued, "Yes, I'm sure an exhausted pregnant girl, a sickly prince, and a lady who is getting on in her years could beat a man in his prime. Besides, who said it was only me?"

From the corridors hidden in the shadows came three figures. Having nothing and being unable to move, Ella could do little more than hold up her hands in defense as she backed away so she wouldn't have her back to the new enemies or to Lord Fox. "What is your plan? Why are you doing this?"

"You want me to reveal my plans to you like a second-rate villain?" An amused smile played across his face as he continued to watch with excitement in his eyes. "Kill the boy, capture the others; they may have some use. Besides, it's not like they would kill me. The Fan Society is above all that."

The shake of his head showed exactly what he thought of the mindset of the Fan Society — as idiotic as the woman he had just stabbed.

Grappling with her thoughts, trying to keep ahold of them before the wash of exhaustion pulled them away again, she tried to pull together a plan to get them out of this. Glancing between the men and Lord Fox, Ella wondered if she would go against Fan Society rules and kill someone. Did she want that life on her hands? But she may not have any choice in the matter. Ella doubted that she could do anything against anyone; already, the flame of fever was causing her to shiver violently, and it took all her strength to stand. Could her mother protect her from the men while protecting Adrian? Though her thoughts were struggling to come up with anything, Ella did remember her fight with Fox a few years ago. It had not been easy.

The figures stepped forward and were revealed in the lamplight to be some of the men Ella had avoided during the chase. Two of them were making their way towards her mother and Adrian. Her mother had pushed Adrian behind her, but even though he was behind her, he held his hands at the ready, just as Ella had taught him. The other was making his way towards her.

Adrian caught sight of the man going towards her, "You know she is pregnant, and still you send men after her?"

"If she didn't want to be attacked, then she shouldn't have interfered in the first place," he said dismissively, as he brushed them aside.

Ella shook her head at Adrian's attempt to distract Lord Fox and turned to the man in front of her. Considering her condition, it was going to be difficult. But with her energy gone, Ella couldn't stop the emotions from erupting from her as tears ran down her eyes, blurring her vision. All thought of coming up with a plan had failed, burned away by her fever. The man didn't rush as he grabbed her arm. Remembering her training, she twisted out of his grip by pressing against his thumb. The sudden release caused her to stumble back, causing more pain to shoot through her.

"Stupid girl," the man muttered as he reached for her again. She tried to dodge, but it was more of a stumble as he grabbed her around the shoulders. Ella struggled in vain. She knew how to get out of such an easy hold, but her body refused to listen. Her body was shivering as the warmth of his body burned through her body like a raging fire, reminding her of all the abuse she had put it through. She could only hope that her baby survived all of this. Yet again, emotion overwhelmed her as her pathetic struggles did little, and the man's laugh echoed in her ears.

Adrian watched in horror as his wife was attacked. He had tried to slow down whatever Lord Fox had planned, but it was useless. Yet again, he was being protected by his mother-in-law. His breathing turned to a wheeze as he helplessly watched his wife stumble back. A grunt near him caused him to turn as Nora expertly fought off several attacks with whacks from her fan. The two men were crowding in on her, but she held them off, though she had to take a few steps back, causing her to shove Adrian further behind her. Stumbling with the sudden shove, he fell beside Clementine. Her eyes were flickering open, and a bead of blood had dribbled down her hairline, revealing why she hadn't been moving. Hurriedly, he untied the ropes, though it was difficult with the moisture in the air. Memories haunted him of a darkened church, and Clementine was injured yet again. The clashing around him changed to the sounds of rioters pounding on a wooden door. Fire licked around his face, and the metal candlestick burned his hand.

But it wasn't. It was only Clementine's hand touching his face and the fan she placed in his hand. In his waking nightmare, he had somehow managed to untie Clementine's ropes. She leaned in close to his ear. "Help Ella."

Then she fell forward as the last dregs of her consciousness fell away. Once again, cursing his uselessness, he gently laid her on the ground as he searched for his wife.

"To think she would wake up for that short amount of time."

Adrian shivered at Lord Fox's words. He turned to look at him. A smile lit his face as he watched the chaos unfold, like watching a show or a play. Adrian was going to try to speak to him again, but he wouldn't be able to reach someone with so little humanity.

"If you want to save your little fan girl, you should save her now. Things are not looking so good for her. Though it would be interesting to see what you do, considering I ordered them to *kill* you."

Lord Fox seemed rather unconcerned by his words, causing fear to burn through him as he finally found his wife. She was dangling in the arms of the man who had accosted her. Another fear came this time, one that stuffed out the fire to a frozen statue. What could he do? He was no fighter. For all the tricks that Ella had taught him, most of them were only for escaping or slowing down opponents; none of them were for real fighting. He was useless in fighting, and already his chest was tightening, making it difficult to even walk, let alone fight. Adrian couldn't stand it. He had to help Ella. Glancing around, Adrian looked for anything that could help him. His eyes fell on the thing that Clementine had handed before passing out. A fan. The heavy iron kind that the members of the Fan Society use. A weapon. Could he use it? Could he walk to what was most certainly his death to save Ella? Looking at his captured wife, he knew his answer. Even if it was an exercise in futility, he would try to save Ella and their unborn child. All he had ever wanted to do was help her. Maybe he would be able to do something or at least buy some time for Nora to defeat her opponents. But he would try.

He stood wielding the fan. If he hadn't held the weight of the fan when Ella had trained him, he might have dropped it, but instead, he held fast. The man was dressed in rags and wet from more than grabbing soaking Ella. His scarred arms held her on the throat and stomach as Ella sagged against him unconscious. Adrian stood in front of him and wheezed, "Let go of my wife."

The man looked as if he was going to let go, and panic filled Adrian as Ella would have been dropped to the ground, but instead, the man just laughed. Anger threatened to fill Adrian but worry for Ella cooled the flames. Remembering what Ella had taught him, he stepped forward to the hand that held her throat. With his right hand, he used the heavy iron fan to wallop the funny bone. Reflexively, the man relaxed that arm as he howled in pain. Adrian, using his left hand, wrenched the man's other hand backward by the thumb fully releasing her into his arms. Her weight pulled on him, and they crashed to the ground. However, Adrian had his arm wrapped around her to keep her off the stone. He barely noticed the pain in his back as he struggled to sit with Ella cradled in his arms. The coolness of the damp tunnels had made him chill, but they now felt like fire as his skin touched hers. Fever burned across her like wildfire, yet she shivered violently like she had been dumped into a freezing lake.

His attention turned from her as the man he walloped turned a fierce gaze to him. Cursing, the burly man aimed a heavy-booted kick at Adrian's head.

He ducked, covering Ella with his own flimsy body, there wasn't much else he could do. He was now stuck. With the weight of Ella in his arms, he was stuck on the stone floor, an easy target for a well-muscled worker. Adrian had gotten himself into trouble.

Again.

No. He looked to the fan that he had dropped in his efforts to catch Ella. No. He was not a fighter, and there must be some other way that he could help her. Though he could not move, there was something that he could do. He had poured over every newspaper and every bit of information so that he could help Ella and pass information to Ella from Drina. He had more information about what was going on than everyone else. Adrian had the information he needed, but what was it? He turned to the man, and he noticed his scarred arms, which looked very similar to his own burned hand. Drina had told him about the repercussions of the burning of the parliament building and how it had grown so fast and destroyed many important documents. Remembering the business deal with Lord Greenwood and how everything was in his brother's name. Lord Fox's name. Business information had been burned — information that would connect Lord Fox to Lord Greenwood's misdeeds.

Pain spread across his face as he had been so lost in thought that the man had attacked again. The taste of copper filled his mouth as blood dribbled down his cheek.

"Keep sitting there, prissy boy, and I'll make your end quick."

Adrian had to push past his pain to speak. But already, he was struck again. He had to speak his words. Pain has been his constant companion, he could handle it. He had been born and raised in pain, dancing on the edge of death. It was a familiar sensation. He decided to take a chance that his gut was correct. Forcing the words through his sore jaw, he spoke, "Was Lord Fox upset that you survived the fire?"

The fists stopped their blows, giving Adrian time to spit out the blood that had pooled in his mouth. This time, speaking clearly, he said again, "Was Lord Fox upset that you managed to survive the fire? The one that started in the Parliament Building in October of last year."

The man stepped back, footsteps shaking on the stone. "How . . .?"

Adrian sat up, woozy from the blows, trying not to shake his head so his thoughts wouldn't turn to mush. Trying not to sigh with relief that his insight proved true, he turned to Ella. Ignoring the man's stutters, he gently wiped drops of blood that had fallen on her face as his fingertips burned from her warm skin. Pulling her into a hug, he whispered, "I'm going to protect you this time."

Then, turning to the man who no longer was shaking with fear, as his face had turned to anger, "What do you know?"

Adrian watched as the man flicked his gaze to Lord Fox, who had done nothing during this exchange. Uneasiness filled him as Lord Fox watched with an amused expression on his face yet again. They would have to deal with him later.

Turning back to his assailant, he said, "The burning of the Parliament building has had lasting effects. Seems it also burned far faster than anyone expected, including you."

He turned away, rubbing his burned arms as if a memory played through his head. Adrian knew that you never could forget the searing sensation or the smell of his own burning flesh. Trying to put his own memories aside, he continued, "Do you also think that killing commoners is the best way to live your life?"

"I have done no such thing!"

It seems Adrian was on the right track. This man was just a grunt for Lord Fox. Someone to be used and then thrown away. The glint of enjoyment that was in Fox's eye hopefully meant that Adrian could change things before he interfered. "Then what were you doing in the water?"

"My job!" The man growled. His face blooming to a ferocious shade of red, letting Adrian know he only had a few moments before his chance to save his life, and Ella's, was gone.

"I'm sure you are doing a fine job with it. Did you ever notice that after you did your job, people in that area got sick?" Adrian was walking on a fine line. No one ever liked facing the truth. Even if you never intentionally tried to hurt people. So, before the man could act on his growing anger, he continued, "I don't think that you knew what you were doing. I doubt you would intentionally try to hurt your family and friends, but I'm certain you would know who does."

Adrian tilted his head in Lord Fox's direction. The man growled as his burning gaze turned towards Lord Fox, "Did you just use me?"

"Of course, you are my employee. I am free to do as I wish."

It was a perfect noble answer, one that a commoner with an anger issue didn't want to hear. His face turned red as he rushed towards Lord Fox like a bull.

A heavy sigh escaped Lord Fox's lips as he shook his head at the oncoming man, "I had thought this would have turned out differently."

Just as quickly as he did with Agatha, he took a step forward and stabbed him, leaving another body at his feet.

"He was your own man."

Adrian hadn't realized he had spoken out loud until Lord Fox turned to look at him. A smile flashed across his face, which would have looked genial except for the bloody knife in his hand. "One can always sacrifice a pawn."

The frozen feeling of fear crept up his veins that was only softened by his wife's burning fever. He may have stopped the man from attacking Ella, but they were still in danger.

Chapter Thirty Three

Since Adrian couldn't move out from under Ella, he turned to look for Nora. Though she tried to hide it, even in the shadows of the tunnels, he could see her labored breathing from facing two attackers. No longer having the stamina she once did, he could tell that the long night and multiple fights were wearing on her.

Using her weakness, they were cornering her as fewer and fewer of her attacks made contact. Or at least that was what he thought. They had pushed her closer toward Lord Fox, and when they made a move to grab her, she dashed between them. Flicking her fan open, its damaged fabric no longer hiding the blade beneath, she held it to Lord Foxe's neck.

The sounds of battle froze, other than the sound of heavy breathing and the groans of those who lay on the ground. Anger and pain filled her eyes as Adrian could see Nora resist looking down at her once friend that lay at his feet.

In the silence, Lord Fox laughed. It was a belting laugh, though it lacked the humanity that a laugh should have. Chills ran down Adrian's spine as he laughed, unconcerned by the bladed fan leveled at his throat. "My dear Lady Nora, you are just like your daughter. She once held her fan to my neck, just like you. But I know you, and I know your group. You won't kill me. It goes against your code. It's the very reason why dear little Agatha was kicked out. You wouldn't want to be a hypocrite now, would you?"

When he spoke of Agatha, Adrian could see how much she had to hold back her anger, but his words were correct. She would be a hypocrite if she killed Lord Fox.

In a steady voice, laced with a steal, she said, "I may not be able to kill you, but I can find evidence, and I will throw you in prison and make you go insane."

He pushed aside her fan, "Lady Nora, I have already made myself resistant to your little poisons. And there is no evidence to be found. Even if you did, no one would believe you, and those who did would not say anything. I am involved with everyone in high society, and they see me as amusing entertainment whose connections are too valuable to give up. With the populous now ripe for a riot, the new queen won't last much longer."

The hand holding her fan dropped to her side. Lord Fox motioned for the two men still standing to grab her, and they started to take her away. How would he be able to fight against a man who doesn't care about others and sees everyone as pieces in a game? An observer.

Glancing down at Ella and seeing the bodies strewn around him, Adrian realized something. Lord Fox wasn't just an observer.

Adrian knew the words that he said to Nora when Ella held her fan against him. It was when she was on her way to save him during the riots. He may have even been the one to go after Viscount Edmund and who knows how many others. Because though he felt as though he could control others, a person as smart as him would realize some things were better off done with his own hands. He wouldn't want some riffraff mucking up his perfectly laid plans.

That thought reminded him of the document that Drina had given him not long ago. In the revelation of information and with the fighting, he had forgotten it. But when or how was he going to use it? It was then that he caught some movement among the fallen that helped him. Now, he just needed to buy time and hope that Nora was wrong and the support they called would come soon.

"If you are just an observer, then why did you attack Ella during the riots?" Adrian asked.

Lord Fox shrugged, "It was better for me to do it."

His eye gleamed with a far-off look of remembrance as he spoke those words, which hit Adrian with inspiration. The problem is a well-laid plan and being smarter than everyone else.

"Aren't you bored?" Adrian asked, pulling Lord Fox's attention to him.

"Why would I be bored? I get to watch as everything falls into place." His eyes showed a glint of interest, as if the pawn was doing something improbable. "I'm an observer watching as all my pieces do as I have planned."

He seemed so proud of this fact, but Adrian knew what it was like having to sit on the sidelines. Though he doubted Lord Fox would ever admit it, it is never as much fun to watch a game as it is to play it. Considering that he had personally gotten himself involved earlier, he was eager to show off how good he really was. He also enjoyed killing those who personally got in his way, just like Edmund. Seems like he is on the right track. "I'm sure that I did exactly as I had planned. You didn't do anything."

Fox raised his brow, "Are you really trying to get me to tell you my plan?"

"Why not? You are planning on killing me and taking them prisoner."

"But my plan hasn't come to fruition yet. I know very well that telling can cause problems down the road." Though his words sounded like he was bored, the glimmer in his eyes only grew as they continued to talk. So far, everything had been too easy for him to do everything. He wanted something interesting. Adrian wondered if that was why he found Agatha in the first place, to give himself a handicap. Some deadweight to see if he could do it.

"Wouldn't that make things more fun?" Adrian asked, giving Lord Fox one final push.

"You are right. It would make things more interesting." The bored expression that he had been holding on his face gave way to a smile, "What do you want to know?"

Adrian held back his relief that Fox was talking to him, but the weight of Ella in his arms made him all too aware that time was not on his side. "I know why Agatha tried to kill Queen Drina, but what do you get out of it?"

"I thought you would ask me a more interesting question, but I did say I would answer it. I want to control England."

"But how would you accomplish that?"

Lord Fox shook his head, "I wasn't done explaining. I knew that the Fan Society would save the queen. But who is in control of Alexandria?"

"Drina is in charge of herself," Adrian spouted before he could hold his tongue. He winced, knowing that he couldn't let his emotions get in the way.

Shaking his head, he moved closer to Adrian, "You shouldn't let your emotions get the better of you. You are correct about this moment when

Queen Alexandria is crowned, but who controls her advisers? Who controls the House? And who controls the people?"

Conversations flicked through his head, and his hidden lessons in politics that he secretly took when he was younger. The Society of Shadows is working to make the people upset at the nobles, and even if they get caught, they don't have enough evidence to capture him, only Agatha. Most likely, all the evidence that could be connected to him was burned when he ordered his man to set it on fire. He also had Lord Montague in his pocket, who had connections to all the nobles, and if anything went wrong, he would just cut off the Montagues and start again. And with everyone helping him get things through parliament, what could a young girl do?

"The Fan Society would stop you!" Adrian yelled, putting as much of the fear he had into his voice, just like Ella had taught him.

A laugh erupted from Lord Fox. Adrian had to force himself to wait until the laughter died down, "Young Prince, I apologize for my outburst, but I managed to find out about the Fan Society when I was just a young lad. They are held back by their high and mighty hypocritical values of not killing anyone. They are also forced to use other people and the law to help them. I have no such compulsion. Besides, women are so easy to manipulate."

As he turned his gaze to look at the floor, Adrian spoke up, "What if they had a higher authority than you?"

Lord Fox shook his head, "The Fan Society looks at England as their child. They would never ask for help and never have in their centuries of operation. And they are not going to change now."

"Are you so sure?" Adrian pulled out the document that Drina had given him, "I have a document giving me the authority to have you imprisoned and or killed, as signed by the Queen of England."

It must have been the first time he had truly been surprised since the bored mask with a pleasant expression dropped and showed confusion and anger. Using that distraction, Nora acted. Now that she had some time to take a break, she attacked, instantly knocking the men holding her out.

Growling, Lord Fox pulled out his dagger, ready to fight, but red-faced and shaking, Nora held her fan up to his neck, pressing closer than what was necessary. Seeing his disadvantage, he held his hands up and dropped his dagger to the floor. "Sorry, ladies, did I push too much?"

Though the anger was obvious even as Nora spoke in a calm tone. "Lord Fox, you will no longer get away with this."

"Really?"

The glint in his eye was the only warning he gave as he grabbed her wrist, pushing the fan away, leaving a red line but allowing him to pull her towards him, "My dear, you are too emotional. Isn't that what you told your daughter?"

The line of blood dribbled down his neck like a macabre necklace as Nora struggled against him. But he had not been fighting this whole time and knew every trick the Fan Society taught. Which only became more evident as the fight went on. Tired as she was, she struggled against him as Adrian watched in horror as his plan started to fall apart.

Finally, he captured her in a hold that, in her weakened state, she couldn't escape from. "Thank you for letting yourself be captured. Now, it seems I've overstayed my welcome. Goodbye, dear prince; I hope your wife lives. It was fun playing games with her. Now, I'll take this piece and claim it for my own."

Adrian's lungs clenched in pain as the time he tried so desperately to gain slipped through their fingers. He held his wife close, trying to stop her chills as Lord Fox slowly backed away while still avoiding Nora's attempts to release his grip.

Seeing movement again at Lord Fox's feet, Adrian called out, "We will never let you get away with this. From now on, the Fan Society will be hunting your every move.'

"I would like that. Thanks for the gift."

"That's not the gift," said a voice by his feet. "Here is your gift, you backstabber."

Lord Fox looked down to see Agatha stabbing him in the calf with the dagger that he had dropped. He cried in pain as he released Nora. Kicking Agatha away from him, he then reached down to pull the dagger from his leg.

"Not this time," Nora said from behind his back.

He released his grip on the blade and slowly stood, but this time, she stabbed him in the neck with a hairpin. Not enough to kill him but enough to let the drug enter his system, even though a prick would have been enough.

He dropped to the ground in a heap. It seems like he wasn't as immune as he had thought.

She turned to Ella in Adrian's arms and looked at Agatha on the ground. The concern in her eyes grew.

Nodding to the fallen Agatha, he said, "I've got her; talk to your friend. This may be your last chance."

"I leave her to you." Then, she turned to her fallen friend.

A wet laugh came from the fallen Agatha until she coughed, "How did it come to this?"

"We were stubborn."

"Yes. We were."

The silence was stifling after Agatha said those words, and Nora held Agatha's hand. Only the wet breathing of Agatha and the groans of the fallen could be heard, making the tension grow worse. Now that the action had died down, the ache of waiting for help to arrive was infuriating. He barely noticed his wheezing had turned to a whistle until a hot hand touched his face.

Adrian turned his attention to Ella, who had woken up, the chills no longer raging as much as they had been. Her eyes tried to focus on him as he could see the exhaustion try to pull them close again. "Ella, it's okay. We will get you better again."

A smile grew on her face as she forced aside his worries by grabbing his hand and placing it on her stomach. He felt a flutter of movement beneath his hand as tears welled in his eyes as she said, "You saved us."

With tears falling down his face, he replied, "You saved me first."

He didn't even notice when the royal guard came earlier than expected to take the men into custody or carried out Lord Fox, who twitched as they took him out. He only moved when they came to help Ella out to see the doctor.

Chapter Thirty Four

One Year Later

Drina's coronation had been a fabulous event without any major mishaps. The streets had been lined by the adoring people as they watched the 19-year-old girl be crowned. But that was a week ago. This time, instead of adoring crowds, it was only a few people in a private room. Many had entered via secret tunnels. Including Euphemia, who, considering her role, now had a neutral relationship.

As Ella stood waiting for Drina to arrive, she looked over at Adrian, who was against the wall holding their daughter, Mary. Their little miracle. After the events in the tunnels, Ella had been very sick, but due to the baby being farther along than they had originally thought and them both being stubborn, she was born into the world six months later.

Ella held back a smile as the wall clicked open to reveal Drina or Victoria, as she wanted to be called. Proof of her victory against the confines of her mother. Seeing her confident walk and commanding presence for someone so young, her first name suits her better than her childhood nickname. Bowing in consideration, she waited until Queen Victoria was in position.

She stood when the queen said, "You may rise. Since this is a secret meeting, there is no need for such pomp and ceremony. But I thank you for showing your allegiance to me."

Madame Briar came forward and bowed her head, "Your Majesty, I thank you for forgiving us for keeping a secret from the royal family for such a long time."

"Yes, several hundred years too long, but that is going to change." Queen Victoria looked out at the few Fan Society members who were in the room. "And it's not going to be easy. The reason I forgave the sins of the Society was because I believed that you were trying to do something good. For now, we will continue to have your work done in secret. But I wish to have the people know of your existence. Lady Nora, it seems you have something you wish to say."

Ella looked at her mother; after the funeral for Agatha, she had been stoic. It wasn't until her grandchild was born that she regained her joy. She had gone back to working with Ella since there was a lot of work that needed to be done to find out all that Lord Fox had done. It didn't help that he had managed to escape his captivity.

"Is it wise to tell the populous?" Nora asked. Normally, Ella would have assumed that she was trying to keep everything from the people, but after the events in the tunnels, Ella understood. It could be dangerous if they revealed too much too fast, but her mother had also been one of the first to start working with the young queen and had become one of the bridges to connect the two peacefully. It was the reason why everyone was in this room.

"Lady Nora, I understand what you are trying to say, but I believe the people deserve to be told. For the very reason why you kept things a secret is the very reason why we should tell the populous. For the mess that happened a year ago not to happen again, they must be told. Not every king or queen will be good or do what's right for the good of the people. That is why the people themselves must be able to have some control over their own lives, even if someone more powerful is reigning. If they do not know about it, they cannot fight for their own freedom. Though of course, there will be many things that would still need to be kept secret."

The passion in her voice reminded Ella of all the pain that Drina had due to the control of her mother. With that passion, her mother nodded her head and stepped back.

Queen Victoria gave a courtly smile, a well-practiced gesture, and continued, "Because of this, the structure of the Fan Society needs to change. It is no longer going to be a secret society but an organization that is under the queen. You will no longer be separated from the country. You will be working for the country legally. Though you will be constrained by the laws that will be set before you, I will also expand your operation."

Trying not to furrow her brows in confusion, Ella didn't know what the queen would say next. In all the talks between the Queen and the organization that she had been a part of, there had never been any mention of expanding the operation. However, talks did get heated when Lord Fox escaped before he could be detained. Her mother had cursed herself for not checking to see if the drug worked fully, but the Society couldn't find him. Maybe with the Queen's plan, they would be able to.

"We will be expanding since not all enemies are within. Some are without and should a criminal escape or be working with outsiders, we would need to know. I will have the Fan Society split into those who work on threats coming from within and those coming from without. It will be easier since they will have my authority to help."

Warmth filled Ella as Queen Victoria continued to talk. What the Queen was saying fulfilled the part of Ella that had been itching, irritated at some of the ways that the Society ran things that had bothered her. But if that is what the Queen was wanting, wouldn't that mean that Madam Briar wouldn't be completely in charge anymore?

Turning to look at her, Ella could see age appearing on her face. Though she looked older, she always had a sense of timelessness when Ella had been studying, but now Ella could see the pressure had worked its hand on her body. Maybe in the end, this is the best thing.

The queen must have noticed Ella and gave a slight nod, "Since the organization will be split, I have discussed with Madame Briar what would be best. Based on her suggestions, we will have a head in each department. Lady Nora will be head of blocking foreign invaders, and Lady Arabella will be head of internal affairs."

Raising her brow in surprise, Ella had expected that her mother might be one of the heads, but she never expected herself to be one. But considering the way Adrian had bowed to Drina, he already knew what she had been planning. Ella stepped toward her when the queen motioned them forward.

Drina must have seen her confusion since she asked, "Speak what you want, Lady Arabella."

The Queen was far better than she had originally expected at reading expressions. I guess being Queen at a young age had something to do with it. Not wanting to hold on to her trepidations, Ella replied hesitantly, "I wonder if my being the head would be best, considering how little time I have spent in the organization, as well as my history. I worry that I will fail."

Letting out a snort but quickly regaining her regal demeanor, Drina held Ella's eyes, "You were the first one to be suspicious and notice something was wrong. If it wasn't for your insight, I would have already been dead before I was able to be crowned. I know of no better person to be the head. Though if you are still worried, I also made the decision that Madame Briar would become the advisor to both departments to help support you and Lady Nora during the transition."

With a quick glance, Ella could see Madame Briar curtsy deeply to the Queen. It felt like she was saying something to the Queen, but Ella didn't know what. Copying her mentor, Ella gave a curtsy to the queen, "Thank you for this opportunity."

"From now on, you will no longer be the Fan Society. You will be called the Secret Service Bureau until things become more public."

"Yes, Your Majesty." The Society, now Secret Service Bureau, chorused as they each gave a bow of their heads.

"Then you are dismissed. I'm sure you all know how to leave discreetly." Drina said before leaving herself through one of the secret exits.

Madame Briar gave her a hug, "I am so proud of you. You will do a good job. I always knew you would be a change. I was glad that it was for the better."

The twinkle in her eye reminded her of her time in school, and Madame Briar always seemed to have something planned for Ella, though she never knew what it was at the time. But she didn't think that either of them fully expected this outcome.

"Of course. She is my daughter." Her mother had come up beside her and gave her a hug of her own. Returning her hug, Ella felt love fill her. After everything that had happened, from the search for her mother to finding not what either of them was expecting. And now they were here. Adrian came up beside her and passed her daughter, Mary, to her. Ella laughed as Mary played with her earrings and smiled in delight as they sparkled in the light.

"Are you ready to go home?"

Ella nodded. They made their way through their own route to the ballroom from the party that she had disappeared from previously, while Adrian left on his own way with Mary. It was time for her to go to bed. Feeling the pull of wanting her family as well as wanting to get back home and think everything through, she made her excuses, saying she wasn't feeling well, knowing that her long absence and rush to get home would be easily explained away.

Arthur was waiting for her at the entrance. He had been alive when they had dumped him, his cold body being mistaken for dead. As soon as Clementine was treated, she spent her time watching over him. It wasn't long before he officially asked Clementine to marry him, and seeing the eager look in his eyes, he couldn't wait to see Clementine again.

"Don't worry, your wedding will be soon," Ella said as he helped her into her carriage.

"I didn't expect to have to wait a month until after the queen's coronation."

Watching him, she could see the shaking of his legs, though he hid it well, and his pale skill was more than just the lighting of the evening. He had been pushing himself far too much so that he could see Clementine as much as possible. But he was still technically in the service of Baroness until the wedding and didn't get the chance to see Clementine unless he was helping Ella. And he was going too far. Deciding to help out Arthur for Clementine's peace of mind, she said, "It is better for you to get some rest; you did nearly die not too long ago."

"So did you." He grimaced.

"And I did take a rest until I was better. Next time, let William take your place. I can't have Clementine's fiancé passing out before the wedding. Besides, you will be married soon enough."

He relaxed his shoulders and admitted his folly, "I'll get some rest."

Nodding, Ella said, "Good, I want to see my own beloved."

Arthur nodded, closing the door once she was seated, and headed off. Lost in her own thoughts, she looked out the window as she worried about how she would be able to be the head of the Fan Society, now the Secret Service Bureau. So lost in her thoughts, she almost didn't notice a figure wandering the streets; it was only instinct that made her shout, stop. Before the carriage could fully slow down, Ella jumped out of the carriage and chased after the figure. He was limping as he ran, letting Ella catch up even though she started later. The figure paused to catch his breath, and the light from the moon shone upon him. Then he went down an alleyway and disappeared into the shadows. Ella checked the alley for a few minutes but knew that the man had escaped. Her thoughts held onto the image that she had seen in the light. A scar across his throat that was still fairly new, though it had been healed. A scar that was where her mother had cut him in the tunnels. Lord Fox was still around.

A grin grew on her face as she made her way back to the carriage. It seems that she had found what she needed to do as head of internal defense.

Catch Lord Fox.

Epilogue

Year 2000

The police officer finished putting in all the boxes then drove away once her relief came to guard the archeologist. Driving to the white stone building, Thames House, in London, she made her way to the back entrance. As she drove up, she pulled her glove off and showed her badge. The badge was just a decoy. The real identification was the ring with an open fan and a circle of eyes around it. Once the guard saw it, she was let through. Driving forward, she went to the delivery entrance, an agent let her through, telling her to give the boxes to the woman in the historical room. Hefting a box out of the back, she made her way into the basement. A young, frazzled woman was doing her best not to sneeze as she looked over a brittle document. Her clean lab coat was white except for an insignia on her breast pocket with an open fan and a circle of eyes around it.

"Here are some more boxes. How are you doing?" The officer said as she set the box on a semi-empty table nearby.

The frazzled young woman looked up and sighed, putting down the tweezers and putting away the document. She slumped in her chair and pulled off her cotton gloves, "Oh, I am doing fantastic."

The officer laughed, "That eye-roll says otherwise. How are you really doing?"

"Considering they keep sending me boxes of papers related to my ancestors doing amazing things out in the field, yet I'm still kept behind a desk working on papers, you can see how it is going." She eyed the box that the officer had just brought in.

"Well, your day is going to get worse since that archeologist just found more. And I still have more boxes in the car."

The frazzled young woman groaned and put her head on the desk. Patting her on her shoulder, the officer shook her head and made her way to get more boxes.

Once she left, the young woman lifted her head and sighed, leaning back in her chair. After a moment in that position, she pulled open the drawer and pressed a button to reveal a secret compartment. Inside was a journal, and on its cover was a fan. Running her fingers over the cover, she whispered, "How am I ever supposed to live up to a Legacy like you?"

Hearing her friend return with another set of boxes, she pressed them one last time, following the outline of the fan, and put it away. One day, she will prove herself. She will be the next head of the Secret Service Bureau, just like her ancestors were.